the Wild Ones

A Broken Anthem for a Girl Nation

Nafiza Azad

Margaret K. McElderry Books

New York London Toronto Sydney New Delhi

MARGARET K. McELDERRY BOOKS
An imprint of Simon & Schuster Children's Publishing Division
1230 Avenue of the Americas, New York, New York 10020

MARGARET K. McELDERRY BOOKS is a trademark of Simon & Schuster, Inc.
For information about special discounts for bulk purchases, please contact Simon & Schuster Special Sales at 1-866-506-1949 or business@simonandschuster.com.
The Simon & Schuster Speakers Bureau can bring authors to your live event. For more information or to book an event, contact the Simon & Schuster Speakers Bureau at 1-866-248-3049 or visit our website at www.simonspeakers.com.
Interior design by Irene Metaxatos
The text for this book was set in Lomba Book.
Manufactured in the United States of America
First Edition
2 4 6 8 10 9 7 5 3 1
Library of Congress Cataloging-in-Publication Data
Names: Azad, Nafiza, author.
Title: The wild ones : a broken anthem for a girl nation / Nafiza Azad.
Description: First edition. | New York : Margaret K. McElderry Books, [2021] | Audience: Ages 14 up. | Audience: Grades 10–12. | Summary: After Paheli escapes a terrible fate, a magical boy gives her access to the Between, allowing her to collect other women of color, hurt by men, and lead them when the boy is in peril.
Identifiers: LCCN 2020048799 (print) | LCCN 2020048800 (ebook) | ISBN 9781534484962 (hardcover) | ISBN 9781534484986 (ebook)
Subjects: CYAC: Interpersonal relations—Fiction. | Magic—Fiction. | Fantasy.
Classification: LCC PZ7.1.A987 Wil 2021 (print) | LCC PZ7.1.A987 (ebook) | DDC [Fic]—dc23
LC record available at https://lccn.loc.gov/2020048799
LC ebook record available at https://lccn.loc.gov/2020048800

Dedicated to my sisters, related through blood and soul:
Robina, Farzana, Teng Teng, Rossi, Famiza, Eliza,
Faiza, Zaynah, Shaina, Aliyah, Yashaswi, Jane, Janet,
Arifa bubu, Ashreena bubu, Ashma bubu,
Wahfiqa, Hina, Maureen bubu, and Jasdeep

This work contains themes of sexual and physical violence.
Reader discretion is advised

Four more minutes and I would have
  been lost.
My sorrow
would have consumed me entirely.
As it is, I realized upon a blink
before the credits rolled.
This is not how I want my story to end.

—PAHELI, *The Book of Memories*

Once upon a midday marked by the blooms of pink and purple bougainvillea, she was born.

They named her Paheli. A riddle.

And she was.

And she is.

And may she always be.

A few words of caution before Paheli tells us her story. We would have you know that the tale she weaves may be true or it may be a lie. Or it may be a khatta meetha, sweet and sour, mixture of both.

We don't know.

What we do know is that every story has a beginning. And this is ours.

The Beginning, or How Paheli Became the First Wild One; With a Cameo by Taraana, the Boy Made of Stars.

I lived a life of spark and charm (false, of course) and (manufactured) wit and splendor. I lived my life on my toes, on a precipice, poised to fall. And fall I did.

But let me begin at the beginning.

My mother was a whore. Not a tawaif as she aspired to be, but a whore. Men visited my mother's body as though it was a city they were supposed to conquer. I don't know what circumstances led her to this profession, and she never volunteered the information.

She named me Paheli because she said I was a mystery. Whether I was a result of a yearning or a moment of weakness, she wouldn't say, and over time I learned not to ask.

I know nothing of my father. No . . . that is not quite true. My eyes are the blue of Afghani skies like his must be. My skin is a deep brown like the earth after its first sip of rain. My mother's skin is the color of day-old dough.

We lived in the City of Nawabs in India. Now Lucknow, back then it was known as Awadh. It wasn't just the city of nawabs, however; it was also the city of tawaifs. What my mother wasn't but what she wanted to be so desperately.

I remember the smells of the kotha. The first floor was rank with the smell of cheap perfume the first-floor whores applied liberally. The aroma of food emanating from the kitchens vied with the stench of the refuse that waited for attention right outside the back doors. Below all this was another scent, one that I now associate with despair.

The second, third, and fourth floors of the kotha were the domain of the tawaifs. The air in those rooms was infused with fragrances created exclusively for them.

What is a tawaif if not a whore? A tawaif, sisters, is a courtesan. She is well versed in the arts of conversation and seduction. She is schooled in music and dance, particularly the mujra. She sings ghazals and plays instruments. Her intellect is formidable and her beauty so divine that the moneyed nawabs paid fortunes to partake of it.

Not for her a dingy, dark room in a row of dingy, dark rooms on the first floor at the back of the kotha. She has a scented boudoir, decorated in silk and satin. Men seek pleasure from her; they do not simply satiate their lusts. Grace, elegance, and choice: a tawaif has them all.

I grew up learning to keep my eyes cast down lest I be the recipient of unsavory notice from my mother's clients. I never left the kotha; I wasn't allowed to. Girl children are tender morsels to those whose hunting grounds are the city's pavements. There were other children in the kotha—some were even my friends—but our first loyalty was to our mothers, and our mothers were often embroiled in complicated feuds with each other. Though the kotha was always full of people, I sometimes went days without speaking to a single person.

My mother's face had been disfigured by a childhood illness, which made her dream of being a tawaif precisely that: a dream. Still, the sisterhood in the kotha was not exclusive, and the women would have enfolded her within its arms had my mother been a nicer person. She wasn't, though. She wasn't nice at all. So, she was reviled around the kotha, and the only reason the Malkin, the owner of the kotha, tolerated my mother was because she liked me.

I grew up on scraps of attention thrown my way by the various whores on the first floor. The second, third, and fourth levels of the kotha were forbidden to us children unless we were sent on errands. My mother mostly kept me in that windowless room that served as home, apart from the time she worked. Those hours, from five in the afternoon to two in the morning, I was left to my own devices. When I was young, my mother paid a kitchen maid to take care of me, but after I turned five, I was deemed old enough to look after myself.

What do I tell you of the evenings at the kotha, sisters? I used to slip under a table set on the side in the central courtyard and peek out from behind the overhanging tablecloth at the spectacles that unfolded there every evening. The evening gatherings, the mehfils, were filled with color; each tawaif was dressed in bejeweled finery, and glowing with life and laughter. The sweetness of the ghazals they sang enraptured me. I was too young to appreciate the sly wit in the banter the tawaifs and the nawabs shared; too young, at first, to understand the incomprehensible whispering between two hearts that people fancifully called romance. The nawabs who frequented the kotha were peacocks; knowing that their money alone wasn't enough to attract attention, they seduced as much as they were seduced.

I would fall asleep under the table and wake only when I could no longer hear the bells of the ghungroo the tawaifs wore to dance.

The city outside the walls of the kotha was unknown to me and would remain so until the year I turned sixteen. My mother had been trying to get the Malkin to take me on as a tawaif-in-training but to no avail. My skin wasn't fair enough, the Malkin said. I was fiercely glad. My mother's ambitions for me aside, I had no plans on whoring myself. I didn't know what I planned to do with my life, but I knew with a certainty that my mother's trade was not for me.

Not that my desires meant much to my mother. My blue eyes were a ticket she meant to use to elevate her status. So, she sent me, ostensibly on errands, to the tawaifs' domain, hoping I would run into a nawab and gain his interest. But I subverted her commands at each point. If I couldn't avoid being in the presence of the nawabs, I would wear my most mulish expression and keep my eyes cast down. Would you look at a dandelion in a field of orchids? They didn't either.

I only let my guard down once and only for half a second. I thought I was safe; I thought that no one was around. I *should* have been safe.

It was early in the morning when the denizens of the kotha were all asleep. I had spent the night under a table again, though at sixteen I was a bit too large to properly fit under there. The courtyard was lit dimly by a few glass lamps scattered here and there. I walked, rubbing my eyes, not seeing where I was going, and kicked a ghungroo that had been lying on the floor. I picked it up and shook it, smiling at the sound it made.

When did I realize I wasn't alone? A sense of danger ran a shiver down my spine, and I looked up at the stairs that led to the second floor. A man, still wearing the effects of the sleepless night on his face and his clothes, stood there. His eyes met mine and widened in surprise. He smiled. Startled, I dropped the ghungroo and ran. I should have known to be afraid.

Days passed and I made another unforgivable mistake. I forgot about the encounter in the dark; I forgot about the man. The Malkin told me about a tawaif who had retired and needed a girl to work in her home. I wanted to be that girl. I was full of dreams of escape. Perhaps my mother noticed.

That day, sisters, dawned red. Not that the day has any business with the work of the whores, but nevertheless, the day dawned red. My mother was uncharacteristically kind that day. She told me it was my birthday, and as I didn't know any better, I believed her. She fed me halwa puri, combed my hair, and embraced me for the first time in a long while. Later, she made me dress in a gharara she had borrowed from an acquaintance.

Then, when the first stars of the night were dotting the horizon, she took me to a party on the rich side of the city.

I should have questioned her then, but I didn't. I should have known to be suspicious, but I was bedazzled by the attention she was giving me. So, I followed her to that party. She was my mother. I thought she would never do anything that would harm me.

He was there, that man who had been on the stairs that morning in the kotha. The man about whom I had forgotten. He was there.

You all have known a similar flavor of pain, sisters. Even if I don't put it into words, you know what happens next. The same old tale of the lamb and the wolf. You have heard it before. You have lived it before.

I escaped too late, running out of the nawab's haveli on bare feet. I was bleeding from the gash on my arm, from the scratches on my face, from between my legs. It hurt to run, but it would have destroyed me to stay.

The night was alive and the city streets blurred as I ran without direction, without thought, without reason. I ran and ran and ran and would have run farther still had I not turned a corner and bumped into that boy. We both fell from the impact. His lips were split, and he coughed up a mouthful of blood. He looked as shattered as I felt.

We stared at each other under the pale light of the half-moon. He had a five-pointed star in the pupil of each eye, and his skin glowed gold like he was made of stardust. My reality receded slightly when I looked at him glowing like a desert in the afternoon sun. The boy got to his feet and made to go. Then he stopped and turned back to me. Without warning he tossed me a box. I barely got my hands up in time to catch it. I blinked and he was gone. I was left with the night, left with the pain; left alone, scared, and shattered.

My reality reasserted itself. At that moment, the shadows provided an illusion of safety, but where would I go next? I couldn't go back to the kotha. I definitely wouldn't go back to that woman who no longer deserved the title of my mother.

I looked down at the box in my hands. It was plain brown wood. I opened it and took a deep breath. On a square piece of black silk was a collection of stars. The stars in the box were identical to the stars in the eyes of the boy I had bumped into. I picked one up and placed it on the palm of my hand.

The sound of voices coming from behind me made me tense, and I clenched my hands into fists without realizing. The star dug into my hand, and all of a sudden, a fire flamed in my veins. I squeezed my eyes shut, intensely aware of my ravaged body, the road underneath my bare feet, my torn clothes, and the pain. Always the pain. The skin on my palm stung, and when I looked at it, I saw that the star I had been holding was now embedded there, like a badge or a medal.

I looked up and the world was different. I managed to get to my feet, though my knees buckled once or twice. I put a hand, palm flat, against a wall for support. A door appeared in the wall I was touching. Golden light glimmered from underneath the door.

I didn't question it, sisters. I pulled the door open, and stepped through.

An Introduction; Hold On to Your Hats.

◆ We are the Wild Ones. We are made of whimsy and lemon.

◆ We have the temerity to be not just women, but women of color. Women with melanin in our skin and voices in our throats. Voices that will not be vanquished. Not now, not ever. We will *not* be silenced.

◆ Just in case it needs to be said, all you need to be a girl, to be a woman, is to decide you are one. Your gender is your decision.

◆ There have been many of us over time and between time. We write glimpses of our stories, of the lives we led before we became wild, in a Book of Memories. We share some of our stories, some of its pages, interspersed within Paheli's story.

◆ Our lingua franca? Why, darlings, we speak all dialects of pain.

◆ Paheli's story is our story. We will give it shape, allow it reason, fashion it wings, and watch it fly.

◆ Now. Are you ready? Take a deep breath. Let's be wild.

The Sweetness in the Sugarcane, or The Impractical Nature of Immortality

The air inside the Between smells very much like the air inside very posh hotels: expensive with hints of nature. Ligaya, with hair as dark as an evil witch's heart, walks to a patch of wall and carefully pulls out a plump diamond embedded in it. She places it gently in a small sack that contains other Between diamonds, each one as exquisite as the other.

We don't take many diamonds out of the Between. Just enough to keep us sparkly and satiated. The stars embedded in the palms of our right hands qualify us as the Wild Ones, and, as the Wild Ones, our needs are numerous.

At this moment, we are traipsing silently down the Between. It would be easiest if you thought of the Between as a corridor snaking throughout the world, invisible to human sensibilities and precious to magical ones. The walls of the Between are made of stone, like a medieval castle corridor flanked on either side by closed doors. If you turn the knob on a particular door, it will open to a city. Each door in the Between leads to a different city in the world. This corridor is always illuminated by a golden light, which, if you believe Paheli, is magic. We can feel this light soaking through our skin and filling us up.

It is never silent in the Between. You can always hear voices talking, laughing, screaming, or crying. There are murmured conversations between lovers, confrontations between enemies, mundane exchanges, and illicit whispers that tease your ears. The worst moment is when you hear a voice you think you recognize. The best is when you hear one you wish you did. So, we are silent in the Between because all of us have some voices we wish to hear and others we never want to hear again.

Once in a while, we pass a middle worlder. None of them stop to talk to us or pay us any attention apart from a furtive glance or two. You see, in the Between, we are invincible and middle worlders know it.

Paheli leads us, as she always does. Her steps are soundless, but the skirt of her dress susurrates as she walks. Widad is wearing belled anklets that chime sweetly with each step, and Daraja's yellow bangles make their own music. We need no words to announce our presence.

We come to a stop in front of a pale orange door. Every door in the Between is a different color. Paheli's eyes have a familiar caution in them. A caution that simmers in the depths of all our eyes. We know exactly what kind of monsters hide in dark places and the kind that walk, without fear, out in the open.

Paheli opens the door and steps through. We follow her. The heat greets us like a lover, enveloping us in a tight embrace. Talei beams, luxuriating in the familiar feel of what was once her home. Areum and Etsuko, though, groan their displeasure.

Thus, we arrive in Lautoka, Fiji. You may have heard of Fiji. People speak of it fondly as a holiday destination. Couples who want something more exotic than Hawaii often name it as the place they will honeymoon. Safe in a resort, where the locals are trotted out to perform so their culture becomes a spectacle for those who have money and are willing to part with it.

After all, everyone has to eat.

We are standing in a small alley beside a rather run-down apartment building on the outskirts of Lautoka City. The apartment on the second floor is ours; we bought it through an intermediary ten years ago. The apartment is dusty, and the mismatched furniture looks particularly forlorn. A withered hibiscus plant stands in a sunny corner. The stuffiness in the air tells tales of our neglect.

Areum turns on the air conditioner at the highest setting while Daraja gives her a look and turns it off. She opens the large windows instead, letting the air in.

"There's no breeze, Dara!" Areum whines, flopping down. Her long hair, currently an electric blue, sticks to her skin, and she picks up a lock, giving it a sinister look. "I think it's time for a haircut."

Kamboja, splendidly ignoring her, settles down on the tiled

floor. *Her* hair is shorn short. "I feel every minute of my seventy-five years today."

"You're actually seventy-six," Valentina says, giving her a sweet smile. Kamboja's glare amuses her, and she giggles merrily.

To be a Wild One means to exist partially in the human world and partially in the middle world while not belonging to either of them. Why? Because we belong wholly to the Between, which is not a world but a pathway.

Though the worlds we partially inhabit are anchored in time, we aren't. Time moves forward for these worlds, but we remain stranded at the age we were when we accepted the stars we wear on the palms of our hands. In other words, our bodies do not age, though our minds do. If you want to call this immortality, you are welcome to.

Talei ignores everyone in the cramped living room and opens up all the windows Daraja hasn't gotten to. The noon song of the city pours in, and for a minute, we sit quietly and listen.

Cities have souls, you know. They are alive and sometimes they die. They grow old either gracefully or shamefully. They shrink and they expand. They grieve and celebrate. We have been to many cities in the world. We have learned the languages they speak, and though we cannot speak these languages, we have learned to listen and understand.

Lautoka City, or as it is known among the locals, Sugar City, is full of verve. Not the verve you'll find in, say, New York, but an island excitement. A molasses-slow excitement. The air is heavy with the smell of, yes, exhaust, but also sugar. The sugar mills are hard at work on one end of the city. The magic here is thin and patchy, though. Bigger cities, older cities, have stronger magic.

We breathe deep of the sweet air and let the excitement in it infect us. We are here for the festival after all.

"Mangoes," Paheli announces suddenly. "I must have mangoes."

"I'm sorry to break it to you"—though by the sharp grin on Talei's face, she's really not—"it's not mango season."

"Well." Paheli illustrates her disappointment by sitting down on the floor beside Kamboja.

"Get up." Valentina nudges her with her foot. "We have to go get some money."

"Oh. I suppose I can find ice cream along the way." Paheli perks up and gets to her feet. Her cloud of light pink hair is tied up tightly in a bun. "Who is coming with us?"

Daraja and Talei elect to accompany her while the rest of us pick up the supplies from under the sink and give the apartment the cleaning it desperately needs.

We have been to Lautoka City enough times that her streets are, if not home, then familiar to us. It is late afternoon, and the city is gaining an emptiness that is normal for her. Soon, stores will start closing up, and the night will find the city ready to sleep. Of course, not all stores close. Some, especially those that serve food and offer other entertainment, remain open till late. The only bus station in the city is open for service until six p.m. You are on your own after that.

Not that we are going anywhere outside the city. We couldn't even if we wanted to. We can travel between cities in the Between but not out in the world. Our footsteps can only go as far as the city boundaries. Beyond that is an invisible wall that separates the wild and the city. We can bang into the barrier, but we cannot get through it—not unless we take off our stars.

After ten minutes of walking, we reach a rather shabby store located between a clothing boutique called Makanjee's and a place selling silver pots and pans. The windows of our intended destination are entirely opaque, as if the products inside are too precious to be viewed by the passing riffraff.

A bell rings when we push the door open and pile in; it is a sonorous sound that echoes in the dark interior of the store.

Large canisters full of colored sugar make up the entire inventory of the store. But see, this isn't the sugar you will find in a grocery store frequented by humans. No, the sugar crystals offered by this store have rather esoteric qualities that customers would do well to be aware of. We have, on occasion, sampled some of the sugar from this place. It caused us to stumble into dreams where flowers bled crimson and the sun was a threat in the sky. Another time the sugar gave us wings, and for thirty minutes we flew. Yet another time, the sugar turned us all into stone, and we learned the true meaning of stillness. The effect wore off, but we have a newfound sympathy for statues.

We haven't been to this store in years, but nothing seems to have changed in the time we were away. We wait at the counter, and a minute later the proprietor emerges from the back room with a wary look in his eyes and a weapon in his hands. We look at the staff he is holding with great interest.

Valentina gives Paheli a look, and Paheli looks wounded. "I haven't done anything to him. I swear!"

The not-human man's name is Josefa, and he has always been friendly to us, so the hostility we see on his face is unexpected.

The staff, made of some kind of wood, is hooked at the top and has a vaguely menacing aura. It is a magician's staff; that much we know. We also know that it is used to direct magic to or at anyone the wielder desires. We are of the Between, however, and untouchable, at least by magic.

Josefa relaxes infinitesimally when he recognizes us, and his expression reorganizes itself into something friendlier. He lowers the staff and places it out of sight.

"So, you are not going to try to kill us?" Paheli asks. Valentina pinches her. "I'm just asking!"

"I'm sorry. There have been upheavals recently," Josefa says shortly. He is a tall man with dark skin and amber eyes. His age is indeterminable. Middle worlders, not-human men and women, live longer lives than their human counterparts, but they, too, cannot evade death. Every city we have traveled to has a store run by a not-human person with whom we can exchange the Between diamonds for money that we use in the human world.

"What kind of upheavals?" Paheli asks, the usual joviality absent from her face. What she means is, *How will this affect us?*

Josefa gives us a considering look. He knows that we are of the Between.

"Power has changed hands. That which was imprisoned was set free. The streets have, once again, become hunting grounds. Those without magic are becoming reacquainted with their vulnerability. You . . ." Josefa looks at each of us in turn. "You ought to be careful. *He* has designs on the Between, and you who walk it freely are most in danger." Josefa doesn't specify who this *he* is. Instead, he holds out his hand, and Paheli drops three diamonds into it.

The Between is made entirely of magic. Sometimes excess magic is expressed as diamonds, hard gems made of solid magic rather than the usual carbon. If no one picks them, they are reabsorbed by the Between. And no one *can* pick them apart from us.

You see, middle worlders have to pay a measure of magic to traverse the Between. The amount of magic required is calculated by the distance traveled and paid when they touch the door leading to the city they want to enter. While magic is not exactly sentient, it is particular about certain things.

"This is the amount you'll get in return." Josefa names an amount, and our eyebrows rise. The amount is a lot more than we expected. He looks at our expressions and makes a face in return. "Magic levels are decreasing around the world, so the price for it has gone up."

In the middle world, magic is both energy and currency. Middle worlders cannot function without magic, which also buys services and items. Magic has two states of existence: one is force, and the other is diamonds.

Every middle worlder is born with a level of innate magic. As they spend time in magic-rich places, the level of magic they contain rises until they are carrying the maximum magic they are able to. This is not always pure magic but a sort of abbreviated magic. A filtered magic of a quality somewhat higher than unrefined oil but barely.

Josefa hands over a large wad of local currency in exchange

and cautions us to be careful once again. Immediately after, he returns to the back room, leaving us standing in the dimly lit store.

Daraja and Talei move closer to Valentina and Paheli as Josefa's warnings linger, unsweetened by the sugar in the store. Paheli pockets the money, meets our eyes, and breathes out.

Paheli: The Vagrant Experiences of a Mango Addict

Sometimes I like to stand with my feet pressed to the pavement of a city and feel it breathe. And sometimes I wait till midnight to eat mangoes because mangoes taste the freshest then. Valentina refuses to indulge in my profundities, but she, whom I found on a bridge in Paris, is a star that commands its own planets and disdains mere immortals like me.

I have been a Wild One for a very long time. Too long, my bones grumble, and sometimes there's an ache in me for green things. Not that I would know what to do with a forest if I found myself inside one, but still, I like dreaming.

I look at the faces of my sisters when we leave the sugar shop, and they look as jittery as I feel. The unnamed *he* has struck a chord of familiar terror in all of us. This certainly won't do. We cannot afford fear; we have paid far too much to it already. So, I lead them back to the apartment where we pick up the rest of our mismatched crew, and we make our way to Marine Drive.

I insist on buying ice blocks from a corner store and make short work of the sweet, milky treats that taste a little like heaven if the place was a flavor. Not that I have any hope of gaining entrance there. I lick my fingers when I am done until Daraja stuffs a wet wipe in my hands. We walk, unseen by humans and ignored by the infrequent middle worlders, through the city toward Marine Drive.

Like everything else that doesn't fit within their boundaries of normal, we, too, are naturally invisible to human beings. To become visible, we have to bring together intention and energy. This is not difficult, usually, but it does get annoying, so mostly we don't bother. Everything we touch becomes invisible as well. We pretend it's a superpower, and in some ways, it might as well be.

Ghufran walks next to me, her footsteps still uncertain, as if she's unsure of her right to the ground upon which she walks. She has been with us for a while now, but fear still sets daily in her eyes like the sunset we have come to see. We sit in a line on the seawall, legs dangling on the seaside. The sky is readying itself to perform for us and we, well, we have always been willing spectators.

You would think, considering the transient nature of a Wild One, I would grow inured to the comings and goings of those I call my sisters, but, and you can ask Valentina this, they all leave a bit of themselves within me. Right now, there are eleven of us:

Ligaya, Kamboja, Daraja, Widad, Talei, Sevda, Areum, Ghufran, Etsuko, Valentina, and me. Five years ago, there were twenty.

The sky is soon painted in the crimson shades of a broken heart; it demands all our attention. Sunsets and sunrises are perhaps the only things that still command our reverence. One announces an end to pain and the other indicates a new beginning: two things that are invaluable to us.

"What Josefa said . . . ," Valentina says suddenly, and I look at her. She catches my eyes and becomes quiet. But of course, it's far too late.

"What did Josefa say?" Areum asks.

"He warned us of a new danger," Daraja replies, shivering even though it's a hot day.

Now everyone is looking at me. I glare at Valentina and pretend I have all the answers. I am really good at pretending, in case you're wondering.

"We have no information yet, so there's no use panicking. There'll be plenty of time for that once we know exactly what shape this monster takes," I say. I understand why the girls are spooked. Thus far, we have lived, skirting the peripheries of the human world and the middle world, slipping under the radar of the magical heavyweights. We don't like the idea of having targets painted on us.

"Let's go back to the apartment. We still have a festival to go to! We'll find out more about this person later. All right?" stinky Valentina says, trying to make up for placing her foot in everyone's mouth earlier.

I jump off the wall and wobble. Ghufran steadies me without

a word. I beam at her before I start walking. I wonder if they will have mangoes at the festival.

"Are you really not worried about this new threat?" Valentina says in my ear.

"I'll worry about it after the festival," I tell her, and walk faster.

Cotton Candy Sugar Screams

The Sugar Festival is an annual celebration in Lautoka City. There is a parade, but we are more interested in the festival grounds located in Churchill Park, not far from the city center. The festival grounds boast fair rides, food vendors, game kiosks, and a stage upon which musical performances, both traditional and modern, are held.

We emerge from our apartment two hours after the night swoops down, spilling darkness all over surfaces and shielding the cracks in the pavement from further censure.

The chaos of the coming night is all but shimmering in the air. The evening is full of possibilities, and, despite the warning from the storekeeper, we are eager to realize them. Not many middle worlders make their homes in Lautoka City; the magic here is too thin to sustain them. Middle worlders run on magic created by human lives. Therefore, the more populous a place, the more magic it contains. The middle worlders who do live here, like Josefa, are powerful beings boasting a greater ability to soak up loose magic from the surroundings compared to others.

You might be curious about what draws us back to this humble place, to this humble festival. Is it the scent of sugar in the air that persists no matter how many other smells try to drown it? Or is it the way the lights of the city and the festival push at the darkness that frames heavens heavy with stars?

Yes and no. You see, one of us, Talei, is from Fiji, and Lautoka is the closest she will allow herself to get to home. Her city is on the other side of the island, but she is not yet ready to return to it. So, we come to Lautoka City once in a while so she can taste home in the air, in the night, and in the sense of the wild waiting at the edges of the lights. For now, this is enough for her.

We walk slowly as the island night demands. Humans avoid us without realizing they are doing so. We hear the music long before we see the lights of the festival. The din of excited voices adds to the soundtrack of the night. The smell of meat sizzling on the barbecue grills is acknowledged by the growls in our stomachs. Truth: We do not eat to live. We are sustained by the magic of the Between. Another truth: What is life without food? Our stomachs remember hunger and we indulge them happily.

We enter the festival grounds unseen before appearing in front of the food sellers. We startle them with both our presence and our voracious appetites. We gleefully patronize little booths sell-ing clouds of cotton candy and snow cones in the colors of the rainbow. We play games and win stuffed animals that we pass on to kids who look at us suspiciously before accepting them.

As the hours slip by, the darkness deepens as does our awareness of shadows.

The festival grounds are getting crowded when we return after watching a meke performance by traditional Fijian dancers. Paheli suddenly stops. We recognize her stillness. We follow her gaze and see three men herding a young girl away from the grounds to the back of a stadium located in a cordoned-off area of the park. Their intentions are as obvious as is her terror.

Other people see the girl's distress, but not one of them moves to intercede. Funny how often situations like this occur.

Time shifts and the men succeed in isolating the girl. The back of the stadium is deserted. The music from the festival is a distant thump. The girl whimpers.

We follow and we watch, transfixed. Her terror echoes all our pasts.

We do not hate all men. Just most of them. That old adage, you know? Guilty until proven innocent.

When we invited men into our stories, into our bedrooms, under our skin, and close to our hearts, we didn't expect them to destroy us as a demonstration of their strength, as an expression of their masculinity. But they did. Or at least they tried to.

None of us were saved by any princes. No kind woodcutters passed by when the wolves were making meals of us.

But we survived. If not in entirety, then in fragments.

Paheli moves. We flow behind her, almost as if we are one body, and perhaps in this moment we are.

The men see us too late. They see our bodies, our mouths, our hips, our femininity, and they think us weak.

Paheli steps forward and all attention falls on her. She is like a storm at dusk, our Paheli. Her eyes are the blue of broken hearts and her face is the reason for them. She becomes the only one they can see and the girl is left to flee. She hesitates before some sense of self-preservation pushes her away. The men barely react; it is almost as if they are in thrall to Paheli.

We take a deep breath, and then all of us scream at the same time. The men fall to their knees, their hands around their ears. The lights in the festival flicker twice before returning to their original brightness. The men do not recover. They won't. They will hear our screams in their dreams. The sound will haunt them. They will lose sleep. Their relationships will suffer. Perhaps they will lose their jobs and livelihoods.

The irony of having screams as weapons is not lost on us. Our screams work differently on humans and middle worlders. For humans, the effect is somewhat akin to having an excess of electricity in their brains. For middle worlders, a Wild One's scream means being injected with more magic than their bodies can safely contain. The effect is the same.

"Let's go," Paheli says, and we heed her. We leave the festival before the Sugar Queen is crowned and the city before the clock strikes midnight.

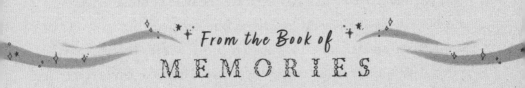

From the Book of
MEMORIES

TALEI
CITY OF ORIGIN: SUVA

Blue. His eyes were blue. Cornflower blue.

Wet leather, carpet stains, corduroy jacket with brown
patches at the elbows. Weathered briefcase and creased
pants.

Shaggy hair, black sprinkled with gray. Crooked teeth
and tanned cheeks. Lean. Thin. Craggy. Complicated.

Love amongst the dusty tomes filled with the words
of long-dead poets. Love behind closed doors, locked.
Love, extra quiet just in case someone heard. Caresses

flavored with guilt. Kisses that felt like despair or maybe desperation. His hands rough on my skin, searching, always searching for the familiar curves of a body that was not mine.

That ring on his finger, damning him, damning me, damning us and what we did. His tears when he thought I was asleep, tired, worn out, exhausted. Love that tasted like helplessness and felt like regret. Love that cursed itself even in the middle of its making.

I saw her once. His wife. Another four-letter word.

She. Blond hair, wide smile, eyes green with laugh lines fanning out. Graceful. Dressed in the soft colors of security. The whole to his half.

I realized it then. I had no part in their equation. *I* was the artificial construct. The Other. The personification of a youth too soon relinquished to duty and marriage and desiring to, once again, thrill. *I* was the sin to be confessed on Sunday to a red-cheeked priest.

She would be flowers on afternoons, jewelry just because, and dinner out with decade-long friends. She is what memories are made of, what the subtexts in poetry whisper of.

And he?

Of the cornflower-blue eyes and fumbling hands?

He was lost in his need both for what he couldn't have
and what he already did.

Our lives are never a measure of possibilities. We are always narrated as tragedies waiting to occur. Our mothers didn't tell us what we could be but expressed once and again what we must not be. We were never told about the roads we could take, but we learned all about the paths we must not wander down. But in the end, their lessons made no difference. Ruin came to us even when we kept to well-lit streets.

Our mothers. Would they love us still now that we have turned into the cautionary tales they used to tell?

"Will You Walk into My Parlor?" Said the Spider to the Fly.

The Japanese have an art of repairing broken things—well, pottery—called Kintsugi. Artists use powdered gold, silver, or platinum to rejoin the broken pieces, making the resulting whole even more beautiful than it originally was. The art celebrates the form as a whole, history and all. Being broken doesn't mean ceasing to exist or remaining broken forever; it means a chance to recover and reconstruct.

Just like the City of Beirut. Just like us.

We can hear Beirut singing through the open balcony doors on our second-floor apartment. A bathtub full of flowers sits in the middle of the living room, and we are arranged in various poses around it. Paheli is hanging upside down from a chair beside the bathtub, her pale pink hair floating in the water with the blooms.

Just because we talk in one voice doesn't mean we are of one mind. We are different shades of one color. We do not represent other girls around the world who might be in situations similar to ours. Would you ask a drop of salt water if it represented an entire ocean?

It is ten in the morning and the city outside tempts. Yet we resist, which is unlike us. Whether we admit it or not, Josefa's warning has spooked us.

The world we live in has three levels. The basic level, the third world, is that of humans who are mostly not aware that they're not the only sentient beings in existence. The second level, the middle world, belongs to the magical beings that appear only as fancies in the literature and other media of human beings. The third level, the first world, is of the divine, and of that we know nothing. The divine is separated from the human and the middle world by an iron curtain that no one has been able to shift. Not for lack of trying either.

We dip in and out of the human and the middle world without regard for the laws governing either of them. Now that Josefa has alerted us to danger, we are skittery.

Still, we can't hide forever. After all these years, we have become the kind of people who poke tigers simply to hear them roar.

"I'm hungry," Sevda announces a little piteously.

Daraja throws a ripe mandarin to her. Kamboja eyes Daraja contemplatively.

"This is the last one and it's mine," Daraja says, peeling another mandarin.

"I didn't say anything," Kamboja grumbles.

"Your face said it for you," Daraja replies, stuffing herself with the mandarin. She saves half of it and passes it to Kamboja, who takes it happily. "My heart is so kind, I impress myself at times."

"Modesty, I remind you of modesty," Sevda says.

"Let's go!" Areum says without moving an inch. She's wearing a bright yellow dress that clashes with her blue hair. It's a statement we appreciate.

Beirut is one of the oldest cities in the world, so the magic here is thick and strong. She was devastated in the last civil war, but Beirut refused to capitulate to the hate and the violence that emptied her streets and shelled her buildings. She wears her scars proudly and stands strong, blooming with the new buildings that dot her landscape.

Her strength gives us hope. Her beauty lets us dream of a time when we, too, will be more than the hurts that seek to define us.

Our apartment is in Saifi Village, an upscale neighborhood, but we see no reason not to indulge. Following Areum's words, Valentina stirs. She walks over to Paheli and pulls one lock of her hair. Paheli promptly slides down the chair she was hanging from and onto the floor. She opens her eyes.

"If you have finished being a monkey, we would like to go exchange diamonds for money. Some of us want to do more than just sit in one place letting the moss grow." Valentina has a bite. The gold tips of her black hair are the exact shade of her eyes. She's the tallest amongst us. She weaponizes her height against us and looks down her nose at us with a flair none of us have yet been able to match.

Paheli raises a hand and gestures, lazily, to the door. "By all means, go."

"We won't go without you," Valentina replies. "You know that."

"Why not?" That's the question, isn't it? Have you wondered too? Why do we stick to Paheli? To each other? It took us a long time to understand why we insist on a sisterhood when the language we speak most fluently is pain, and pain usually insists on solitude.

The reason is simple. We see ourselves reflected in each other's eyes, and we are reassured of our existence in worlds that turn unfamiliar with the passing of the years. We anchor each other, if not in time then in existence.

"Because," Valentina replies evenly, with a steely look. Paheli sighs and gets to her feet. Apparently, that is answer enough.

We take to the streets dressed in colorful outfits. All of us, yes, every single one of us, are devotees to sartorial splendor. We take pleasure in putting together outfits that are bursts of color. Tassels? Oh yes. Sparkles? Of course. We wear glitter on our faces and flowers in our hair. Even bees sometimes look to us for dew.

We construct ourselves daily in different types of clothes and brilliant daubs of makeup. We have become so skilled at putting our outer selves together that the cracks in us are barely visible.

Our first destination today is an antiques store located on Hamra Street. We take our time walking there; so many things demand our attention along the way. Some buildings in Beirut display their battle scars with a grim grace while others have new facades to help them face the future. Arched balconies spill over with greenery dotted by multihued flowers.

The city is healing, true, but like us, she is wary and always prepared for the pain to begin anew. A tension simmers in moments. Questions rise with the sun every morning. Will there be blood spilled today? Will the streets echo with the sound of gunshots? Or will the city witness the fanaticism of a suicide bomber? Or suffer the consequences of a corrupt government?

Graffiti, bold and beautiful, covers the walls of abandoned and inhabited buildings. The street art is defiant, seeking to reclaim the city from those who would see her burn again. Li Beirut, as the singer Fairouz names the city, is no maiden who hides her blushing face. She is an embattled matriarch, looking the world in the eyes, daring it to look away.

We look around as we walk, catching glimpses of the middle world here and there. That glint you see in the corner of your eye or that time you thought you saw something move in the shadows is the middle world. The store you swore you had never seen before, or the alley that springs up suddenly one day only to be gone the next. Human beings are, as a rule, completely blind to the middle world. Even when they see middle worlders who are not at all human-looking, their brains normalize whatever they are seeing. They are unable to see the true selves of middle worlders unless the middle worlders want them to.

The antiques store on Hamra Street is full of shadows, dust, and memories. Each item in the store contains the memory of an experience. Should a consumer purchase one, they will be able to relive the experience as if they were the one it occurred to. In

Beirut, all memories smell of smoke and have the taste of tears. We once asked the proprietor, Idrees, about the kind of people who purchase the sad memories. He told us that there are beings in the world who desire to remember what sadness feels like because it is during emotional turbulence that a person is most alive.

Idrees is out in the front when we enter. A seemingly frail not-human man, his white beard and stooped figure hide the strength in his body. He glances over at us without saying anything before returning his attention to the customer he is currently serving. We look at her and she turns, as if sensing our gazes.

Not a single word is spoken, but the air suddenly takes on an electric charge. We draw close to each other and to Paheli, the sun around which we orbit.

Idrees's customer is unlike any middle worlder we have ever seen before. Her hair is made of dappled feathers of various lengths. Several of these feathers are missing, and her scalp is covered with either scars or baby feathers. Her eyes are the silver of mercury. Her skin is dark like the night, and when she smiles at us, she reveals teeth with sharp points. We thrum like the strings of a guitar; our senses flood with warnings of danger.

"My name is Assi," she says. "I bear you no ill will." We remain unconvinced. She walks closer to us and we tense. "Will you show me your palm?" She addresses Paheli directly, but we all hiss, putting our hands behind our backs. Paheli tilts her head, looking at the woman without betraying any of the tension we are stiff with.

"Why do you need to see my palm?" she asks the middle worlder.

Assi, if indeed that is her name, gives Paheli an inscrutable look. "I am searching for a group of girls who call themselves the Wild Ones."

"To what end?" Paheli again.

"I heard they frequent Idrees's store, so I came to leave a message for them. What serendipity to meet them here." The woman smiles. With all her teeth.

"You haven't answered my question," Paheli says.

"I have an invitation for the Wild Ones," Assi replies. She really doesn't want to answer that question.

When Paheli doesn't respond except by silence, the woman continues. "In two days, there will be a gathering in Byblos. The stars you wear in your palms—the one to whom they belong will be present at the gathering. He asks to meet you there."

Paheli starts at the middle worlder's words. Her eyes narrow and a quicksilver expression of panic freezes her features.

"Will you attend?" she of the sharp teeth asks. We look at Paheli.

"We might," Paheli replies very reluctantly.

"Excellent. I will tell him to expect you," Assi says. Without another word, she disappears, leaving us unsettled and curious.

The Best Ice Cream in the World, Teddy Bears, and a Tree Creature.

Hanna Mitri in Beirut, according to various sources, sells the best ice cream in the world. After our run-in with Assi, we find ourselves in severe need of sustenance of the sweet kind, so we make our way to El Saydeh Street, where the ice cream parlor is located. It is a small, unassuming place, manned by an elderly gentleman who cannot quite control his surprise when we pour into his shop and fill it, almost to bursting. The walls are white, the television set in a corner is old, and the oven has bullet wounds.

We pay fleeting attention to the details and concentrate, instead, on the ice cream. The flavors on offer are apricot, rose water, milk, lemon, peanut, strawberry, chocolate, and croquant. After we have been served, we leave the store as suddenly as we entered it. And the ice cream? It is everything the newspapers, the food blogs, and the social media posts boasted it would be. Rich, milky, ice-creamy.

We walk silently around the city with no destination in mind. Conversations flow around and through us, but we are quiet, none of us wanting to ask the question all of us want the answer to.

"Well?" Valentina is the first to break. She is an impatient sort, so we are surprised she has held out for this long.

"Shh, shh. Let's not spoil the taste of the ice cream with conversation," Paheli replies. "Give me a minute. No, an hour. Perhaps a week?"

"Paheli." Valentina flicks her with a manicured nail. Her nails, if you are curious, are red.

"All right. Fine." Paheli finishes her ice cream, licks her fingers, and leads us to the painted Saint Nicholas Stairs. She flings herself down on a step near the top of the stairs while we arrange ourselves on the lower steps. She gazes down at us, much like a queen gazing at her misbehaving subjects.

Some of us flinch and turn away, not wanting to see her displeasure. Others meet her eyes warily. She is our savior; without her intercession, we would have been lost. We will never forget this.

"Stop with the theatrics and tell us. Are we going to Byblos?" Valentina, of course, has no such compunction. She has been a Wild One for the longest time after Paheli. She takes liberties when none of us would dare.

"I have to. I don't want to, but I have to," Paheli says softly, looking down at her hennaed hands.

"We don't have to do anything we don't want to," Valentina replies.

"This person, he was the one who gave me the stars. He gave me and thus you the escape without which . . . Where would we be right now?" Dead. Either by our own hands or someone else's.

"So, we are going to waltz into what could potentially be a trap?" Etsuko says. She has sharp cheekbones, and a tattoo she doesn't ever talk about peeps out from the short sleeves of the bejeweled shirt she is wearing.

"I owe him a debt. I need to hear him out," Paheli says, and pauses. "It is not necessary that we all go."

"Of course it is," Sevda replies with a roll of her eyes.

"I have never been to Byblos," Ligaya says.

"None of us have," Valentina says, then stops and looks at Paheli. "You've been around long enough to have visited, right?"

"Are you calling me old?" Paheli stands up and puts her hands on her hips.

"You *are* old," Valentina replies. "But like cheese . . ."

"I think you can stop there," Kamboja says. The rest of us snicker at Paheli's disgruntled expression.

We turn our sights to Beirut once again. The ice cream, delicious as it was, has been eaten. The decision has been made. We are going to Byblos or, as it is now called, Jbeil. Before we do, though, we have to find out more about the *he* Josefa mentioned.

Valentina accompanies Talei, Ghufran, Ligaya, and Widad back to the apartment as they are not comfortable with the creature the rest of us are going to meet. Our destination is not too far, so we decide to walk. It takes us an hour instead of the usual thirty minutes because Paheli keeps getting distracted by the shops along the way.

When we reach Bourj Hammoud, it is early afternoon and the air is spiced with the aroma of food emanating from the nearby restaurants. Before Paheli decides she's hungry, we march her to a patch of greenery found between Armenia Street and Mar Youssef. The pavement surrounding the greenery is a checkered pink-and-once-white. The pink is pervasive in the area. Narrow buildings, tightly squeezed together, also boast a pale pink color.

The green patch is not just a median strip but also contains umbrellaed tables where people can seek shelter from the sun. Though the day is bright, apart from one or two old men, the place is empty. A few flowers wilt sadly on one side of the strip while some art installations do their best to bring culture to the space. We head straight for the tallest palm trees growing near the tables and chairs.

Sevda breathes deeply of the air that admittedly smells little like a forest. Of all of us, she struggles the most with the lack of green in our lives. We are currently invisible to humans (and thus more comfortable), and so we garner no attention from the people sitting at the tables.

Paheli pokes at the trunk of the tallest palm tree and we wait. Nothing happens. She deflates and pulls Sevda to the front. "You do it. He likes you best."

Sevda wrinkles her nose and touches the bark softly. Sure enough, there is an immediate response. A thin sheet peels off from the bark; it has two eyes and fleshy lips. Paheli dumps a bottle of water on it, and with a pop, it gains a vaguely humanoid form. An unclothed humanoid form. He is short, barely up to our shoulders. His hair is a bright green and his tummy is a large pouch hiding his genitalia.

Not all middle worlders have human forms; we have learned to accept them in all the ways they express themselves.

"Oh?" The creature we call the Greenich looks at us with eyes full of avarice. "Look at what the wind blew in." He blows a raspberry at us. "If you want information, you need to pay."

"If you want magic, you need to give us something worthy of it," Paheli replies promptly.

The Greenich chuckles. His long tongue snakes out and he licks his eyebrows. Okay, we lied. Some things are easier to accept than others. No one should have a tongue that long. "I was wondering when you would get here."

"Why?" Sevda asks.

"How much will you pay me?" The Greenich won't budge.

"One Between diamond," Paheli replies.

"Two," the creature counters.

"One. If you don't want to trade, there are others who will tell us what we want to know," she says to him with a firmness we are not used to.

"Oh fine. You are stingy as usual," the Greenich says with a huff.

"Thank you," Paheli replies with a sweet smile. "Talk."

"Here's what I know," the Greenich says. "A predator has emerged from the depths of the dark where he was imprisoned for a long while. Don't ask me the details because I won't say. I *can't* say. All you need to know is that those who imprisoned him have disappeared, though whether it is by their own design or his is unknown."

"What does that have to do with us?" Kamboja asks.

"He is obsessed with the Between, or to be more precise, the Keeper of the Between. You are of the Between, and thus, he is interested in you. Don't let him catch you, girlies. He will chew you up and spit you out before you know what's going on." The Greenich looks us up and down and shakes his head as if grieving. We hiss; we are no one's prey. The sound carries enough magic that the creature loses his color. He rushes back to the palm tree, perhaps to disappear into the tree trunk once again, but Paheli grabs him by his shoulder.

"What about a creature with very sharp teeth and feathers on her head instead of hair?" she asks.

"A Cheraj?" The Greenich turns back, his eyes wide and his fear forgotten. "Have you seen one? If you have, pluck a feather from her head!"

"Why?" Daraja asks. She sounds horrified by the idea.

"A Cheraj feather is said to attract luck! Pure luck! Guaranteed luck! Maybe pluck two feathers and give me one?" the Greenich wheedles.

With a curl of her lips, Paheli takes a Between diamond out from a bag and throws it to the creature. Without another word to him, she turns her back and walks away. We, of course, follow. None of us look back.

This is not the first time we have sought out the Greenich for information, and it probably won't be the last. But this is the first time he has given us information that has so thoroughly disturbed us.

"Oh look. Stuffies." Areum stops and points. We look. We don't know who Jack is, but we buy stuffed animals from his gift store, ostensibly for Ghufran, but the truth is, we all need a hug right now.

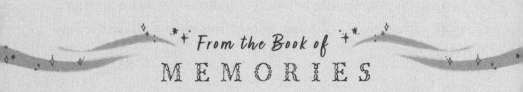

From the Book of
MEMORIES

SEVDA
CITY OF ORIGIN: MARMARIS

Listen.

This is a story about a careful construction of helplessness. Of futility

dressed in blue.

I? Merely am. But you? You are plural. You are in my hair, in my eyes. You are of tomorrow and you linger from yesterday. You remain while I become ephemeral.

You appear in front of me with your hands already dipped in blood and ask,

"How shall I break your heart today?"

And I, dressed in blue, stand up to die.

These are the wanderings of a mind prone to winter.

You see? I built this helplessness in three stages.

First: I let myself love you.

Then: I perfected the art of crying without tears.

And finally: I learned to like the space a broken heart occupies in a chest.

I.

Why can't we look into mirrors without flinching?

Why can't we look at our reflections without finding things that could be thinner, smoother, or prettier?

Why is meeting our own eyes in the mirror an exercise in despair?

Why are we never enough as we **are**?

II.

Here, have this with your cup of tea:

They come for you in the dark or in the light, but only when you are alone, isolated from anyone whom you can call an ally. Even though you want to yell when they take you, you are too frightened to make a sound. Because what if this is your fault? What if, somehow, you are the architect of your own misfortune? What if it was something you said or did? Or didn't say and didn't do? What if it is the clothes you are wearing or the smiles you gave them or didn't? You know what people will say.

It is too late when the pain becomes worse. Your lips already know the shape of silence. Your voice has shrunk to a gasp. You are left with a mouth full of screams and a silence that binds them within you. The screams you didn't scream echo in your mind and in your body. They remain long after the incident. They pollute your days. Take the luster from your sunshine. Until all you can hear are the screams you didn't scream. The rest of the world goes on, oblivious to the din in you.

The Reappearance of the Boy Made of Stars and the Plight of the Girl by the Oleander Lane.

The City of Byblos, now known as Jbeil, is about thirty-seven kilometers from Beirut. We cannot, of course, travel there in any other way except by the Between.

We exit the Between in the historic quarter of Jbeil. The City of Byblos is one of the oldest cities in the world and one of the only cities that has been continuously inhabited ever since she was built. If cities had voices, Jbeil would have one like good wine, with layers, notes, and depths granted to her by her age.

Perhaps it is due to her age that Byblos was declared a sanctuary city by the Magic Council. No middle worlders, no matter how severe their enmity to each other, are allowed to spill blood in Byblos. All conflicts may be peacefully resolved, but no conflicts are to be created here. We don't know what punishment is given to those who break this law, but the ones who govern the middle world aren't known for their grace. The city is as close to safe as the middle world can get.

It is afternoon and the cobbled streets of the historic quarters are filled with sunshine. We breathe deep of the air scented by flowers and spices as we slowly take in the beauty of the city. The old souk is not far from where we are.

But first, food.

We fuel up with shawarma, mezze, and a host of other local delicacies, the most memorable among them, baklava. Licking our fingers and feeling a rare peace with the world, we set out to walk through the streets of the old souk. The magic is strongest in the narrow alleys of the marketplace, so it's no stretch of the imagination to assume that the gathering Assi told us about will most likely be held there.

We pass through an oleander lane on the way. The oleander trees curve toward each other above us, forming a sort of tunnel filled with flowers and green. What can we say about the beauty with which the light fills the lane? Probably nothing the poets haven't already.

Jbeil is rich with stories. Every step we take has been taken by countless others, thick in the middle of their own tales. The history steeped into the stones of the streets gives the place a resonance that young cities do not have. When we emerge from the lane, the sky is streaked with the colors of a gentle dusk. Some early stars glint in the darkening sky. We stop walking to fully appreciate the spectacle of a world clad in the colors of both day and night. At that moment, a soft sniffling sounds, breaking our hard-found serenity.

A girl, about seventeen, is not quite hidden in the shadows of an oleander tree. Her face is damp with tears. The area is deserted of all other humans, but we're sure there are a few middle worlders here. A place this thick with magic would not be overlooked by them. We look to Paheli; do we listen to this girl's story or do we keep moving? The world is full of crying girls, and though we try, we cannot listen to all of them.

Paheli steps forward and at her signal, we shimmer into visibility. She clears her throat. The girl looks up, sees us, and opens her mouth as if her first instinct is to scream. We tend to evoke that reaction in people. In the end, she contains herself and looks at us with wide eyes as if not understanding how we came upon her so suddenly.

"Who are you?" she whispers in Arabic.

"That is not yet important," Paheli responds in kind. "Why are you crying?"

At the reminder, the girl's eyes fill with tears again. Angrily, she wipes them away. "What does it matter to you if I cry?"

"Why shouldn't it matter to us?" Ligaya demands hotly. "Wouldn't *you* ask someone who is crying why they are grieved?"

"Is it so odd that we might be moved to offer you aid?" Etsuko asks, raising an eyebrow.

"Why would you help me?" the girl spits out. "Even my family has no time for me. Why would strangers care?"

"Because we can," Paheli replies. "You are, of course, welcome to reject our help. If you do not wish us to intrude upon your pain, we will leave now." We turn to go.

"Wait!" the girl calls out. We knew she would. "Don't laugh, okay?" She tries to glare at us, but the tears in her eyes ruin the effect. "I have a dream. It's not a particularly impressive one, but it's mine." Her voice slips into a whisper. "I'm good at studying. My grades are excellent. I was at the top of the school the last exam, and my teachers say I will easily get into a top university in Beirut, but my father, he insists on sending my brother to university instead. My brother, who spends his time hanging out with his friends, playing pool instead of attending school. Him." She laughs bitterly. "We only have enough money for one of us to go, and it should obviously be me, but my father, he says that a girl is like spilled milk when married, so he sees no point in investing in me. And my mother, who should understand me best, says that if I win in this, I will start wanting other things. Why is it so wrong to want things? Why is it so wrong to win in things?" She looks at us. "Is it because I'm a girl?"

"What do you want to do?" Paheli asks instead, her question curling around the breeze in the air.

"What *can* I do?" the girl bursts out. "I live in this small place with no jobs I can do. If I don't go to school, I will be married off to some man who will think I am a replacement for his mother or his maid. I will have children and spend the rest of my life wishing for all the things I didn't do and didn't learn.

"I thought about running away, but where would I go?" the girl asks. "I do not want to bring shame to my parents. I love them. I just want to study more. Why is that too much to ask for?"

If you are a woman, any desire you have that is yours alone

is too much to ask for. Everything you do must benefit the family, the community, the country, or the world. You never simply belong to yourself.

"I don't know why I'm telling you this. It's not like you can help me." Her voice falters in the darkness.

Paheli takes out the pouch in which she keeps her money. She removes two bundles of cash from it and holds them out to the girl. "This should be enough for your tuition."

The girl gapes at Paheli's outstretched hand. "How can you just give this to me so easily?"

"Money is one thing we don't have to worry about. Take it," Paheli urges. "You might change your mind about school. We don't mind if you do. Consider this a gift."

"I . . . How do I trust you?" The girl makes no move to take the money.

"Look, if you don't want it, don't take it," Kamboja says impatiently. "We are not asking to move in with you or anything. We just want to help you in the only way we know how. We can only give you the money, not fight your parents for you."

"Also, we aren't asking you to trust us." Talei is gentler. "In fact, you will probably never see us again after today."

"I pay my debts," the girl says, taking the money. "I will repay this one too."

"What is your name?" Valentina asks.

The girl hesitates, then looks at us and says, "Sadia."

"Well, Sadia," Valentina says, "if you consider this money a debt, you can repay it by helping some other girl who needs it. Give her your faith, love, or money when she needs it. Like we have helped you, help her. When you do that, your debt will be repaid. Sound good?"

"I . . . thank you," Sadia says. The sound of the azaan breaks into the darkness, and the girl starts. "I have to go!" She turns to us, her face a canvas of questions, gratitude, and disbelief. "I don't know what will happen in the future, but I will never forget what you have done for me. I *will* pay the debt I owe. Thank you." She looks at us one last time and slips off into the darkness, gone as suddenly as she appeared.

We stand silently for a bit.

If all the troubles we seek to resolve were of the financial kind, our work would be so much easier. Still, it cannot hurt anyone if we consider this encounter a success.

A few minutes later, we walk farther up the path and enter the souk. Most of the human vendors have closed up for the night, though a few eateries remain open. Light spills out from open doors and lamps placed at intervals; the cobbled streets glisten softly. The power in the stones of this place takes our breath away. The Between pulses behind the walls; the barrier between it and the old souk is very thin.

As the evening deepens, magic asserts a stronger presence. The smell of it, like freshly cut grass, becomes prominent. Humans think they are alone in this souk, not realizing that the stranger who just passed them has skin the color of the sea at noon or the person they just smiled at is dressed in clothes made of cobwebs. Slowly, the souk empties of humans and fills with middle worlders. We stand, leaning against a wall under the shade of a tree heavy with purple blossoms, ready to bolt into the Between at the least provocation.

Opposite us is a human-shaped middle worlder whose skin is made of the silver scales of a fish. We do not intend to find out if he smells like one too. He keeps a marked, but fixed, distance from us. We, who have worn all shades of danger on our bodies, recognize his stare for what it is. He fancies himself a predator and thinks us prey. However, bound by the rules of this city, he can make no move on us.

A few minutes pass and the streets get busier with middle worlders.

We see Assi first, or perhaps she sees us. Paheli is practically thrumming with tension. Valentina and Talei stand protectively on either side of her. Assi, the creature with silver eyes, feathers instead of hair, and a mouth full of sharp teeth, moves toward us with a smile, perhaps of welcome, on her lips. Behind her is a motley group of middle worlders, each wearing their battle scars on their faces or their bodies. One of them has a gouged-out eye, the empty socket inviting both horror and sympathy. Another one has green thorns around her neck; she winces with each step.

"Follow me," Assi says. When we don't move, she looks back at us and her lips quirk. "We mean you no harm."

There's absolutely no reason to believe her, but we do anyway. She leads us to a small house with a walled garden. It seems empty of people; the windows are dark. The fierce middle worlders accompanying her don't speak, so we make no attempts at conversation either.

The night is soft and pliant. We fill the garden of the small house, leaning against the wall without care for the empty garden beds beneath our heels. We keep a distance from the group of middle worlders, not an unfriendly distance but one marked by caution.

They, in turn, seem more at ease once the gates between the house and the streets outside are closed. As we watch, they shift away from each other. It is then that we see the boy they were hiding in the middle. He has dark skin through which pinpricks of light peek out. Each of his eyes has a five-pointed star gleaming in its dark depths. His face is beautiful, and his attention is trained solely on us.

We look at Paheli and find her with a shuttered face. No light sparkles in *her* eyes. She has retreated somewhere deep inside.

Paheli: An Interlude in Blue

What do you do when your past pops up into your present to say hello? If you are me, you pretend you don't see him for at least three whole minutes. A lot can happen in three minutes. Lives can get ruined. People can disappear. What was right can become wrong. When it becomes clear that none of these (especially the second) things is going to happen, I change my strategy. I try to blend in with the scenery. What is one more girl in a madness of girls? Right?

It is not my night.

The boy's eyes calmly assess all of us. When it is my turn, he looks as if he is peering through my skin and bones right into that dark place where I hide all the things I don't want to remember. The stars in his eyes brighten. He recognizes me as that broken creature he offered an escape to so many years ago. How, I don't know. I don't exactly resemble her anymore. She is gone now, that broken girl.

I am lying.

She is still here. Slumbering in the depths of me. Pro tip: You don't ever get rid of your broken pieces. You just bury them as deeply as you can.

The boy and I stare at each other for a long moment. He is beautiful, so looking at him is no hardship. I notice that he has scars on one side of his face. I have scars too, though mine are all in places not visible to the eye. He is taller than I remember. Slender but solid. He moves with a fluidity that is kin to flowing water.

"I saved myself," I tell him in lieu of a greeting. I might as well get it over with now. I don't want any man taking the credit for my fight, for my life. He just opened a door for me; I stepped through that door all by myself. Actually, he didn't even open that door. He just gave me a key.

The boy's lips quirk and oh my goodness, he is dazzling. There is something broken about his smile, though. Like his lips aren't quite at ease with what they're doing. I know the feeling.

"I am glad you did," he says. His voice has a bit of the night in it.

"What's your name?" I can't keep calling him "boy." That's rude. I'm a very polite young-old woman.

"Taraana," he replies softly, as if he's telling me a secret. Oh no, I am going to swoon. Wait, no, I am calm. He comes to stand beside Assi, who looks very much like his bodyguard. I bet she makes a good one with those sharp teeth of hers. Actually, all the middle worlders accompanying Assi and Taraana look like they could hold their own in a fight. One that doesn't include screams. We could totally beat them.

"My name is Paheli," I say brightly, keeping a smile on my face. "Starting from the right are: Widad, Daraja, Kamboja, Areum, Talei, Valentina, Etsuko, Sevda, Ghufran, and Ligaya. Collectively, we are known as the Wild Ones. . . ." He listens with rapt attention. It's embarrassing. I clear my throat. "Thank you for the stars. You gave a chance to escape not just to me but to all my sisters. We owe you something. Ice cream?"

Something like wonder slips into the boy's—sorry, Taraana's—face as he looks at all of us once again and stays for a second before fading. He doesn't seem to know how to respond to my gratitude. For some reason, this makes me like him more. But that's not important at this moment. I narrow my eyes. What if the reason he called us here is because he wants his stars back?

"Why did you want to meet us? Why now? You could have reached out to us, to me, at any time in the past, but you didn't. Why?" Perhaps my questions seem too aggressive, because Assi and her companions bristle. My sisters gather closer to me, and I wonder if I'm going to be handling blood. I hope not. I am wearing one of my favorite dresses.

Taraana places a hand on Assi's shoulder and the woman glows. Whoa. I wonder what their relationship is. Or maybe the boy makes everyone he touches glow. He seems like he would.

"I will tell you, but . . ." He pauses, so I seize the chance.

"But not here," I say. I look around the dark garden, bare of any flowers. The dark house promises ghosts, and I'm not in the mood to entertain hauntings. I want to talk to this boy but not in this place.

"It is not safe to talk elsewhere," Assi says before the boy, Taraana, has a chance to respond.

"Why?" Valentina asks.

"That . . . ," the boy says, looking at Assi, hesitating.

"What if I promise that we'll keep him safe?" I say, and my sisters look at me as if I've just announced that I'm giving up desserts.

"How can we take your word for it? Do you think you're strong enough to resist the monsters chasing him? Chasing us?" the middle worlder woman with green thorns sticking out of her neck says.

"Do you want a demonstration of our powers?" Our hotheaded Ligaya takes umbrage at the woman's words.

"Fine, if you're not willing, we'll leave," I say, and nod at Areum, who lays her open palm on the garden wall.

"Wait," Taraana says, and we all look at him. He tugs at his collar and lowers his head. "I'll go with you."

"No, you won't." Assi immediately overrides him.

"Yes, I will, Assi. I need to do this." His voice is firm, and the feather-haired woman's lips flatten.

She looks at me, and her gaze promises to tear me into thin strips before she roasts me. Her gaze is very eloquent. "Keep him safe and bring him back."

I look at the boy and raise both my eyebrows. He doesn't seem to find her domineering. Huh. I wouldn't like her attitude if I were him, but I'm not and I never will be. I just need to know what he has to say, and then I can return him to her and continue on my way. No big deal.

The boy walks over to me. He looks so lost that he reminds me of my girls. I grab his hand, intending to comfort. It's an unconscious action and I mean to let go after I squeeze it, but he latches on. Great job, Paheli. He's going to become a duckling and follow me around.

"Okay, let's go. We'll bring him to you once our conversation is done," I tell the glowering Assi, and ignore the other middle worlders.

Areum places her right palm on the wall we were leaning against, and a second later, the lines of a rectangular door dissect the wall. She opens it and we follow her into the Between.

Besieged in the Between

We breathe easier in the Between. We are safer here than anywhere else in any of the worlds.

Widad suddenly hisses. "Look at the boy!"

As we turn to him, the golden light of the Between flickers and the hum of it grows louder, *warmer*. Taraana is enveloped in this golden light; it enters his skin and seems to flow through it so he looks like he's going supernova.

Taraana looks back at us, the stars in his eyes so bright that we wonder if they will spill over. His face has a pained expression, which strangely enough is reflected on Paheli's face. Then we see that he is squeezing her hand tight.

"Oi." Paheli pulls her hand out of his grasp. "Are you having a moment?"

Daraja gives Paheli a look and asks Taraana kindly, "Are you okay? Is this the way the Between always reacts to you?"

He nods jerkily. "It sort of feels as if someone has called you on the phone, and though you can hear their voice, you can't understand a word they are saying, even though they are speaking your native language."

"We cannot stay here," Valentina says, ignoring the other two. "That fish-scaled middle worlder concerns me. It felt like their motive was more than casual observation."

"Where do we go?" Talei turns to Paheli.

Before Paheli can speak, however, a voice we haven't heard in a long while says, "I'd like to go to Jiufen." It is our Ghufran. Her voice is a wisp.

"Then we'll go to Jiufen," Paheli replies. "Let's move."

Taraana doesn't seem to have much of an opinion on our destination. Even if he does, he keeps it to himself. He looks like he is ill at ease in the Between; his shoulders are drawn together as if he is suffering some kind of pain. Paheli, in a rare act of mercy, allows him to hold her hand again.

Sometimes the Between splits off into different passages leading to different places in the world. While the distance we walk is not comparable to the distance the cities are from each other in the physical world, there is a relative distance between a door leading to Jbeil compared to a door leading to Jiufen. The magic directs us to the door we want to go to. Sort of like a GPS system without the annoying voice.

We have been walking for an hour when the doors around us all open at the same time. First comes the odor of two-day-old fish going bad in the sun, and then we see the creatures to whom this reek belongs. At first glance, these middle worlders are identical to the fish-scaled man we saw in the old souk in Jbeil, but an unavoidably closer look pronounces the marked difference between them. The middle worlders surrounding us have fish eyes and no noses, just gills in their necks. Their bodies *are* scaled, but not silver. The scales are a dirty gray, and covered by a thick mucuslike substance.

They surround us, and we in turn surround Taraana, making a wall between him and these middle worlders.

"What do you want from us?" Paheli asks one of the scaled men. His fish lips open and close, but he doesn't say a word. Well, okay.

A minute into the siege, we hear footsteps. The fishy middle worlders on the right move apart, and we see a human-shaped middle worlder standing at a distance from us. Even with the space between us, we can feel the contempt he has for us. He is tall with broad shoulders and hair liberally sprinkled with gray. His cheeks are heavily scarred, so the beard on his face is uneven and patched. He is wearing a plain black shalwar kameez. Sooty eyelashes ring eyes that are unlike any others we have seen before. Even Taraana's starry eyes are overshadowed by the strangeness of this middle worlder's eyes. You see, a river flows in this man's eyes.

That doesn't make sense, does it? But that's exactly what his eyes feel like. Everyone else's eyes are still pools, but this man's eyes move like the surface of a river. The malice in his inhuman eyes is practically a scream in the still air. The voices in the Between fade a little, as if the corridor, too, is paying attention.

This, then, is our as-yet-unnamed villain. He looks through

us at Taraana, who stumbles as if reacting to the man's gaze.

The man smiles. It is not a pretty sight. "It has a been a while, boy. Have you enjoyed playing outside?"

His voice is gravelly, and we all never want to hear it again. Alas, we aren't going to be that lucky. We look at Taraana and find him frozen, as if his ability to talk has suddenly disappeared.

"What, have nothing to say to me? I'm hurt." The man smiles again, enjoying Taraana's distress. We bristle, but it is as if we are invisible to the middle worlder.

"Bring them all to the Bhool Bhulaiyaa," he says to the scaled middle worlders, and turns to go.

"This is the Between." Paheli speaks before anyone can make a move. "You should leave us alone." Her voice is the quiet before a storm.

"Or what? You think you have enough magic to oppose *me*?" The man scoffs. Without another word, he lifts a hand and sends a force, composed of magic, our way. However, we are made of the same stuff as the Between, and the Between is made of magic. Magic won't harm itself. Space shrinks around the man, and the magic force he exerted returns to him, boxing him into a small sphere without any air in it. He gasps for breath.

Seeing his situation, the scaled middle worlders move toward us. In response, we scream. When we scream, the Between shudders. Our screams melt into each other, so sharp and piercing, they become a weapon. The scaled middle worlders collapse and turn into liquid while the man, with his hands over his ears, opens the nearest door and escapes through it.

Tea, the City of Stairs, and the Story of a Boy

Jiufen is a small mining town not far from Taipei. We follow Kamboja out of the Between into a narrow alley that leads to the stairs that Jiufen is mainly composed of. The sun is nowhere to be seen, but a glance at a clock reveals the time to be a little after ten in the morning. A light rain is falling—not that this deters any of the tourists that fill the old streets of the town.

We walk up many flights of stairs, through twisted alleys, stopping every so often to sample some snacks from the many food vendors (the barbecued mushrooms are delicious), until we finally arrive at a long, dark tunnel. Taraana looks apprehensive, but we sail through it, determined not to give in to the fear stalking our heels. It is not every day that our travels are interrupted by murderous middle worlders, after all. On the other side of the tunnel is a multileveled teahouse that belongs solely to the middle world and is patronized only by beings of the magical variety. This teahouse sits on one of the peaks of Jiufen and boasts views not possible at any other place in the vicinity.

We have been frequenting this teahouse for decades now; the owner, a not-human woman we call Ah Mei, is a friendly sort as long as you don't ask her any questions. The teahouse is deserted at this time of the day, so Ah Mei seats us at a coveted spot on the balcony facing the bay. She gives Taraana a once-over, looking at his starry eyes a bit longer than we are comfortable with. But she doesn't say or do anything else and leaves us to deliberate over the menu.

The view of the sea and the little islands dotting the horizon is obscured today, but the rain provides an atmosphere more conducive to the conversation we are about to have. All of us are reeling from our experience with the man in the Between; Ghufran is shaking, so Daraja and Sevda sit on either side of her, giving her comfort and security with their proximity.

Taraana draws away from Paheli for the first time since we met him and sits a small distance from the rest of us. He lifts his trembling fingers to touch his face and takes a deep breath before raising his head. We meet his gaze without speaking. Before we talk, we order, and a little later our tea, accompanied by small plates of mochi, sesame crackers, and green tea cakes, is served. We sip the fragrant beverage from ceramic cups and wait. What we know, but the boy made of stars probably doesn't, is that the tea served here makes conversations flow easier. He looks like he needs all the help he can get.

Taraana clears his throat and takes a sip of the tea. The lights in his eyes are dim. He has this habit of folding in on himself when he wants to deflect attention. When we made our way through the long winding streets, strung with large red lamps and full of humans, he walked as if he were made of air. *We* walk as if the roads and the paths we take should be glad we chose them. Then again, we had to learn not to apologize for the space we occupy in the world.

Taraana clears his throat again; his cheeks are flushed. "Earlier," he says, "I could have taken care of myself. I . . ." His voice wobbles.

"Being afraid is not a weakness, Taraana." Paheli wraps her hands around her cup of tea. "In our world, feeling fear is being intelligent because fear keeps you sharp. Fear keeps you ready." She pauses and looks at him. "Fear keeps you alive."

Taraana bows his head and shuts his eyes as if letting her words soak into him. Then he looks up and we glimpse the smile on his face. It devastates us, not only because it is beautiful but also because it is made of so many broken things.

"Before I tell you my story, let me ask you what you know about the particularities of the middle world," he says.

Valentina looks askance at him. "You mean how the not-human men and women are organized in the middle world?"

He nods. Valentina glances at Paheli.

"Aren't they divided into clans according to the element from which they harvest magic?" Talei asks suddenly. "Eulalie has some books about the middle world in the house library. I read that each clan has a keeper who has the power to harvest magic from a specific element or a natural metal or stone like copper or gold. These keepers have the responsibility of distributing the magic they harvest to all their clan members. The book said there are keepers of land, sea, air, metal, river, and whatnot."

"The mark of their office is in their eyes," Ligaya adds, and we stare at her. "What? I read too, you know!" Yes, if forced. But we are nice and say nothing.

"So that man in the Between . . ." Etsuko raises an eyebrow at Taraana.

"His name . . ." Taraana stops and swallows. It doesn't seem to help, so he gulps down some tea and tries again. "His name is Baarish. He is the Keeper of the Rivers and Lakes in Uttar Pradesh. He is also known as the Dar."

"Ah!" Widad blinks. Her curls are out of control in this weather. "Dar from the Urdu word 'daria'?" When we look at her, she explains. "'Daria' means river in Urdu and Hindi."

"Yeah." Taraana nods. "Being the Dar means being the head of a clan that functions primarily on magic harvested from rivers and lakes."

"So why does this Dar, this Baarish, want to capture you?" Paheli asks.

"To tell you that, I need to tell you the story of a boy. Will you listen?" he asks. We lean closer and do.

Taraana was born to human parents in a small village in India. They knew nothing about the middle world that existed around them. They had no idea their child was made of magic and had a fate beyond what they imagined possible. Taraana grew up in abject poverty, surrounded by hungry siblings and helpless parents until he was about six years old. His life took a turn for the worse shortly after his sixth birthday.

"There was a lake near my village," Taraana continues. "I used to spend hours on its shore, playing. People left me alone there, you see. That day, I remember it was raining, and my parents told us to stay home while they went out to beg from house to house with my youngest brother. It was stifling at home; we lived in a one-room shack that leaked and had no windows. My brothers played rough, and I was often on the wrong side in fights. So, I ran away to the lake. I didn't mind the rain.

"I stayed by the lake for hours. I hunted for sticks, ate some berries, and found shelter under a peepul tree. I fell asleep there. I don't know how much time passed before some voices woke me up. When I walked back to the lakeshore, I found"—he stops again and squeezes his eyes shut for a brief moment—"two men standing there. One of them was the man you saw earlier."

"What did he do to you?" Ghufran asks, and we are surprised by her voice all over again.

"You see the stars in my eyes?" We nod. "Apparently the presence of the stars marks me as the Keeper of the Between. . . ." He scoffs.

"Is that why the Between was flooding you with light?" Paheli asks.

"I don't know. I don't know what a Keeper of the Between does or is. All these stars have given me is grief," Taraana spits out. "I hate the Between."

We exchange shocked glances. The place is like home to us.

"But why did Baarish want you? Or rather, why does he still want you?" Etsuko asks. When she sees Taraana flinch at the question, she grimaces and mutters, "Sorry."

He shrugs away her apology and continues with the story we derailed him from. Baarish recognized Taraana by the stars in his eyes, something usually only visible to middle worlders, and bought him from his parents, who were only too happy to exchange one of their children for monetary compensation.

"Because I was human, my rights as an individual, as a living, breathing person, didn't . . . don't matter to the middle worlders. What happened with Baarish . . . Forgive me, I still can't speak about it," he whispers. "Those stars you wear in your palms? They are my tears. When I am in more pain than I can endure, I shed a tear that is the purest form of magic that can exist. They're the reason Baarish wanted me. Wants me. If consumed, one tear can fuel a middle worlder clan for years. Baarish intended . . . *intends* to use me to harvest as many tears as he can before my body breaks and I die."

The tea turns cold in the cups. None of us speak. None of us are able to.

Taraana tells us that the chance to escape came once. A little girl, a granddaughter of Baarish's, felt sorry for him, so she set him free when the Dar wasn't around. Taraana took the box of tears and ran.

"I didn't think I would get away with it, but how could I not try?" That was the day he met Paheli. He tossed her the box right before he was recaptured because he was damned if he would let Baarish use the tears.

"Why didn't you just escape into the Between?" Etsuko asks.

"I didn't know what the Between was then. I was completely unschooled in the ways of the middle world. I had seen doors to the Between, but I was never brave enough to open one and walk through," Taraana confesses.

"Not even once?" Valentina looks disbelieving.

He shakes his head. "I had learned that what seemed like it could hurt me, usually did."

We are silent for a while after this.

"Baarish took advantage of the fact that no one knew of my existence. He kept me in a cage for a decade. The girl who helped me escape once did so again when the coup happened—a month after I was recaptured—and Baarish's enemies came into power and imprisoned him. This time she led me to a wall, guided me into opening a door to the Between, and all but pushed me in. My time stopped from then on. Just like you, I'm stuck at the age I was when I first entered the Between.

"I have spent a lot of time hiding. Learning about the middle world. Trying to figure out what I'm supposed to be. All I can find out about the Keepers of the Between is that they always begin as human beings, and I suppose that's why they're considered expendable. No matter how much I searched, I couldn't find any other records of them." Taraana leans back, looking as if the telling of his tale has exhausted him.

"Why haven't we seen you before? Why haven't you contacted us before?" Paheli demands. "I always wondered who you were! I looked for you everywhere!"

Taraana flushes. "I spent most of my time hiding in towns and cities with thin magic, hoping to remain out of notice of middle worlders who would try to exploit me if they knew who I was. I knew you"—he gestures to us all—"existed. Every time someone wears my stars, I can hear echoes of their hearts. But being with me would have meant being in danger. In fact, I am risking you right now." He ducks his head apologetically.

"So, the reason you have approached us now?" Valentina prompts.

The light leaves Taraana's face, and an end tries to write itself in the depths of his eyes. "Baarish will pursue me until he captures me. Once he does, he will torture me. This time around, I won't submit to the pain. I refuse. This time around, I will end myself rather than go through that pain, that humiliation, again. I don't know what the consequences of my death will be. I don't know if the tears you wear will be affected."

So Baarish dreams himself the architect of our end?

Paheli snorts. "As if we are going to allow him or you to do anything of the sort."

"No one can stop him. No one ever wants to," Taraana says, his words soft enough to be mistaken for the sound of the raindrops falling on the wooden railings of the balcony.

"We have had enough of being victims," Kamboja spits out.

"What can you do?" Taraana asks. "Unless I stay in the Between and never venture out, he will capture me. Even if I stay in the Between, he will find a way to take me. He has resources that I don't. His family and his allies are more than I will ever be able to claim."

"We are your family now. We are your allies, and we will be

your resources. You helped me when you didn't need to. You helped all of us. Your fight is our fight." Paheli drains her cup and looks at Taraana. "We haven't had enough of living yet. We are not willing to give up. Are you?"

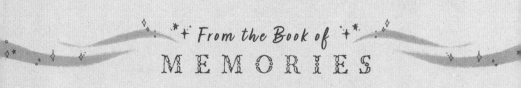

From the Book of
MEMORIES

GHUFRAN
CITY OF ORIGIN: BAGHDAD

The inimitable truth of loss creeps up on her like the sun rising in the morning—only without the light. She is made up of yellow ribbons dipped in blood and memories of fear and filth. When the sunlight brushes the leaves of the date trees, she stands at doors listening for her own footsteps and wonders if there is a curve in time where she can meet herself. Escape from her thoughts is impossible except on Fridays when the muezzin calls the world to prayer and she finds peace, briefly, from the blue in the sky. But the afternoon nearly always finds her weeping behind the curtains of her sister's house.

She has poetry, a dirge or two, scribbled in henna black on her sand-scarred arms. Her palms are full of lines that talk of lives shorter than the last film someone smuggled in across the border. Her kisses, and she is stingy with those, taste like goodbye and her eyes are continually searching the crowd for faces she knows she will never see again. She hides her hair and her body in voluminous material the color of a shroud. Her toes curl bashfully in the sand, remembering the ground her feet will never walk on again. Mismatched bangles clang on her hands and her lips shape questions that will never be answered.

She has the scent of the desert, the madness of the desert, and the sorrow of it. She has screams in her mouth and blood on her hands. She is what they removed to find space for the liberty they gifted, this woman.

Heartbreak, Stone Buildings, and Tandoori

We accompany Taraana back to Jbeil and leave him safe with Assi before, with a pause in between to gather our spirits, we walk toward the next door, our next destination. After some discussion, we decided that if we are going to fight Baarish, we need more information about him. As such, we are going to go to the city in which he lives to do some reconnaissance.

Paheli opens the door to Agra without much thought, but the Between must be hiccuping, because the city on the other side of the door is definitely not Agra. For one thing, it's snowing in this city. She closes the door and then turns to us, her eyes confused.

"Try again," Valentina commands. Paheli silently obeys, and this time the door opens to the city it is supposed to.

We pile out of the Between and out into a courtyard in front of the Taj Mahal. After spending a few minutes staring at the monument, we leave quickly and enter the city proper. Agra, built on the banks of the Yamuna River, is eminently suitable to be the location of the residence of the Keeper of the Rivers and Lakes in Uttar Pradesh.

We become visible to humans and make our way to Kinari Bazaar to exchange money. It is a shrill Saturday morning, and the sun is entirely without mercy. The market is bustling with people and purpose, colors and smells. Vendors hawk their goods in raucous voices. People haggle over each cent they unwillingly spend. In a corner of the market, right beside a vendor selling fragrant bunches of gajra, is a very old woman sitting in the middle of countless corked bottles. At first glance, the bottles seem empty, but a closer look reveals a smoky substance inside. Nobody stops at her stall; nobody even seems to realize she is there.

We linger in front of her cart and wait for her attention. At first, she seems disinclined to give it to us, so Paheli takes out a Between diamond and holds it up to catch a spark of the sun. The old woman's eyes flicker, a reptilian blink, and one side of her mouth creeps up in a ghastly facsimile of a smile.

"Well, well, well," she says. All right, she speaks in Hindi, so she doesn't say exactly that, but bear with us. Some things are lost in translation. While not all of us know Hindi, Taraana's tears in our palms let us communicate in all the existing languages in the world. It's a perk we enjoy. The woman licks her lips. "What have we here?"

Paheli steps up. "We would like to exchange some Between

diamonds for local currency," she says carefully. She's wearing a festive blue dress, and thanks to Kamboja, her light pink hair is arranged in complex braids.

"Let's see what you have." The old woman leans nearer. An unpleasant odor wafts toward us. Something dark and decaying. We stand our ground. Paheli takes out five Between diamonds. The woman's eyes widen and her smile grows, crawling up her cheeks. She licks her lips again with a black tongue and names her price.

Paheli stares at her for a very long moment before returning the diamonds to the pouch they came in. "We will try our luck with the human merchants."

We turn to go.

"Wait!" the woman says, half-rising from the rickety stool she is sitting on. The decaying smell grows stronger. "I will give you more."

We don't react.

"I will give you the going rate," the woman says, and this time we stop, turn around, and do business.

Afterward, Paheli gestures to the corked bottles with her chin. "What do you sell here?"

A sly look brightens the woman's eyes this time. "Heartbreak. All different kinds. To give to your rival or take yourself. Can I interest you in one?"

"No, thank you," Widad says before we drag Paheli away just in case she becomes curious.

Three rickshaw rides—with two stops for mithai and one for pani puri—later, we arrive at the posh hotel we plan to stay in.

The hotel employees are anxious when they realize their much-lauded luxury and Koh-i-noor suites are going to belong to us for the next few days, though their unease melts into pleasure when we tip them lavishly.

We settle into rooms that are richly and tastefully decorated in pleasantly contrasting, vibrant shades. Paheli and Valentina share the Koh-i-noor suite, claiming seniority among the Wild Ones, and we gather into its large living room after freshening up in bathrooms with walls the color of the Mediterranean Sea. The doors leading to the balcony in the living room are open, and we can see the domes of the Taj Mahal gleaming in the distance. We arrange ourselves on the chaise, on the chairs, and on the rug in the middle of the room.

Valentina walks out of the bathroom, wearing a towel as a turban. She stares at Paheli, who is eating a mysteriously sourced mango with glee. "We need to talk."

"Room service," she replies to our unasked question. She glances at Valentina. "Aren't we talking now?"

"I mean about Taraana," Valentina says, sitting next to Sevda on a settee.

Paheli finishes eating the mango, washes her hands in the mini kitchen, and returns to the living room. She sits on the floor beside Talei. She, too, has showered and is wearing a shapeless yellow lounging dress with large red flowers embroidered on it. With her light pink hair, blue eyes, and dark skin, she looks very much like an exploded rainbow. We don't tell her this, of course.

"Do any of you disagree with my decision to adopt Taraana?" she asks, looking around at each of us. All of us feel a thrill of recognition when her eyes rest on us. "Please feel free to tell me frankly."

"I don't disagree. . . . It's just that I'm scared," Sevda finally says. Widad, Daraja, Talei, and Kamboja don't speak, but the fear on their faces needs no words.

"We are not helping him. We are helping ourselves," Ligaya says, lacing her fingers together. "If he dies, won't we, too? How can I disagree with that?"

"Right? Besides, we owe him," Etsuko adds. "This Baarish has a lot more power compared to us, but the magic he is so proud of doesn't work on us. Doesn't that give us an advantage?"

"I'm scared too, Sevda. There's nothing wrong with being scared," Areum says, the bracelets on her wrists noisily chiming. "It's just that fear cannot be the language in which we make our decisions."

Paheli raises an eyebrow at Valentina. "And you?"

"We're already here." Valentina rolls her eyes. "Besides, I am always ready for a fight."

"Ghufran?" Paheli asks very gently.

"I am tired of being afraid," she replies, rearranging the veil she always has on her head.

"All right. If, at any time in the following days, you feel like you can no longer participate in this battle, if that's what it is, please leave. You can stay with Eulalie in New Orleans until things calm down. I don't know what the future holds, but you have my word that I won't begrudge you your need for safety. It is *never* a bad thing to put yourself first." Paheli looks around the room. "Is that good?"

We all nod.

"Okay! Tomorrow, we are going to go around the city to find out more about Baarish from the middle worlders here," Paheli says.

"How are we going to gather information when asking questions here is like painting targets on ourselves?" Talei asks.

"We don't ask questions," Valentina replies. "We guide conversations."

"What exactly are we looking for?" Sevda asks. She has a frown on her fair face. "Can't we ask someone else to gather information on him without putting ourselves at risk?"

"We could . . . ," Paheli says slowly. "But what would be the fun in that? I'm joking, don't pinch me, Talei!" She stops and glares at Talei. "We know that Baarish is scum. We are just going to see how much of a scumbag he is. Does his scumminess extend to other people, or is it exclusively reserved for Taraana? How does he treat the other people in his clan? What about his family? What's their relationship to Baarish? How do they treat people? We're looking for Baarish's unofficial profile, the one that wouldn't appear on the website of Keepers of the Middle World."

"Why do we need to know about the way he treats his family or how his family treats others?" Daraja asks.

"Well, if we can remove Baarish from power, someone else will have to step up. If we know what his family dynamics are, we may be able to guide someone who doesn't want to kill Taraana to fill Baarish's position. It seems prudent for us to see what kind of people his family are, as well," Paheli says.

"Isn't this going to be dangerous?" Sevda asks. She's sitting on the edge of her seat, looking ill at ease.

"If you don't feel up to it, you can stay behind tomorrow," Valentina reminds her.

"No, I was just asking," Sevda says, a blush staining her cheeks.

The conversation falters for a bit, and we turn our attention to the Taj Mahal gleaming in the distance.

"It's so beautiful," Widad says, sighing. "People call it the greatest testament to love."

"People need to remember it's a tomb." Kamboja sneers. "A *tomb*, in case you didn't hear me the first time."

"How did the empress die?" Areum asks. "Don't look at me like that, Talei. The lives of dead royalty are hardly the most important parts of the history I need to know."

"She died giving birth to her fourteenth child," Daraja answers her.

Fourteen children. That poor woman.

"He should have loved her a little less so she could have lived a little more," Etsuko muses out loud.

"What is love, do you think?" Areum asks.

"Mangoes. Unlimited mangoes," Paheli promptly replies.

Valentina rolls her eyes. "Love is peril."

Paheli nods. "And mangoes."

"I miss going out on dates," Sevda says softly. "And meadows filled with flowers."

"I can ask Eulalie to magic us a meadow," Paheli offers.

Sevda shakes her head. "It's okay."

"You know what I miss?" Ligaya asks, leaning against a chair.

She doesn't give us a chance to answer. "Periods."

We stare at her.

"Periods?" Areum chokes.

"Periods." Ligaya nods.

"Kick her out of here," Kamboja says, standing up. "Take her star!"

Areum pounces on Ligaya, tickling her, and the rest of us join in, until Ligaya is screaming for mercy. Our periods stop as soon as the stars embed in our palms. Time stops for us biologically, so periods, too, become a memory.

Does the absence of periods make a question of our femininity?

Observations, Conversations, and Hot Parantha

After the tandoori is devoured and Ligaya is tickled, we engage in a dance-off to the beats of Bollywood music. None of us claim to be Madhuri Dixit, but Paheli is particularly lethal on the dance floor. She has two left feet, and anyone dancing near her will be tripped. We go to sleep late and wake long before the roosters and spend some time battling private demons. Later, the hotel provides us with a far grander breakfast than it should be able to in the wee hours of the morning. We spare a thought, and some money, for those whose fate writes them into hot kitchens for far less than they deserve.

In this moment, a capricious energy connects all eleven of us. We cannot stay still, so we don't. We spill out of each other's rooms, sprawl over sofas and chairs, sing, and whisper to each other or ourselves. Now that we have an immediate purpose, we are more alive and more clearly present in each moment. We suddenly have meaning. We, who were abandoned by those who meant the most to us, suddenly are important to someone. It is a heady feeling that occurs less in words and more in the feeling of looking into someone's eyes and knowing you are being seen.

We leave the hotel just as the first rays of the sun hit the Taj Mahal's domes and turn them incandescent. The city still has patches of darkness. The murmur of people on their way to act out the daily struggle of making a living is gaining momentum. We pause in front of a chai wallah and purchase eleven cups of hot masala chai from him. Looking around as we sip our tea, we see many middle worlders in this sea of humans. Most of them are physically identical to humans, but there are some who aren't, who present themselves in the human world anyway, relying on the human brain to not comprehend their not-human features. For example, a middle worlder with the body of a human but with the yellow legs of a bird is standing right next to us. He is talking merrily about his wife to the chai wallah, who notices nothing different about him.

Another middle worlder in a purple sari that is a touch brighter than her equally purple skin walks coolly down the opposite street, turning heads but not for the reason you'd think.

We are visible to humans today, and as long as we don't give it away, middle worlders cannot tell that we aren't human either. So we pretend that we don't notice the middle worlders who express themselves more fantastically than others. This is an added layer of protection we have carefully cultivated.

The city is waking up to a new day. We pause a minute, appreciate the heat already pronounced in the air, and then plunge into the chaos. The middle worlders whom we think safe are the ones we follow. Initially, they think us human and ignore us, but when we insist on talking to them, they realize we see them for what they are. Some of them question us, curious about who we are and what we're doing in Agra. We give them nonanswers or elaborate lies.

We ask our own questions, like where to find the most delicious sabzi, which shops to go to, and, most importantly, who to be careful of in this city. We listen to what they say and we hear what they don't.

Many middle worlders congregate in places thick with magic, and so we travel by rickshaw to monuments that serve as homages to human brilliance; we go to the Red Fort and spend a few hours walking around the Sheesh Mahal, wandering through the Anguri Bagh, and drinking in the hallowed splendor of Nagina Masjid. We find pockets of middle worlders, and all of them have something to say about Baarish. We do not even need to direct these conversations. These places we mention, though just words on a page to you, are steeped in history and memory. How can we hope to convey even a tiny bit of that to you? Due to the many lives lived and lost in these places, the magic is potent here, like deep wine. Those of the middle world who linger here are full to the point of spilling over from the power in these places. They speak far more easily than middle worlders hungry for magic would.

In a dim, crowded restaurant, over a silver thali containing little bowls of sambar, tamarind chutney, sabzi, and potato-stuffed parantha, we listen to a not-human girl tell us about Baarish's grandsons (he has more than five) and her escape from them. It is not a pretty story, and she doesn't dress it up as such. She shows us her scars.

On our way to yet another place with deep magical wells, we see a little human girl holding a broom in the doorway of a shop, staring at a bunch of giggling schoolchildren with such naked longing on her face that we pause, unsure how to respond. In the next moment, a woman comes and drags her inside by the ear.

In the late afternoon, we pass a market and we see a young woman holding plastic bags filled with groceries in one hand and a little baby in the other. Two little ones hang on to the pallu of her sari. She walks behind a man who swings his empty hands while walking, whistling as he ogles the women he passes.

When the sun fades into red streaks in the sky, we return to the hotel.

Paheli: The Spies Who Came In from the Between

Sometimes, when I am walking along a street in a city somewhere, and the skies are the blue of a bruise three days after the hurt was first received, I feel a twinge of homesickness for a place that never existed. When I see people returning home at the end of the day, I, too, wish I had a place to return to. A forever home.

When we return to the hotel after our day of reconnaissance, which yielded far more fruit than I thought it would, it is already early evening. Tired, we call for room service after we finish our ablutions and gather in the living room of the Koh-i-noor suite. The doors to the balcony are open, inviting the warm attention of the night outside. The heat is kept at bay by the air conditioner.

The best thing about being in Agra right now is the abundance of mangoes. They are peeled and diced and, most importantly, they are sweet.

"Are we going to go meet Taraana tomorrow?" Areum asks with a kulfi in each hand. Ooh, the kulfi looks good too.

"No," I reply, my attention still on the kulfi. I know Valentina's looking at me. I can feel her gaze boring a hole through me from across the room. "We found out a lot about Baarish, but I feel like there's still something more we can find out."

"She was watching a spy movie in Beirut," Widad whispers loudly to Kamboja. "She had *that* look in her eyes." I ignore them.

"Baarish has an estate in Khandari, which is not too far from here actually. I'm going to go undercover as a housemaid," I tell them.

"Do you fancy yourself Mata Hari?" Ligaya asks, sitting up. Her short hair is sticking out in all directions, making her look like a bristling chick.

"Of course not!" I am offended. "*She* got caught!"

"What happens if you do?" Valentina demands.

"First, magic is useless against us, and no one can rip the stars from our palms. I won't remove them willingly, so magic will remain useless against me. Second, like you all, I can scream. Oh, I can also use the invisibility to work for me," I say.

"We are vulnerable to violence, Paheli," Valentina reminds me. Ah. Yes. So we are. But I am willing to take the risk and say as much.

"I will go with you," Widad says suddenly. She squares her shoulders when we look at her. "It's much better than letting

Paheli go by herself," she says with a sweet dignity that hurts my heart. I don't know why my sisters think I'm so unreliable, but their nagging is how they express their affection, so I let it go.

The next day, very early in the morning, Widad and I take a rickshaw to Khandari, one of the more affluent neighborhoods in Agra. We get off a little way before we reach Baarish's mansion. All the houses in this neighborhood are sprawling havelis, each of them a little more palatial than the last. We peek through the guarded gates for glimpses of them.

Humans, to whom we are currently invisible, work at these havelis, maintaining the gardens and cleaning the insides. The middle worlders living here walk among the so-called elite in the human society, pretending to be just like them, defined by the amount of money and assets they have. A person's worth in this society is calculated by how much they have and not who they are inside.

These middle worlders, just like their human counterparts, export chefs from expensive culinary schools, have foreign cars chauffeured by soft-spoken and well-educated drivers; they wear clothes specially designed for their bodies. The rest of the world may be struggling to make ends meet, but these 1 percent show their worth by the amount of food they discard daily.

· There is beauty in this world, of course there is, if you have time to see it and the money to afford it. Most of us, whether human or middle worlder, don't. Most of us are machines, programmed to wake up and work, to live facsimiles of lives, and to what purpose? Why are we the background scenery, the extras, for those chosen few who have taken this world, and us, hostage? Where our breaths, pain, and sweat fuel their lives and we, fools that we are, don't even realize it.

Anarchy sometimes appeals to me.

It doesn't take us long to reach Baarish's mansion; it is, unsurprisingly, the biggest estate on the street. The tall fence and the guarded gates show that he takes his security seriously. He probably makes a new enemy every time he breathes. We linger at the gates until a milkman shows up and they open to admit him. Thankfully, the guards and the milkman are both human and thus unable to see us as we slip in. Widad looks nervous and I squeeze her hand. She gives me a tremulous smile.

We walk up the long driveway, taking our time to admire the roses blooming in the garden. Gardeners, dressed in white dhotis and kurtas, are busily pruning the rosebushes. Sprinklers are whirring around the gardens, giving the morning dew a helping hand. The vista is ridiculously peaceful. Who would say that a monster resides within the four walls of this house? Since when have monsters started liking roses?

Widad pinches me and I come to attention. We follow the milkman to the back entrance. The plan is to pretend we are housemaids; we have certainly dressed for the part in drab saris. Wigs and contact lenses make us less noticeable. The wig itches like I'm wearing a moth-ridden woolen coat on my head, but I endure. We are invisible to the humans but visible to the middle worlders. So the human servants won't see us, while Baarish's family will (hopefully) assume us new additions in their service. This is a risky strategy, and I'm not sure if we're going to be able to pull this off, but there's no harm in trying.

I keep Widad with me, and we attach ourselves to a group of

maids carrying brooms and rags. The mansion has two wings and three floors. On the wall in the central living room is a large, rather complicated family portrait including everyone except Baarish's lone granddaughter. Baarish's sons and grandsons look very much like younger versions of him. We do not see Baarish, but his sons and grandsons are at home. They stalk around the house as if they own the world; they speak in loud voices and expect everyone else to cower. They sit with their legs spread wide. They command the servants, expecting immediate obedience, and punish those whom they consider subversive. Some maids they leer at, but others, who don't meet their standards of beauty, are ignored. We are lucky to be among the latter.

Their wives and mothers do nothing to curb their behaviors. From what we observe of their interactions, they enable their husbands and sons. With feather dusters in our hands, Widad and I make our way through the mansion, attentive to anything that might help us with the Baarish problem.

Three hours later, our efforts pay off when we see Baarish's youngest son walk into the house looking furtive. He is carrying a box in his hands, and, avoiding the rest of his family, he walks swiftly to a room on the ground floor in the left wing. I grab Widad's hand and pull her outside onto the veranda wrapped around the house. The windows of all the rooms on the ground floor are open, so we walk along the veranda, hoping that luck is on our side. And it is.

So, we eavesdrop on the conversation Baarish's son is having with his wife.

They speak of their daughter and Baarish's only granddaughter,

Tabassum Naaz. Hmm. She must be the one who saved Taraana, twice.

"How long does my daughter have to live in exile?" Baarish's daughter-in-law asks, her voice low.

"It's better for her to live in exile than be dead!" her husband replies in a whisper.

Wow. How exciting.

The woman suppresses a sob. "Can you be sure she's safe in Istanbul? If your father catches her . . ."

"He is too busy looking for that keeper to bother with Tabassum right now. Call her. Tell her to lie low and not draw attention to herself," Baarish's son replies.

"I want to see her! She's my only child!" The woman sobs.

"It's better if she stays far away from here, Gulnaaz," the son replies. "You know that."

They don't say anything more, so I pull Widad away. Back in the house, we linger around the empty living room next to the entrance, dusting the stone head of a rather ugly man half-heartedly. We should leave now, but I can't help feeling there's more to be learned here.

Ten minutes pass and I am forced to concede. However, before we can take more than two steps, someone comes down the stairs. The back of my neck prickles and I immediately turn, keeping my eyes cast down. I squeeze Widad's hand. I feel her tremble.

"Girl." I recognize the voice in the way you recognize things and people you really wish you didn't. When did Baarish return to the house? Why didn't we see him earlier? My heart starts dancing in my chest.

"Ji, sarkar?" I reply, even though it isn't clear which of us he is talking to. Bollywood movies have given me a dialogue for this scene. I delivered the "Yes, sir?" in the perfect tone. Valentina will be proud of me right before she kills me for taking this risk.

"Bring a cup of tea to the study," he says, and continues on his way down the stairs and into what I assume is the study at the end of the corridor just by the living room. He didn't even wait to see whether I followed his orders, so confident is he of the obedience of his servants. We sag against each other when he is gone; I remind myself that I am stronger than I was. That I, and not my fear, control this situation.

Then I wipe the cold sweat on my palms and we make our way to the kitchen, which is in the expected state of controlled chaos. Due to the constant demands of the family, there's a kettle of chai simmering all day on a stovetop. I gesture to Widad to wait on the side and wade into the chaos.

I pick up a cup, saucer, and tray from the sideboard; they become invisible as soon as I touch them; perhaps they become imbued with a fantastic flavor not meant for human eyes. I fill the cup with tea and arrange the items on the tray, making sure not to bump into anyone.

"Are you really doing this?" Widad stops me when I emerge from the kitchen.

"Yes," I tell her with a smile I don't really mean.

"What if he recognizes you?" she demands.

"He won't," I say, more confidently than I feel. "He needs to look at me to do that, and he won't. He thinks I'm human, and humans are beneath his notice."

"If you don't return in ten minutes, I am screaming the house down," Widad warns me before I go.

Perhaps she changes her mind about staying behind, but Widad comes at least halfway with me. She hides in an empty sitting room while I willingly walk into the monster's mouth.

I know, all right? This may not be the best idea I've had, but if I walk away right now, I will always wonder if I missed something that would have helped me help Taraana, help us. I am cobbled together by foolish ideas and reckless behavior. It has kept me alive so far.

Baarish's voice bids me enter when I knock, so I open the door with one hand and awkwardly maneuver my way into the study. One of Baarish's sons—I recognize him from the portrait—is in the room with him, and I freeze, wondering if I should have brought another cup, but no one pays any attention to me. I put the tray on the desk, glance at Baarish, and turn to go. I am almost at the door when Baarish speaks.

"Girl." The scream I keep in my throat is almost out of my mouth, but I manage to keep my lips closed until it is pressed down again.

"Ji, sarkar?" I turn around, my heart pounding.

"Is there sugar in the tea?" he asks.

"Yes, sir," I reply in my most subservient voice.

He nods and waves at me to leave. It takes me three steps to get out of the study, but I don't leave the area. Instead, I stand right next to the door and press my ear against it in the conventional eavesdropping pose.

Baarish doesn't look like a monster at home. He is wearing a cotton white shalwar kameez, looking like someone's grandfather. It is difficult to believe that someone who looks as benign as he does could torture Taraana.

Baarish and his son talk about people I am not familiar with for a long while. I am wondering if I should leave when Baarish's son mentions Taraana.

"Abba, did you really find that boy?" The man's voice is muted through the door. It is obvious who the subject of their conversation is.

"I saw him, but I wasn't able to capture him. He has found some girls to hide behind," Baarish says, the scorn in his voice loud and clear. "He will return to me eventually. How can he escape?"

"What if he does? What if one of the others catches him first?" The man sounds anxious.

"You don't need to worry about him," Baarish says. His words are nothing less than a command. "What was the cause of the disturbance yesterday?"

"People in our clan are complaining about the amount of magic distributed to them," Baarish's son replies. "They seem to think the Dar is keeping the quota that is legally theirs. Abba, is the magic really decreasing?"

"If not, what? The decreasing magic has everyone around the world worried. Even the magic that is harvested is of poor quality," Baarish says. They are silent for a bit. "Don't worry. As long as I get the boy, we will have more than enough magic. Until then, keep the people in control. No matter what it takes." He pauses. "Is the stock ready to be shipped?"

Stock? What kind of stock is Baarish selling? I listen harder.

"We had to move them. One of the children ran away and managed to reach the human police," the son says.

"And?" Baarish's voice is sharp.

"We paid them enough to buy their silence." Baarish's son chuckles. "It was an easy transaction."

"Where is the stock now?"

"The warehouses near Shaheed Smarak Park," the son says. "Jugul is waiting for us there right now. He wants to try the experiment before the stock is shipped."

"Very well. Let's go." I hear the sound of a chair being scraped back and straighten.

I run to the empty sitting room Widad is hiding in a minute before the door to the study opens. We cower behind the closed door of the room until they are gone. Until we can no longer hear their footsteps.

Baarish, he sells children. He is involved in child trafficking.

The monster under the bed is no longer under the bed. He is standing in front of me, and I must decide whether to confront him or run away.

The question is, if I run away, how will I retain what remains of my humanity? I haven't been human for a long while now, but some light in me still persists. I cannot bear to extinguish it.

Widad looks at me. "What is it?"

"I have to follow Baarish and his son," I say. "You don't have to come with me. Things may get more dangerous than you've signed up for."

"Why? What's happened? What did you find out?" The series

of questions rushes out from her and lingers in the air between us. If I were kind, I wouldn't answer.

But kindness is a distant skill. I don't care to claim it too often.

"He sells children," I say. Widad's face loses whatever color it had. "I heard him talking about stock. He meant children. Widad, he sells children."

Her hand clutches mine. It's shaking. I squeeze it, but I need comfort myself.

"You . . . You are going to go to the place they're holding the children?" she asks, even though she knows my answer. I nod anyway. She falls quiet, thinking. "I'll go with you. No, don't say anything. Hear me out." She squeezes my hand, and I get some of the comfort I need. "I'm scared, of course I am, but now that I know, how can I pretend I don't?"

Nothing else needs to be said.

We leave the mansion quickly. Luck is on our side as the gates are open; we slip out, unseen by human eyes. After flickering into visibility in the shadows of a mango tree, we find a taxi willing to take us to the park named by Baarish's son. It is a little after noon, and the sun is at its zenith; the heat crawls on our skin. The taxi driver drops us at the park, and after asking around, we find an enclosed area nearby containing a number of warehouses.

We stand outside, invisible to humans once again, looking at the sun glancing off the corrugated tin roofs of the warehouses. To tell you the truth, even though it reveals me as the coward I am, I wish we had left before I heard what I did in Baarish's study. I wish I hadn't eavesdropped on them. I wish I could go back in time and tell myself not to.

People talk a lot about courage and its expressions. But sometimes courage isn't enough. Sometimes, no matter how much you yearn to do good, you cannot make yourself take that first step.

I go down on my haunches and bury my head between my knees. I *know* I will have to see this through just as I know that what I will see in the next hour will destroy me a little. I can't endure it when people exploit and hurt children, and here, they're doing both.

Hah.

Widad says nothing, but I feel even guiltier. I should have thought harder before I brought her here.

"Let's go," she says when I remain unmoving for five minutes.

That first step is one of the most difficult ones I have taken. We walk softly but we needn't have. No human guards stand at the gates, which are closed but not locked. The entire place has a deserted feel to it that would only fool the humans. You see, *we* can feel the magic.

It leads us to a warehouse at the very end of a line of warehouses. The faint murmur of voices alerts us as we approach the building. We slow our steps and creep into the shadows cast by the empty warehouse right next to it. There are middle worlders standing at the entrance to that warehouse, watching something on their phones and blocking the way in. Though they are situated as guards, there's a marked lack of caution against anyone trying to infiltrate the area. I, of course, have to take advantage of this carelessness.

We move soundlessly into the alley between the two buildings and through it to the back of the warehouse. To our surprise,

an unguarded small door is propped open at the back, perhaps
to ease the heat inside. Signaling to Widad to stay behind, I slip
through the door and into the warehouse. If I am seen, things
will get troublesome. There's no easy entry to the Between here.
I could end up a prisoner, and Valentina will be forced to rescue
me before she kills me.

What's living without risks?

I blink in the dark interior. At first all I see are shadows,
abstract colors, which then coalesce into cages on the uncovered
cement floor, containing children, mostly girls, but some boys,
too. Naked light bulbs dangle from the ceiling, barely illuminat-
ing the large space. As far as I can see, there are five children
crammed in each cage. Their faces are streaked with tears, and
their clothes are dirty and torn. They are skin stretched tightly
over bones. Their eyes . . .

Have you ever seen eyes without hope, without life?

This is not the first time I have seen children stripped of their
humanity and locked up as products for sale. It probably won't
be the last, either. But every single time I come across something
like this, I lose a little of myself.

Baarish, dressed up and hiding the monster inside, is walking around the warehouse, inspecting the cages and nodding
in approval. His son preens beside him. Are the children inside
invisible to him? How much of yourself do you have to lose to
become this evil?

Another middle worlder, a not-human man, stands beside the
two with a staff that looks very much like Josefa's in his hands.
He moves to the front of a cage, raises the staff, and intones what

sound like incantations. Nothing happens. After consulting with Baarish, he opens a cage and drags a child out. A girl. He takes out a dagger and I stop breathing. The need to march over and snatch the child from him almost overpowers me. I can't make a move. Not yet. The man slices the girl's arms, and she wails in pain. He anoints his lips with her blood and retries the incantations. Once again, nothing happens. With a scowl, he throws the girl back into the cage. She curls up in a corner and cries.

The Dar and his son exchange a few more words with the magic user before exiting the warehouse. They are soon driven away by the chauffeur of their imported car. Left behind are the magic user, the few guards, and the children. The middle worlders clearly don't expect anyone to make trouble for them. They must have done this many times before; their actions are relaxed, betraying no guilt, horror, or caution.

I return to Widad, thankful that she had stayed behind.

"What did you see? What do we do?" she whispers as soon as she sees me.

If we scream while invisible, our screams will only affect the middle worlders. All right. Finally, something is going right.

"I will scream while you go to the park and send all humans you see in this direction. Tell them to call the people they know. Tell them to call the media. Can you do that?" I ask her.

"Why don't we call the police?"

"They're unreliable. Some of them have already been bribed to look the other way."

"All right." She glares at me. "Don't take risks."

"I would never." I find a smile for her. "Go!"

Once she's gone, I slip back inside the warehouse and find a particularly dark corner. I ready myself and take the biggest breath I can. I feel the scream swell up inside of me; it rushes up my throat, into my mouth, and out. My scream, heavy with magic and sharp with anger, pierces through the air and into the unwary ears of Baarish's henchmen.

First, they will be surprised. Then, elated because their bodies are filling up with magic. Horror will come quickly, however, because their bodies will fill beyond capacity. Finally, they will feel pain. Pain as they've never felt before. Pain as they will never feel again. They won't die. I refuse to give them that satisfaction. I have been a Wild One for a very long time, you see. Even Valentina's scream cannot match the lethality of mine.

My throat is raw and my cheeks are damp when I finish and open my eyes again. All the middle worlders are on the floor, jerking as if they've received an electric shock that has cooked their brains. Well, that is not exactly incorrect. The children are frightened, and were I someone else, I would offer them comfort. But I don't because I can't. Because I won't. I return to the alley, lean against the wall, and wait.

I don't wait long. Two middle-aged women, dressed in bright saris, arrive first. They march into the warehouse and scream at the sight of the children. In the next moment, they're on their phones. Other humans make their way over in the following minutes, and soon there's a brouhaha brewing. The media arrives before the police.

I find Widad near the gate leading out of the area.

"You did well," I tell her. "Let's get out of here."

We take a taxi back to the city center, and Widad leads me to a dessert store where we order too much mithai and two glasses of mango lassi each. We are jittery with shock. Or perhaps adrenaline.

I am sure of one thing, though. I didn't save the children. I just removed the obstacles so someone else could.

"Do you think he'll know it was us?" Widad asks between sips of her lassi.

"I don't know. Perhaps?" I drown my sorrow in a gulaab jamun.

"Will you tell the others what we did today?" Widad asks next.

I think of Valentina's rage, and I shudder. "Drink your lassi."

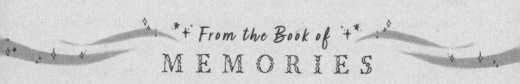

WIDAD
CITY OF ORIGIN: LAHORE

Dear Dead Boy,

I read that you died. It was quite by chance that I saw that conversation. Friends from high school were talking about it on social media, expressing shock, sharing stories. One of us is dead. Well. You're the fourth one, actually. Two boys have already died. One girl. All tragic, but you were the only one out of them all that I touched. It has been more than a decade since that day. I had forgotten. I wonder if you had too. You used to sit in your corner of the classroom not looking at me, and I used to sit in mine pretending your coldness didn't hurt. We fought, heated whispers, absolute hate because there were these feelings and neither of us knew what they meant or what to do with them. So we hid behind stinging words and cruel looks. We expressed these feelings in the only way we knew.

Did you remember that afternoon after school? You caught me behind the school building. It was almost the end of the school year. You took my arm and tugged me into the shadow of the wall where we weren't visible to the rest of the world. You pressed your body against mine. I remember your warmth from that afternoon. It scared me. My white scarf fluttered to the ground, and you stared at me as though you were going to consume me whole.

It wasn't only you, though. I wanted to kiss you too. I wanted to feel your lips on mine. I had dreamed about it. So, I let my fingers touch your face. Feel your skin. I broke all the rules then, yours and mine. Moments stilled and pooled; the heat of your skin warmed me. But someone called your name. Then someone else called mine. We broke apart. You turned away. I picked up my scarf. You stifled a shudder. I took a breath.

We never spoke of it. That almost-kiss. It was as though it had never almost happened. Maybe it didn't. Maybe I dreamed it up.

Some days grief catches us unaware. It strips away all our carefully constructed facades and leaves us as freshly hurt as we were when we first became wild. Our roads become impassable, and we cannot turn one damn page because our stories are stuck in that same rank darkness, and we cannot move, we cannot think, and we cannot be anything other than the pieces of what we once were.

Would giving specific names to our tragedies make you know us better? Get black paint then and mark us victims of rape, sexual, physical, and verbal abuse. Stalked. Sold. Made destitute. Abandoned. Hated. Silenced. Do these words make us more or less to you?

Some days we are so sad, we want to drown the world. Some days we are so angry, we want to set it on fire.

When we become wild, the first thing we do is throw ourselves away. Or rather, we throw away the pieces of us that remain after whatever tragedy that tries to define us occurs. Then we throw away all the people we held dear because, ultimately, these people failed us. After that, we unearth ourselves, carefully digging up the roots that we sank into the place we first called home. Last of all, we throw away time.

This is more difficult to do than it should be. Paheli never talks about the time she threw away. None of us do. But though it doesn't show on our surfaces, our bodies record the passing of hours in different ways. Our smiles gradually get brighter, warmer, and even though we are the furthest from normal we will ever get, we start feeling like people again.

The French Quarter, the Spanish Half, and Eulalie

I.

We leave Agra the evening Paheli and Widad return from their day of spying. They tell us nothing except that we have to leave immediately, so we do. Settling the hotel bill on our way out, we find an expanse of uninterrupted wall a few streets away. Talei lays a star-embedded palm on the wall, and a second later, a door to the Between glimmers into existence.

We are three-quarters of the way to the door leading to Arijejen in Nauru, where Taraana is staying with Assi and her group, when the Between's lights flicker violently. A minute later, we see Taraana sprinting toward us. Behind him are three silver-scaled middle worlders, Baarish's minions. Taraana has a split lip, a blackened eye, and cuts on his arms and face. His knee is battered and his clothes are torn.

It will be a long time before we can forget the look on his face the moment he glimpses us. He flings himself at us and we catch him and bring him in, shielding him with our bodies. The hum in the Between deepens—an ominous sign. Anger, a furious storm of it, rises in us.

The scaled creatures see us and hesitate. They know we are not to be trifled with. "You should let him go," one of the scaled creatures says. There is an odd quality to the way he shapes words, as if his tongue is not used to speech. "You cannot keep him safe forever."

Taraana shudders at his words.

"How can you be sure?" Valentina raises her chin at the challenge in the creature's words.

"Do you think the Dar is alone in his desire for the Keeper of the Between?" another scaled middle worlder asks with a smile we can only describe as fiendish. "He is but one of many."

"So? Are we supposed to hand Taraana to you based on that?" Kamboja scoffs.

"Enough," Valentina says. In the next moment, entirely without warning, she screams. Like the last time, the creatures fall into themselves, ending as liquid, which might be water but we're not going to get close enough to truly identify it.

"You! Give us some warning so we can cover Taraana's ears!" Daraja scolds Valentina.

"Our screams don't affect him." Valentina rolls her eyes. "Do you think the Between would let us scream if they did?"

We look at Taraana; he looks shell-shocked but otherwise fine.

He flinches when Paheli takes his hand before he realizes it's her. When he does, he holds on. Tight.

"What happened?" Valentina asks him as we turn around and make our way to our next destination.

"I was betrayed." Taraana's voice is flat.

"Assi?" Areum asks.

He shakes his head immediately. "Not Assi. It was Jam, someone she rescued. He told me . . . told me . . ." Taraana shakes his head and stops talking. "I ran into the Between to lead them away from her. She can fight better when I'm not around her, and plus, I thought they'd all follow me."

"Did they?" Paheli asks.

He shakes his head. He licks his lips, then gasps when it stings. "No. She . . . She . . ." His eyes are shiny and he is breathing in short, shallow gasps. "I don't even know if she's still alive. She's the closest thing to a family I have, and I can't even go back to her." He shakes.

Paheli slips her arms around him, and he stands rigidly in her embrace before his control wavers and he crumples. We support his weight as he cries racking sobs that shake his slight frame. He might have cried for a minute or many, but finally his sobs taper off and he lifts his head, his cheeks stained by a blush and his eyes lowered.

We do not say anything more. Nothing that will break his eggshell composure. Instead we resume walking until we reach the door to the next city. Valentina reaches out to open it, but for some reason the doorknob won't turn, and when it does, the door won't open. She pulls at it, exerting all her force without being able to open it. Finally, Taraana reaches out and tries, and, confounding all of us, the door opens up easily, revealing our destination on the other side.

II.

New Orleans, Louisiana. Also known as NOLA, the Big Easy, and Nawlins. You may have heard of it. The books say it was founded in 1718 and named after Philippe II, the Duke of Orléans. Like all good cities, it has a complicated history replete with revolutions, war, and hurricanes.

The city's magical history is just as complex, and we have barely scratched the surface of it. Here is what we know:

The magic pours off the pavements here. It is strong, sticky, and lasting. You breathe the magic in and you breathe it out. It keeps you warm on winter nights and cool during summer days. New Orleans is not the only city in the world that has an influx of magic, but it is one of the more accessible ones, and so creatures who live in the middle world crowd it, hoping to get as much of the magic as possible.

For that reason, New Orleans boasts many more magic users than a lot of other cities in the world. We have said before, haven't we, that magic is the currency of the middle world? However, very few middle worlders can actually use magic. Sort of like how everyone can hear music, but only a few people can make it. Similarly, all middle worlders can reap the benefits of magic, but very few can actually shape it. This is why magic users are extremely valued in middle worlder circles.

The French Quarter is the oldest section of the city and is refulgent with magic, so, obviously, we invested in real estate here. From outside, the place we bought looks like a one-level shotgun house painted a sunflower yellow. A porch, surrounded by black wrought-iron railings, wraps around the outside of the house. The front yard is closed off from the sidewalk by a white fence. A garden full of hibiscus and other rioting blooms is interrupted by a path that meanders its way to the five steps leading up to the front porch.

We walk up these steps light with relief at being in a place where we can perhaps be safe for a bit. The door, spelled to respond to Paheli's hands, swings open and we enter the house. The middle worlder who manages the house for us appears in the parlor the front door opens to. She utters a short, surprised sound when she sees us. Two steps later, she is pulling Paheli into an embrace. Paheli suffers the contact for a brief minute before pulling away. She smiles to soften her action, but the not-human woman doesn't seem to mind. An almost maternal affection lights the woman's eyes when she looks at Paheli.

Her name is Eulalie, and she is one of those rare magic users we mentioned previously. We keep her supplied with a liberal amount of Between diamonds, and in return, she shapes our house to be as big on the inside as we need it to be. We each have a room; there is an excess of them here. The house also boasts a pool, a library, and even a conservatory, all of it invisible to human eyes.

Taraana stands uneasily in the very feminine parlor, looking around in the same way a mouse does when it doesn't know which direction the cat is going to attack from. He starts when he sees Eulalie, her rich brown skin glowing with health and magic. She, in turn, goes still before a strangely gentle expression settles on her face. She takes a step toward him and Taraana takes two back, his fingers clinging to Paheli's. His fear is written on his face in the cuts and bruises that decorate it. We move closer to him, wanting him to be at ease, hurting for him.

"The Keeper of the Between," Eulalie whispers, as if scarcely daring to believe his presence in our parlor.

We stare at her, surprised. No one other than Baarish (and, perhaps, the others the scaled middle worlders mentioned) has been able to recognize him for who he is until now. Taraana, on the other hand, looks panicked. We understand his feelings, of course; the majority of the middle worlders who have recognized him thus far have had less-than-pure intentions.

Eulalie sketches a deep bow to him. "I'm honored." She is entirely serious. We look at Paheli, not sure how to react to this new development.

"Is the Keeper of the Between like a unicorn? A rare sighting?" Paheli asks Eulalie. She doesn't seem worried about Eulalie recognizing Taraana. We don't quite understand the specificities of the relationship she has with Eulalie, but she trusts her. As such, we do too.

"Unicorns are far more common," Eulalie replies, her eyes still attached to Taraana.

"Lalie, if you keep staring at him, I'm going to think you mean him harm," Paheli says without a smile. "As you can see from the state he is in, we've had . . . interactions with others whose intentions are downright evil."

"I apologize," Eulalie says, grimacing. "I've heard of the Keepers of the Between, but I never thought I'd be entertaining one." She frowns at Paheli. "How did you meet the keeper? Who is after him? Why didn't you tell me you were coming?"

"Sorry, I meant to call you, but things happened," Paheli replies. We do use human technology; Talei has an Instagram with followers numbering in the thousands, and Valentina boasts a large Twitter following due to her poisonous wit centering around social commentary. "Are we interrupting something?"

Eulalie has her own set of rooms in the house. An entire floor of them, in fact. She doesn't invite guests to her rooms, preferring her privacy and respecting ours. "I do have a gathering to go to shortly." She looks at Taraana again and frowns slightly. "Please stay inside until I'm able to equip you with spells. The keeper will be in danger if anyone recognizes him."

"His name is Taraana," Valentina says. "Please use that instead of calling him Keeper."

Eulalie nods. "Thank you for correcting me." She glances out the window. "As much as I want to stay and listen to how you met him and what circumstances have led you here, I have to go fulfill my obligations. We will talk when I get back." She gives Paheli another hug and exhorts us to be safe before leaving.

"I am tired and hot. I want a shower, a change of clothes, some food, and some rest," Kamboja announces, sprawling on the sofa in the parlor. "Not necessarily in that order."

It is midday in New Orleans, and despite our fatigue, the day outside beckons.

"Taraana doesn't have any clothes, and I don't think he'll want to wear any of ours," Etsuko points out.

We look at him and he shrugs. "I don't care."

"As much as I would like to see you trying on our clothes, I reckon it is not the time for such hilarity," Daraja says. "We will go get you some clothes and other necessities. We need to get some human currency anyway. Should we cook or should we go get takeout?"

Takeout is a unanimous decision.

We look at Taraana. He has not moved from his position by Paheli. He clings to her like she's the rock to his barnacle. Excuse the analogy. We've had a trying day. She is reading something on Valentina's phone and doesn't appear to mind his proximity.

That gives us an idea.

Valentina clears her throat softly. Etsuko looks at Daraja and smiles widely. It is not a kind smile. Daraja nods and pinches Sevda, who nods and looks at Ghufran. Ghufran smiles her acquiescence and grabs Talei's hand. Talei looks confused before she sees us glancing at Paheli and Taraana. She nods and pulls Areum over. Areum signals to Ligaya, Kamboja, and Widad and they get to their feet, looking extremely casual.

"Well, we're off to shop for stuff. You stay here with Taraana," Valentina tells Paheli with a look that announces her schadenfreude.

"What? Why are you leaving me behind? I will go too." Paheli frowns. Belatedly, she appears to notice how close he is to her and inches away. "Why can't someone else stay with Taraana?"

"He prefers you. Don't you, Taraana?" Etsuko asks.

Taraana nods in answer.

"Taraana is too tired to know what he wants," Paheli says, and crosses her arms.

"Don't be mean, Paheli. We can't leave Taraana alone here. Didn't you hear Eulalie? You need to stay here and protect our keeper." Valentina beams and Paheli's cheeks suddenly flush a becoming red. Hah, we knew she isn't as indifferent to Taraana as she pretends to be.

"I can protect myself!" Taraana protests, though not very confidently.

"No, you can't," Ligaya tells him nicely.

Before Paheli can say anything else, we leave the house, locking the door behind us.

Paheli: The Eggplant Overture

They leave me with the boy and a silence so thick, you could cut it six ways for tea and still have some left over for dinner. He is sitting right next to me. So close that his arm touches mine and I don't hate it. I don't, but I move away because to not move away means admitting I don't hate it and goodness, I need to breathe.

I am breathing.

He looks at me, the stars in his eyes gold, and he sees through me, inside me, as if my secrets have no shame and lay themselves bare for his perusal. Shameless secrets. What am I without my secrets? Who am I without my secrets?

"What is it?" I demand, at odds with the world.

"Do you like eggplants?" he asks, and I stare at him.

"The purple vegetable?" I wonder if I heard wrong. I am pretty old. It would not surprise me if my ears were the first things to go, considering how much I enjoy loud music.

"Eggplants are actually fruits, and sometimes they are white," he replies.

"Oh. Fruits. Well. I don't hate them. Why?" Why is he talking about eggplants? Why does he keep looking at me?

"No reason. I just wanted to know." He tries to smile but ends up wincing when his split lip reminds him of the pain he is currently in.

"Come on." I get up and grab his hand, pulling him along behind me. He holds on tight. Wait. Why did I hold his hand? Clearly there is something wrong with me. Didn't I decide, not twenty minutes ago, to keep a distance from him? Did I forget? Is my memory going too?

"Are you okay?" I ask him as we walk up the stairs.

"Because of earlier?" he says, and I nod. He shrugs. "I'm used to it. When you live in a glass house, you learn not to ever get too comfortable." That is the saddest thing I have heard in a while.

I take him to a washroom on the second floor and open up the cabinet to reveal a first aid kit. I get him to lean down, and I swab as gently as I can at his cut lips. He bears through my ministrations with only a grimace, and as a reward I give him a candy. He stares at it.

"You put it in your mouth," I tell him helpfully.

He looks at me. The stars in his eyes brighten as if I have just amused him. I don't think I care for being secretly laughed at. I bid him to follow me and take him to an empty bedroom on the third floor that he can use while we are in New Orleans. He doesn't talk much.

"Do you want to rest until the girls get back?" I ask him, awkwardness creeping back between us. I might start wringing my hands if I don't get away from him soon. He makes me feel very uncomfortable. As if my skin is too tight for my flesh. As if my heart has grown legs and wants to go on a vacation. Anyway, I don't like this feeling.

"No, I don't want to be alone," he replies. He is looking at me. I can feel his eyes on my face, but I can't, for the life of me, meet his gaze. So, I hold my breath because it seems like a good idea. It's not like I'll die.

He slips his arms around me and holds me while I try not to die because I'm holding my breath. I gasp noisily and he pulls me closer to him.

"Hold it," I squeak, my face smooshed against his chest. He smells nice. Like the sunshine. The boy made of stars smells like sunlight. Hah. His heart is racing.

When do I realize that he is terrified? I don't know. It just dawns on me. Hard. Like a sledgehammer dropping on an unsuspecting head. He is shaking.

"Are you all right?" I ask, when clearly, he is anything but.

"No," he whispers into my hair. I don't remember when I last washed it. I hope it doesn't smell too terrible. "I will be, though. For some reason, being near you reassures me."

I can't be close to anyone. This is the first time a man has held me like this since . . . since that time. Maybe it is because Taraana is as broken as I am. Maybe it is because he saw me at my worst moment and didn't turn away. Maybe it is because I can sense he is not a threat. Or maybe it is because he wants nothing from me at this moment other than comfort. I allow him the liberty of holding me.

He pulls away after a minute. "Thank you," he says. "I promise to be stronger."

I shrug. "You're still alive, aren't you? I reckon that means you are strong enough."

"It doesn't feel like it." He sits down on the bed and looks around the sizable room. It is elegantly furnished with wide doors that open up to a balcony. All our rooms have balconies; magic does have its uses. He glances at me, a little shyly. Oh dear.

"Can I ask you something?" he says.

"You already are." He gives me a look and I relent. "Go ahead."

"What have you been doing in the years since I threw the box of stars to you?" he asks. I sit down beside him. I wish he hadn't asked me this question.

"Why do you ask?" I croak.

"Do you not want to answer?" His voice is so gentle, I might hit him. I don't want to be treated like I'm glass.

"I don't want to answer," I tell him. He nods.

"What do we do now?" He moves on quite easily, this boy.

"What do you want to do?" I ask.

"I want to explore this city, but I suppose that wouldn't be a good idea." His defeat is almost palpable. It hurts me. He picks up my hand, like it belongs to him, and turns it up to look at the star embedded in my palm. He kisses the star and dammit, I stop breathing again.

"You!" I snatch my hand away and he grins.

"Sorry."

"Are you really?" I look at him suspiciously.

"Not really."

"Why did you do that?" I ask him, sweating. He is moving too quickly. I can't keep track. After so many years of not allowing anyone near me, his attentions are confusing. I am confused. Slightly intoxicated. And possibly dying. Or dead. Whichever. "This is the third time I am seeing you. You don't kiss girls after seeing them three times."

"I didn't kiss you. I kissed the star." The grin is still in his eyes. Then his smile dims. "I don't know why I'm acting like this. No. Actually I do. I'm scared that I will die when I've only just started living. I want to do everything because I feel like I never will if I don't seize the chance right now. I haven't kissed anyone before." He ducks his head, blushing. "I'm sorry. I won't do it again."

"No. Wait. Stop. I'm not sure I don't want you to do it again. I just don't understand what this is. What is this?"

"I don't know either."

"Great." This is a case of the blinder leading the blind.

We are silent for five minutes before Taraana stirs.

"Can you show me around the house?"

"I can do that. There is a conservatory. Did I tell you that?"

"No. Does the conservatory have eggplants?"

"Let's go find out."

Sunny Jelly Beans, Po'Boys, and "Alouette"

When we get back to the house, Paheli and Taraana are arguing over a jar of peanut butter. He thinks it's disgusting, and she thinks *he's* disgusting for thinking that. This is not how we thought their relationship would progress, but it will have to do for the moment.

Daraja has stocked up on jelly beans from the store at which we exchanged Between diamonds for money. These jelly beans are all yellow and all contain bursts of sunlight that brighten up your day no matter how desolate you are feeling. We are addicted to them.

We hit the mall right after getting moneyed, glimmering into visibility for an hour and a half as we swanned into human stores and picked up clothes for Taraana. Can there be anything crueler than trying out clothes in a changing room with mirrors on all four sides castigating your imperfections while outside well-dressed mannequins judge you smugly for being more flesh than plastic?

Taraana looks dubiously at the bags of clothes we hand him and turns to Paheli for help. She pops a spoonful of peanut butter into her mouth and turns her nose up at him. He sighs softly and gets up, resigned to the fashion show we beseech him to do. We settle in a parlor by a dining room on the second floor and wait for him to grace us with his presence.

A few minutes later, he comes into the room wearing the light green shirt Daraja lobbied for. He pairs it with sleek white dress pants, and the effect is dazzling. We roar to show our approval, but it is Paheli he looks to. Our Paheli is heartless, however, and refuses to give him the satisfaction of a reaction. But even she cannot hide her pleasure when some outfits later, he comes back wearing an overlarge sweater in soft gold paired with tailored black pants that mold to his shape. Widad guessed his size perfectly.

Taraana carefully smooths his hands down the soft wool of the sweater and smiles. We swoon. Paheli clears her throat noisily.

"I am hungry. Did you bring food?"

"You were just eating," Valentina points out reasonably.

"That's not food," Taraana says disdainfully.

"Don't you start again," Paheli warns, shaking her spoon at him. He looks away with a sniff.

"We bought food," Ligaya says in a peaceful tone, signaling our move to the dining room beside the parlor. We left the packets and containers of hot food on the table, awaiting our attention. We transfer the food from the containers to the pretty china and elegant utensils we bought for everyday use before we claim chairs and plates around the table.

The table strains under the weight of dishes containing jambalaya, shrimp étouffée, gumbo for those who don't mind okra, muffuletta from Central Grocery, and, as an alternative, po'boys. For dessert, there are sugar-sprinkled beignets and coffee that will ensure we do not sleep until the wee hours of the morning. The conversation at the table is light; we prefer to concentrate on the intense flavors of the food.

Afterward, we clean up the dining room, take showers, and rest for a few hours. When the clock strikes eight, we gather in a different parlor, this one on the third floor. Outside it is dark and a soft rain is falling. The warm light in the parlor, the colorful cushions on the soft chairs, and the braided rug provide a backdrop for the conversation we will eventually have.

Outside these walls, our fate has become nebulous, and our survival subject to the strength of an enemy we are barely acquainted with. Within these walls, however, we are safe. At this moment, we are safe. Though this safety might be an illusion, it is one we will cling to. What is life if we cannot lie to ourselves?

Taraana is sitting on the floor, leaning against the chair Paheli is curled up on. She is trying to braid his longish hair idly. Neither of them is aware of our scrutiny. Paheli has never shown any romantic interest in anyone before. We don't yet know what she feels for this boy made of stars, but we are certain her feelings are more than the usual kindness she shows us.

While we wait for Eulalie to return, we listen to Widad sing. She refuses to sing love songs, so we are left listening to nursery rhymes in a variety of languages. She is halfway through "Alouette" when the door to the parlor opens and Eulalie enters. We all turn and look at her, and she stops, suddenly hesitant. "Am I intruding?"

"No, we were waiting for you." Paheli straightens up, her hands falling away from Taraana's hair.

Our frivolity melts away with Eulalie's arrival. What words do we use to tell you how we feel? Scared? Angry that we haven't yet outrun fear? Predatory because anger makes beasts out of us all? Alive because danger reminds us that we are still alive and we want to remain alive? A mixture of all four and perhaps more? The mixture of our emotions makes a potent drink, and we are all drunk from it.

First, Valentina fills Eulalie in on everything that has occurred, starting from Assi's invitation all the way to the abduction attempt we interrupted in the Between.

"Can you do something for us?" Paheli asks after Valentina is done.

"Of course, ma chérie," Eulalie replies immediately. Warmly.

"Will you find out what happened to"—Paheli glances at Taraana—"Assi?" She gestures for Taraana to fill in the details.

"I . . ." He hesitates, then takes a breath. "Assi and I met on a crisp blue September morning when we were both running for our lives from middle worlders who think our bodies objects to exploit. In the beginning, what we had wasn't friendship but a forced companionship. Or perhaps charity. She is stronger than me in all ways, plus, she has a good heart that refuses to see me fall to the same demons that chase her. I owe her a lot, but this isn't the first time I have failed her." He squeezes his eyes shut in some private anguish. "As time passed, our group of two gradually grew as we took in others targeted by those stronger than them. I fancied that I was growing a group just like . . ." He looks at us. "You."

"What happened?" Valentina prompts after a few beats of silence.

"We were betrayed by someone we considered our own," Taraana says. "He came to Jbeil with us and figured out my identity. He later approached one of Baarish's creatures to cut a deal with Baarish. He told me he had no choice. Siding with Baarish guarantees his survival while allying with me is like trying to survive on a tightrope." Taraana looks up. "Perhaps I shouldn't blame him?"

"No, you should. You should totally blame him," Kamboja says, her eyes blazing.

"Blame him to death," Areum adds, her red lips snarling.

Taraana ducks his head, stealing a moment. Then he continues. "When Baarish's creatures attacked, Assi did her best to get me into the Between before they could drag me away. I wanted to stay and fight, but she told me I would be hindering her ability to fight. So, I ran like the coward I am."

Paheli flicks him on the forehead. "Trying to survive isn't an act of cowardice."

"Are you worried that they might have caught Assi?" Eulalie asks.

"She said she would much rather die than be captured," Taraana replies. They seem to share that sentiment.

"Ah," Eulalie says. "I shall find out what happened to her. Give me a few days and I will have some news for you."

"Thank you." Taraana looks straight at Eulalie, perhaps for the first time.

"All right. Let's talk about Baarish now," Paheli says without letting another minute pass.

The air in the parlor loses its warmth, and we gather closer together to deconstruct the monster to find the man within.

Our days of reconnaissance led us to some inviolable facts about Baarish: He straddles the fence between the human and the middle worlds, dipping his thumbs in both pots. All testimonies that we heard from the middle worlders in Agra tell us that Baarish subscribes to an old-fashioned code of honor that precludes humans and women. His power means everything to him. He will exploit anyone he can, even if they are related to him. Even little children do not escape his quest for money and power.

Uttar Pradesh, which includes Agra, and other states were ruled by one of Baarish's enemies for a long while. Baarish was imprisoned during that time. However, there was a recent coup, which led to a change in rulers. The new administrator of the region is not just Baarish's closest and oldest friend, but also his brother-in-law.

"Who fulfilled the role of Dar while Baarish was in prison?" Eulalie asks with a frown knitting up her eyebrows.

"Baarish's youngest brother," Ligaya replies. "Ask me what happened to him. Quick!"

"Baarish killed him the day after he was released from prison," Etsuko replies to the question that wasn't asked. "He doesn't share his power with anyone."

"Hey!" Ligaya wails.

"Children," Daraja says.

Baarish has had three wives, four—well, now three—brothers, five sons, fourteen grandsons, and one granddaughter. None of his family members have a lot of magic, but all of them believe they are entitled to large amounts of it. As the only magic user in his family, the patriarch holds tightly to power and has not yet chosen his heir, though his grandsons are all hopeful.

"A lot of the middle worlders complained about the gradual decrease of the magic in places that used to be full of it," Kamboja says. "It seems that the rivers and lakes that Baarish is in charge of yield far less magic now than they used to."

Eulalie has a dark look on her face. "He is not the only one facing this problem," she says. "I attended a meeting today regarding the very same thing. The level of magic in New Orleans is decreasing at a significant rate, and we don't know why or how to fix it."

"So perhaps this is the reason his pursuit of the keeper and you girls is so fierce." Eulalie shoots Taraana a look. "The stars are pure magic, even purer than the Between diamonds. One will fuel a middle worlder for decades." She turns to Paheli. "Let me see it again."

Paheli holds out her palm, but Taraana catches her hand with his and holds it. It seems he is still suspicious of Eulalie. Paheli glances at Eulalie, who shrugs and doesn't insist.

"First of all, let's address the issue of safety," Eulalie says. "Baarish won't easily attack you here. This is not his territory, and appearing here without explicit permission from the ruler of this region will be seen as an act of war. I'm assuming this is a risk he won't take lightly. However, Baarish isn't the only middle worlder to be wary of. Anyone who knows about Taraana's stars will want to acquire them . . . him. Fortunately, not many people are aware of the Keeper of the Between. I will draw up a spell to mask Taraana's eyes—"

"Magic doesn't work on me, either," Taraana interrupts Eulalie.

"Oh." Eulalie seems stumped. "In that case, I recommend sunglasses."

"I'm sorry to interrupt," Ghufran says, and we thrill again. Every time she speaks is a victory for us. "We know very little about the Keeper of the Between. Do you know if there have been any before Taraana? What do they do?" We look at Eulalie for answers. She is part of the middle world, after all. She will have *some* answers.

"I'm afraid I have to disappoint you," she says, looking apologetic. "What I know about the Keeper of the Between is only enough to fill a thimble. I do know that there has always been one . . . and that's about it."

"The thimble is almost empty, Lalie," Paheli says.

"Sorry," Eulalie says with a grimace. "Here's what I can do, though. One of the people attending the meeting today was an old friend of mine. She's the Keeper of the Green of New Orleans. Her magic comes from nature, trees, and other plants, to be specific. She is very powerful and will be a fount of information for you. I can arrange a meeting between you and her, if you desire. There's also someone who used to be a librarian in the middle-world version of the Library of Alexandria. She may know a lot more about the Keepers of the Between than my friend, but she's nomadic, and locating her will take some time. Do you want to wait to meet the librarian, or would you like to talk to the Keeper of the Green first?"

We look at Paheli and she looks at Taraana. "I would like to meet the Keeper of the Green first, if you don't mind," he says after a moment.

"All right. I will ask Mama Magdaline and let you know what she says," Eulalie replies.

A few moments pass quietly. "Will we be safe here? Will I be endangering you all if I stay here?" Taraana asks suddenly.

"There are few in this city who would break into a house I call my own, child," Eulalie says. The mien she has maintained so far of a good-natured not-human woman falls away, and a creature with teeth peeks through. "I have set up wards outside that will warn us should anyone try to trespass. So yes, we are safe here."

Taraana looks slightly reassured. We understand. Sometimes you can lock yourself in a fortress and still feel vulnerable.

"Well, since we have discussed all the somber things we can tonight, let's get back to singing!" Areum says brightly.

"You *want* Widad to go back to singing nursery rhymes?" Sevda demands incredulously.

"Oh yes!" Widad perks up and clears her throat. "I was singing 'Alouette,' wasn't I? I shall start from the beginning!"

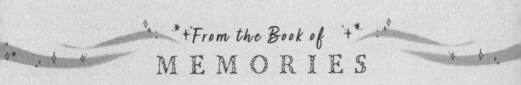

From the Book of
MEMORIES

LIGAYA
CITY OF ORIGIN: CEBU

It was midnight. Or a smudge past twelve.

The darkness was held together by broken fragments

of nowhere poetry. I-don't-care poetry.

I was there. My soul bared and vulnerable to the
mockery

of the empty page. Constructing a house (and home)

from the cutout pictures of the Ikea catalog.

I was draining out of myself gradually. Like water

draining out of a swimming pool. I was walking

blind. Emptying out. It's important that you understand.

One need not be made of glass to shatter.

The Keeper of the Green and the Mysteries of Magic

The Keeper of the Green accepts Eulalie's invitation to come to tea. After further discussion, we decided against letting her know about Taraana and his identity ahead of time. Not because we don't trust her—well, actually, we don't. We don't know her, so the question of trust isn't even a question at this point. We also don't trust the people around her. Avarice is a universal middle name.

The day of the meeting is sunny with nary a cloud marring the pristine blueness of the sky. We attempt to help Eulalie in the kitchen but she shoos us out, calling us nuisances. She is busy whipping up meatballs, deviled eggs, coconut shrimp, cakes, and a host of other goodies we get our hands slapped for. The entire house smells like a feast. The rules of hospitality demand that no one leaves the house they visit with an empty stomach. Eulalie means business.

The front parlor on the first floor, where the meeting will take place, is cleaned and polished till it shines. Colorful cushions grace the chairs, mahogany gleams, and little white doilies soften dark surfaces. Vases full of freshly cut flowers are placed around the room. Curtains are pulled apart to allow the sun to whisper its way in. When the room is done, we look to our toilette. We put on our prettiest clothes and our pinkest lipsticks. With some persuasion, Taraana puts on one of his new outfits and combs his hair back. He looks uncomfortably debonair. At ten minutes before the meeting hour, we are in the parlor watching the clock count down the minutes.

"I feel like we're meeting royalty," Valentina says, fussing with the headpiece she is wearing.

"I object to the deification of a human being simply on account of that being's privileged birth," Talei says.

"The Keeper of the Green isn't human," Kamboja points out.

"I'm not talking about her," Talei replies.

"So, you wouldn't mind the deification of a human being if the human being did something to deserve the deification?" Etsuko jumps into the conversation.

"Look, all I'm saying is that we're all overdressed," Valentina says, bringing the conversation back and earning several dirty looks in the process.

"What I'm more worried about is how I will feel if, after all this fuss, she doesn't show up." Paheli's light pink hair is in a tight French braid, emphasizing the bones of her face. This face is currently furrowed up in a frown.

"Mama Magdaline always keeps her word and her appointments," Eulalie says, a reprimand in her voice. She wheels in a breakfast cart almost tipping over with dishes full of food and gestures for Paheli to bring in the second cart that contains a teapot and matching cups. She glances at Taraana, who sits silently on a settee in the center of the parlor. "Do not fear, child. Mama Magdaline will do you no harm."

"How can you be so sure?" Taraana asks Eulalie.

"Hmm, let me put it this way. She has more than enough magic of her own to require yours."

"There is no such thing as enough magic for middle worlders," Taraana bites out, more bitter than we have ever experienced him being.

Eulalie opens her mouth to reply, but at that moment, magic, as we have never felt it before, washes over us. We stiffen and, moving almost as one, gather beside Taraana. The doorbell rings.

Giving us a look that begs us to behave, Eulalie goes to open the door.

Our first inkling that Mama Magdaline is not your usual middle worlder is the fragrance that precedes her. A scent of roses fills the parlor long before Eulalie opens the door. Then we get our first look at the Keeper of the Green.

Middle worlders are generally long-lived. Not the century that humans call a long life, but a millennium, though we haven't met any more than five centuries old. Or perhaps we have and didn't realize it. We comprehend time in different ways from humans and middle worlders, after all.

Mama Magdaline is . . . for a lack of a more delicate way of putting it, really old. Her age is a skip in our hearts, a burning in our eyes. Or perhaps that is the effect of the power that rolls off her. She is not a tall woman, but with the magic she contains, she may as well be a mountain. Her face is delicate; she wears her age in fine lines around her full lips and eyes. Oh, her eyes . . . like Baarish's eyes, Mama Magdaline's eyes give away the position she occupies—her office, so to speak. Her eyes are deep pools of green that occasionally reflect trees—trees that are nowhere in sight in the real world. The effect is unsettling.

We watch her approach, as do the flowers in the vases. They bloom brighter in her presence just as we sit straighter and quieter. She comes alone, needing no entourage to buoy her presence. When she has settled in the settee across from the one we are sitting on, she looks at us. Well, more like she glances at us before her attention falls on Taraana with all the grace of a hammer falling on a glass window. Her face freezes and surprise, like a typhoon, sweeps through her features. She observes Taraana carefully, cataloging the bruises on his face, the look in his eyes, the grip of his hands on Paheli's.

"Child, is this the Keeper of the Between?" Mama Magdaline asks Eulalie, who is standing beside the breakfast cart.

"Yes, Mama," Eulalie replies. Her voice is soft and her tone reverent.

"Explain to me what the Keeper of the Between—no, what these children—are doing in your parlor?" the Keeper of the Green demands without moving her eyes from Taraana. It's almost as if she's afraid he will disappear if she stops looking at him.

We watch with great interest as Eulalie squirms. She has always treated us as the children Mama Magdaline calls us, but this is the first time we have seen her being treated as a juvenile. All of us, except for Paheli, hide our smirks. She has no such compunction.

"I've told you about the child I picked up in the Between, Mama," Eulalie says, erasing Paheli's smirk easily. "That's Paheli. The rest of them are her sisters."

Mama Magdaline's eyes leave Taraana for a short second to look at Paheli, who bristles at the attention.

"You may call me 'Grandmother,' child," the Keeper of the Green tells us, and Paheli offers her a weak smile in response. "Now, I very much doubt you've invited me over simply for tea. Not that I mind tea." Eulalie takes the keeper's words as a signal to serve food and puts us to work.

"Would you tell us what you know about the Keeper of the Between?" Paheli asks her, an unfamiliar shade of respect coloring her words.

Mama Magdaline looks at Taraana, and once again, her eyes show her surprise. "Before I tell you what I know about the Keeper of the Between, tell me what you know about magic."

Magic, huh. We have never cared to deconstruct the magic around us. It is important to us, but we don't question it. We know what is commonly known about magic, but we know nothing about where it comes from nor how it is created.

Mama Magdaline doesn't seem perturbed by our silence. In fact, she seems to take our lack of knowledge for granted.

"Despite the arrogance and superiority evinced by middle

worlders, they, *we*, cannot survive without human beings. Isn't that funny?" No, it really is not, but okay. We continue listening. "The magic middle worlders need to live is generated by human lives. Specifically, the life and death of human beings generate magic that is eventually used by the middle worlders for energy, sustenance, and as a form of currency. With me so far?"

We nod. Mama Magdaline pauses to eat a scone and sip some tea.

"However, the magic generated by the life and death of humans is like crude oil. For it to gain a form usable by middle worlders, it needs to be refined. That is where the Between comes in. The Between is much more than a magical corridor; it is the source of magic in the natural world. Like an oil refinery takes crude oil and separates it into different forms of usable oil, so does the Between take the original magic and refine it into magic found in the natural world. Do you follow me?"

Our wide eyes and arrested faces answer her.

"The refined magic is further refined by the rivers and lakes or green and growing things, or metals and gems, to create different varieties of magic, but the point is, all of these magics share a point of origin, and they all require the Between to process the original." Mama Magdaline takes a breath.

"And the keeper?" Areum prompts.

"I'm getting to the keeper, child. Patience." The rebuke falls short and Areum grins unrepentantly.

"The last Keeper of the Between that I remember walked the Between when I was a child. It has been a long time since then." Mama Magdaline's expression is softened by nostalgia, not that she shares what she is remembering. "The blood of the Keeper of the Green has the essence of green and growing things. The blood of the Keeper of the Rivers and Lakes is filled with the essence of the rivers and lakes, just like the Keeper of Precious Gems has the essence of gold in their blood. The Keeper of the Between, however, always has the blood of a human being because their job is to facilitate the conversion of the crude magic into refined magic. The Keepers of the Between always begin as humans."

"If the Keepers of the Between are so important to the flow of magic, why is Taraana being hunted like this?" Valentina demands.

"Because most people are not aware the Between even has keepers. Powerful middle worlders have, for centuries now, exploited the Keeper of the Between for their own gains, without caring for the consequences to the middle world. But I fear we will all realize the danger that comes with neglecting the needs of the Between soon." Mama Magdaline sighs and a sharp scent of green rises in the room. "Once I would have brought along forests with me. Now, I am forced to scavenge for magic in the roots of old trees."

"The Between is failing?" Eulalie sounds scared.

"Indeed. Were we not talking about the decreasing levels of magic in the natural world last night?" Mama Magdaline sighs again. "I fear that this is the beginning of the end."

"Can't you speak to other powerful middle worlders? Have them make laws that protect Taraana? If the Between fails, won't the middle world end?" Paheli frowns. "Can you not warn the other keepers, the Dar who wants to capture Taraana, of the consequences of his actions?"

"I have tried. But I can only speak to other beings in positions of power if they are willing to listen, child. The recently freed Dar from Uttar Pradesh is only one of your enemies. This won't sound pleasant, but Baarish is the only active pursuer because he has claimed you." Mama Magdaline exhales.

"Who are these others, do you know?" Paheli asks.

"Everyone who sits on the Magic Council with Baarish is a potential enemy," Mama Magdaline replies. "I have seen them, gorged on magic, and full of the arrogance too much power brings, talking and planning."

"Is there nothing I can do to keep myself safe?" Taraana asks.

Mama Magdaline thinks for a while. "You need to bond to the Between, child. That is when you will truly become the Keeper of the Between and gain the powers of the office. I'm not sure of the specifics, but I know for certain that the Between-bonded keepers don't lack power."

"How do I bond to the Between?" Taraana's question is a little desperate.

"That I do not know. I'm sorry to disappoint you, child." Mama Magdaline takes a deep draft of sweet tea. She puts her cup down on the table between the two settees. "To bond to the trees and green, I had to find the first place the magic flowed in the area I call my own—I had to find the oldest tree in existence and mix my blood with its sap. Perhaps you need to find the door to the oldest city in the world and bleed on it? I'm not sure. But for all our sakes, I hope you find the way soon."

Having said this, Mama Magdaline proceeds to ignore our existence and devotes her attention to the sumptuous tea Eulalie prepared. We hold out for a minute before we join her. It is, of course, rude to let a guest eat alone.

Blood and the Between

Mama Magdaline left after eating her fill of Eulalie's food. Though she is gone, the smell of roses remains, and the sunflower growing outside pokes its leaves in through the window Ghufran just opened as if searching for her. We are draped over the furniture in various poses of repose, recovering from Mama Magdaline's overpowering magic. Well, all of us are exhausted except for Taraana.

He sits beside Paheli (which is not a surprise at this point), with his chin cupped in the palm of his hand, his elbow of which is resting on his knee. He is deep in thought.

"What do you plan to do now?" Eulalie nudges Daraja over and sits next to her on the settee Mama Magdaline was sitting on. Valentina and Paheli, who were whispering to each other, look up at her words.

"It depends on what Taraana wants to do," Paheli replies. "I'm still thinking about the best way to defeat villains."

"With a giant vat of boiling oil," Kamboja suggests.

Paheli pauses, tilts her head, and narrows her eyes. She seems to be considering the suggestion.

Widad sighs loudly. "Be serious."

"I don't know how you can get more serious than a giant vat of boiling oil," Kamboja huffs.

"I will not dignify that with a response," Widad replies.

"But you just did?" Ligaya points out.

"Have a jelly bean." Daraja takes out her stash and places it on the table.

Before the chaos can fully descend, Taraana clears his throat. We fall silent and look at him.

"I would like to see if I can bond to the Between," he says. His voice is too soft, as if he's not sure of his right to make noise. We will have to give him screaming lessons.

"It's not easy to figure out which city is the oldest one in the world. I mean, there are speculations but nothing certain," Talei says.

"We can try as many as it takes . . ." Taraana's voice is hesitant.

"You mean you want to find the doors to all the oldest cities and bleed on them just in case one of them is it?" Paheli says, her voice containing no censure.

"Do you have to word it that way?" Taraana asks with an annoyed expression.

"Yes," Paheli replies.

Taraana sighs. "Yes, well. That's what I want to do. Bleed. On doors."

"Okay. We can help you do that. It will be safer if not all of us accompany you, so we will use New Orleans as a base. Does that sound good to you all?"

We nod at her question.

The next day, before Paheli, Talei, and Areum accompany Taraana into the Between to search for the door to Varanasi, Eulalie stops us and hands a phone to Taraana. He takes it with a questioning look before he puts the phone to his ear and hears the voice on the other end. His expression crumples and he sobs out a name. "Assi." He doesn't ask her where she is or if he can go see her. We know why. We have all learned to let go.

Taraana's forays into the Between are unsuccessful, but he doesn't give up. He bleeds on the doors leading to Cádiz, Thebes, and Larnaca. In between those days, we give him secret looks at the New Orleans we know. The day before the trip to bleed on the doors of Thebes and Larnaca is a sunny one, so Paheli, Daraja, and Talei take him for a picnic in the City Park where Paheli hugs trees and Taraana tries not to be jealous.

When some of us (Kamboja, Valentina, and Paheli) accompany him to bleed on the door to Athens, we run into Baarish's minions in the Between. This time, the scaled middle worlders make no attempt to capture Taraana or hurt him; they do nothing that can be construed as explicitly malicious. In fact, there is always a careful distance between us and them. All these scaled middle worlders do is look, but somehow it is a violation. Paheli chases them off, but the damage is done. Taraana's sense of security is eroded again.

When we return to New Orleans, he is shaking with fear. That night the cobblestones are slick with rain and the air full of music. We accompany Taraana through the hours of the night, singing, dancing, covering all possible surfaces where loneliness and pain may fester with our presence. We ply him with chocolate and ice cream. We move from one room of the house to another, up and down the stairs. We coax Valentina into playing the saxophone and Paheli into singing, something she rarely does. Her voice has all the broken notes of a tragedy and echoes long after the song is done. We climb into bed only when the darkness turns to blue and Taraana has regained the faint edges of the smile we've worked so hard for. He perseveres and ventures out into the Between again, but like a bad stench, Baarish's servants are there every time he does.

Two weeks pass like this. Taraana's hands are now filled with pinpricks from which he squeezed out blood, but he refuses to give up. He tries the doors leading to Balkh, Kirkuk, and Tyre, all of them old cities.

When none of these are successful, Paheli rebels and refuses to let him bleed again. They argue and she locks herself into the study with Eulalie, leaving Taraana to us. Daraja feeds him yellow jelly beans and Areum brings him some beignets from Café du Monde. Between warm, buttery pastry and confectioners' sugar, we coax Taraana out of his shell, which is a lot more fragile than we thought.

You see, while our tormentors were human and our escape more solid, he lives his life poised to fall, anytime, on a sharp blade. He may not see his enemies around him, but he knows they're always there, waiting. He only trusts us because we wear his tears on our palms and he can read our hearts to a certain degree.

We wonder what he reads in Paheli's heart, but he refuses to say, claiming some things are his alone.

He likes eggplants, cotton candy, and mangoes. He likes to read, and were he allowed to live a normal life, he would write books in which all the monsters die.

"I would write impossible things like happily-ever-afters, requited love, and freedom," he says with a smile lighter than his words deserve.

The first day Paheli locks herself away, we watch American television: a commercial that states good cologne is all a man needs to attract women; a music video of a song with lyrics that dissect the character of a woman while the singer surrounds himself with girls who are little more than accessories; the news that talks about how the promising futures of several young men are suddenly in jeopardy because a high school freshman made them rape her. We turn off the TV and bury the remote control.

Paheli emerges at noon on the second day and tells us we are leaving New Orleans. We make preparations, but she suddenly insists on visiting Marie Laveau's House of Voodoo first. She won't say why she needs to visit the store, but she won't be denied. Eventually, we give in and accompany her. The place is not far from where we are, so we walk over. Taraana, as always, walks in the middle. The store is beautiful and crammed full of things we itch to touch but know better than to lay a finger on.

You see, human conjury is the antithesis to the magic we are familiar with and are immersed in. Eulalie says this is because human conjury is transient, unlike middle-world magic. Magic is a state of being, while conjury is a placement of intention into an object. Human intention, like human lives, is short. If magic were to haunt a house, it would haunt it forever, while conjury would haunt the same house with the same conditions for a week at the most. Real human conjury is very rare, and when it meets middle-world magic, explosions occur.

Paheli has a particular obsession with conjuries. We've accompanied her as she's searched for it in many different stores in many different cities. This time is no different. She is about to waltz into the store when Taraana catches her hand.

"You can't go in there," he says.

"I totally can," she replies with a sunny smile. "I just need to take one step, and I will be there!"

"Assi said human enchantment unravels middle worlders," Taraana says. "She told me to stay away from it."

"But, Taraana, you aren't a middle worlder. Neither am I." Paheli pulls her hand away from him. "You don't have to come in with us if you don't want to."

So, he doesn't. Talei, Valentina, and Ghufran stand on the sidewalk with him, waiting for us to come back.

We walk gingerly inside the store, trying to move without touching anything. Most of these things are fake; in our experience, conjured objects, conjuries, have a purple aura, a sheen that is a poor cousin to the glow of the magic that we are used to. Human conjuries depend largely on faith; sometimes we wonder if the reason we see so little of it is because we do not believe in it.

Paheli looks around the shop with a frown on her face before finally picking up a flask filled with water. She swirls it around and looks at the gleaming liquid inside.

"This is lake water sourced from India. It is supposed to open your senses to magic," a shop assistant says, appearing beside her. "Would you like to try it?" Paheli stretches out a hand in response, and the shop assistant uncorks the flask and sprinkles some of the water onto her outstretched palm. The water falls on the embedded star and immediately turns into steam. Paheli looks at the shop assistant blankly. "It's not supposed to do that. . . ." The shop assistant gives her a suspicious look and, making an excuse about stocking, leaves.

We wait for some tragedy to befall us, but nothing happens. "It wasn't a true conjury," Paheli mutters, turning around to look at some bird skulls. Ten minutes pass as she examines everything on the shelves.

Suddenly, we hear Talei's piercing whistle. We exit the store to find that clouds have taken over what was a clear sky just a few minutes ago. Taraana is frozen, his eyes on the sky.

"What is it?" Paheli asks, and grabs his hand.

"He travels by thunderstorm," Taraana whispers.

"Show-off," Paheli grumbles just as thunder shakes the old bones of the House of Voodoo and the store's wooden sign lurches in the sudden wind. "Let's go."

We take a few steps out of the cover of the store awning and rain hurls down, punishing in its fury. Humans run for shelter while we look around for a wall uninterrupted by windows. We find a wall separating a garden from the sidewalk, and Paheli runs her fingers down the cement.

"Call a door," she tells Taraana. She could do it, but she chooses to make him take the first step.

He cannot stop shaking.

"Taraana," Paheli says, reaching up and cupping his cheek. "Listen to me."

He blinks as if emerging from a trance. He lays a trembling hand on the wall. A door with its edges gleaming in gold appears. Thunder booms again and the skies crack open. We watch Baarish descend from a staircase made of what look like clouds. Before he can reach the ground, we are gone.

Some days we don't get out of bed. We can't. We fold in on ourselves and retreat from the world—and each other. We do not smile, joke, or pretend that everything's okay. Some days we let the dark we carry inside slip out and cover all the colors we surround ourselves with. We cry softly and loudly—a broken anthem for our girl nation. On these days, the minutes stretch into hours and the hours become small eternities. We sink to the very bottom, and because we are among comrades, we emerge unscathed but for the wounds on the inside. The wounds that will never heal. The wounds that we have learned to live with.

The Library of the Lost and the Stories of the Silenced

I.

We slam the door to the city behind us and stand still in the Between for one charged moment. All of us are drenched from the rain, but the reason we are shaking has very little to do with the cold. Taraana's fear is catching, and all of us are nearly drunk from the force of it.

"Follow me," Paheli says, and walks ahead, pulling Taraana behind her.

"We were betrayed," Valentina says. She doesn't move a step from her spot. Paheli stops and half-turns to her. "Eulalie—"

"Eulalie wouldn't," Paheli cuts her off.

"How can you be so sure?" Valentina demands. We look between them uneasily.

"Think on it, Tina. If it were Eulalie, she would have granted

Baarish access to the house when we were sleeping and at our most vulnerable." Paheli shakes her head. "It wasn't Eulalie. . . . It was probably me." She looks chagrined. "The voodoo store clerk sprinkled some lake water on my palm. The palm containing the star, I mean. She said the water was from a lake in India, but I didn't think—"

"That's the problem, isn't it? You *never* think." Valentina's voice is cold, and the air in the Between is colder.

Paheli nods and a smile blooms brilliant on her face. "That is correct. I never think. Thinking is vastly overrated."

The lights of the Between flicker suddenly, and we look at Taraana. He has stopped shaking, but he refuses to relinquish his hold on Paheli's hand. The magic in the Between covers him so he looks like he is made of coruscating balls of light.

He looks at Paheli for a long moment but doesn't say a word. Instead, he slips a hand around her waist, touching her more easily than any of us have ever dared. Paheli meets his eyes and looks away, the smile on her lips fading slightly.

"Let's go." She starts walking again and we follow her, keeping our counsel. The only person willing to fight with Paheli is Valentina. We don't know where Valentina gets the courage from, but Paheli never responds to her provocations.

We pass many doors and turn several corners before arriving at a solid black door we have never seen before. We turn to Paheli, but our questions simply compound when she brings up her free hand and knocks on the door in a complicated pattern.

We have never before needed to knock on doors, as we operate on the assumption that none will ever fail to open for us. Half a minute later, this door is pulled open by a brown-haired, hazel-eyed boy of about nineteen. We look at him suspiciously, but he merely nods at us and smiles warmly at Paheli.

"I didn't expect you back so soon," he says to her, and we lean forward, puzzled. He stands aside and gestures for us to enter.

The door does not lead to a city but to what, at first glance, seems like an immense library that contains not just books but various objects as well.

"This is Qasim," Paheli says, nodding at the boy. "He is one of the librarians here at the . . ." She pauses and looks at the boy. "Perhaps you ought to introduce this place."

Qasim smiles at us. His gaze encompasses all of us without judgment or rancor. There are other patrons in the library, but none of them look toward us or display any curiosity at our entrance.

We are standing beside the door to the Between, which, unlike any other door we have encountered, seems fixed in place, on a small platform from which a staircase descends to lower levels. The middle of the library is an atrium, and around it are many levels that are enclosed by railings. We are standing on the highest level.

The boy moves toward the railing and gestures to the space beyond him. "Welcome to the Library of the Lost and the Silenced. We do not curate works of literature, carefully crafted and revised, but the lives of people clumsily lived and easily ended. The stories of the silenced occupy positions of honor here at the library. Follow me."

He leads us down one level to a section labeled OUT OF TIME

and gestures to a large collection of objects housed in glass cubes. "I am not just a librarian but also a collector of stories contained in the object a person most values. That object holds that person's life story after they move on." Perhaps he notices the skepticism on our faces because his lips quirk. "What, do you not think an object can be read?" He takes out a scuffed leather shoe from a glass cube and brings it carefully to a viewing table nearby. He sets the shoe down and gestures us closer.

"Look at this shoe. Filthy, no? What material is it made from? What about the mud embedded in its sole? Where did it come from? Look at the creases in the leather. This shoe tells a story even to you who do not understand the language of objects, but to me, this shoe tells a tale about a laborer, not particularly old but not young, either. His name was Raoul, and he lived in a vast country not his own. He had a young daughter for whose sake he worked for little pay at a rich man's company. Raoul owned only one pair of shoes, and he kept them clean." The young librarian's face slips into sorrow as his hand traces the creases of the old shoe. "His daughter was killed by bullies who wouldn't accept her differences, and because he was an immigrant, justice for him, for his child, wasn't a priority to those in power. Excuses were made. Without his daughter, the man lost his reason to live. He slipped into despair, and one morning, just after dawn, he walked out onto a busy road and ended his life."

"Are *all* these stories tragic?" Areum asks after a protracted moment of silence.

"The stories of the lost and the silenced usually are," Qasim says in a whisper. Another moment, soft with sorrow, pulses through us. He abruptly turns to Paheli. "I suppose you are here for the objects belonging to the past Keepers of the Between?" Taraana stills at his words, and he, too, turns to Paheli.

"Yes, I didn't finish looking through them the last time I was here," Paheli replies. "I also wanted to know if Master Ferdinand is feeling better now."

"I will get them out for you, if you will wait here? As for the Master, I will go and inquire." When Paheli nods, Qasim leaves.

We turn to her when he is gone. She preempts our questions. "Eulalie told me about this library and taught me the knocking pattern guaranteed to gain me an entrance. She was given this information by Mama Magdaline, who thought this library might contain information about the keepers."

"Why didn't you tell us about this place?" Etsuko asks, her dark eyes demanding.

Paheli's eyes brush lightly over Taraana before she answers, and she shrugs. "I didn't want to get anyone's hopes up before I found something concrete."

"Did you find something concrete?" Widad asks, her question a breathy trill.

"We'll see," Paheli says, and drops into a chair with a sigh, then rubs her face. "I dislike fleeing from places. It hurts my pride."

Ligaya sits down beside her, close enough to offer comfort without touching her. Our Paheli is affectionate, but she doesn't like touching people. Ligaya studies her bejeweled fingernails for a moment before asking, "Why do you think Baarish showed up like that? He had to have known that he wouldn't be able to capture Taraana once Taraana slipped into the Between."

"We're only safe in the Between if they use magic against us," Valentina counters. "Perhaps he thought to use violence."

"But they didn't follow us into the Between," Areum says. Her hair has dried in a cloud of blue curls around her head, so she looks particularly interesting at the moment. She glares at us. "Stop laughing at me."

"Are we not safe in the Between, either?" Kamboja suddenly asks, and we all battle horror.

"I don't know about that. No one has ever attacked us successfully in the Between. When Taraana was being pursued, didn't you feel the tension in the Between? I reckon the Between would have acted if we hadn't showed up," Paheli says.

"That's just speculation," Talei replies.

"It's not like I'm saying that we test it out," Paheli says. "I'm just saying there is a lot we don't know. A lot that we haven't questioned. We move from one city to another, living nomadic lives because this isn't our—no, *your*—ever after. It might be mine. What I'm saying is there is more to the Between and to the middle world than we know, and it is best we don't pretend there isn't."

"Baarish didn't intend to catch us," Ghufran says, breaking the silence following Paheli's little speech. "He wanted to terrorize us. Scare us with his power. His might. He wants to corner us so we lose hope. Why else would he take over the sky?"

"He must be really confident of his allies if he's making such big shows of his power," Daraja muses. While human beings are generally blind to all magical acts, the denizens of the middle world usually try to avoid doing magic that will attract human attention. Middle worlders who continuously do conspicuous magic often find themselves at odds with the regional authority.

"Did you find anything?" Taraana says, speaking for the first time and bringing the subject back to Paheli's mission at the library. Hope thickens his voice.

"Mm, maybe." Paheli shrugs vaguely. "I don't want to speak about it yet. Don't get me wrong. . . . Actually, now that I have said that, you most probably will." She bites her lip. "Maybe listening to the stories of the other keepers isn't a good idea. Especially not for you."

"Do you think I am not strong enough?" Taraana demands, two spots of color high in his cheeks.

"It is not a matter of strength, Taraana. I don't see why you should have to subject yourself to further tragedy."

"Am I supposed to stand back and let you do it for me?"

"Yes."

"Why?"

"Because I want to. Because I owe you."

"You don't owe me anything," Taraana says icily, and turns away as if he hadn't been clinging to her not even five minutes ago.

Paheli glares at him and mutters unflattering things about stupid boys who don't listen to commonsense suggestions when they should. He pretends not to hear.

II.

The librarian brings back six items and a very old man. The six items include: one handkerchief with unraveling embroidery, a comb with several missing teeth, a link of a silver bracelet, a cracked handheld mirror, a chipped mug, and a yellowed turban.

The old man is dressed in white robes that have softened from multiple washings. His face is mostly obscured by a long white beard, and his head is covered by a black kufi. But the age that the lines on his face illustrate cannot compare to the time marked by the depth in his eyes. Even though this man appears human, his age is many times the span of an ordinary person. We do not ask, but we have the feeling that the how and perhaps the why of his age will be revealed soon. Qasim holds on to the old man carefully, and the old man holds on to his cane tightly. His frailty alarms us. We tend to break fragile things.

Taraana rises to his feet when the old man and Qasim come to a stop before him. The old man lets go of Qasim's hand and surprises us all by bowing to Taraana, who looks flabbergasted. Not quite the right response to the obeisance shown him, but we can't really blame him.

"Master!" Qasim is shocked and helps the man straighten from his bow.

"Show him some respect, boy. He is the new Keeper of the Between and our new Master." He turns to us. "My name is Ferdinand," he says in a voice that contains the accumulation of his years. "It is my honor to read for you, keeper."

"He's not the first keeper you have met, is he?" Paheli says while we try to wrap our minds around Taraana being someone's master.

Qasim helps the old man to a chair at the table on which the relics have been placed. The old man lifts a shaking hand to his forehead and rubs it. "No. I knew the last keeper. They were the one who created this library." Ferdinand looks at Taraana. "Sit with me."

We all take seats around the table. "They chose to call themselves Eckle, and they wore their immense power lightly."

"What happened to them?" Valentina asks. She's sitting next to Paheli; the tension between them has disappeared. That's the thing we never understand. They can hate each other one moment and move on to the next as if their argument never happened.

"They chose to fade. They couldn't endure the loneliness of walking the Between by themselves any longer. They were the last keeper to bond with the Between."

We come to attention at these words.

"Do you know how they bonded to the Between? What was the process?" Taraana asks, his words tripping over themselves in their hurry to be out.

Master Ferdinand shakes his head. "It isn't my place to know the details. I didn't . . . No, I *couldn't* ask. To do so would have been a discourtesy."

Taraana ducks his head, possibly to hide his disappointment.

The old man picks up a little glass cube containing a link of a silver bracelet. "This belonged to them, and I have kept it by my side for years, waiting for a Keeper of the Between to come and ask me about it."

"What happened to the keepers who were born after Eckle?" Ghufran asks. There is a peculiar intensity in her eyes that we don't yet understand. "Did all these relics belong to them?"

"The potential keepers were always abducted before we could get to them. Many of them never entered the Between and couldn't understand the middle world. They didn't want to. The others, we reached too late and could only collect their relics," Ferdinand says heavily.

Qasim keeps stealing glances at Taraana as if he cannot quite believe Taraana is real. "Master will read the bracelet, and I will read the rest. Do you have a preference for the order in which they are read?"

"Can you read the bracelet link first?" Our poor Taraana seems entirely overwhelmed by the amount of attention he's getting. His face is a bit too red.

Ferdinand nods and opens the small glass cube containing the bracelet link. He picks it up, his gnarled fingers sketching an ode to the relic with their gentle touch. He closes his eyes and we hold our breaths, all of us, even Qasim, as the moment stretches and the noise in the library fades.

"Is there any information about the bonding process?" Taraana shatters the moment with his question.

"I apologize, keeper. All I see are burning doors in the Between. Burning doors. This is all this bracelet link contains," Ferdinand says.

"Where's the rest of it?" Taraana is furious. And frustrated. We can't blame him.

"Lost to the Between," Ferdinand says. "This library and this bracelet are all that remain of Keeper Eckle."

"Perhaps the other items will contain more information," Qasim says, breaking the bleakness in the air.

So, we settle back and listen to the stories these objects tell, as narrated by Qasim. We learn of the pain these keepers suffered. They spent their lives either in hiding or in the employ of someone who kept on taking more and more from them until they had nothing else to give but their lives. With each tale, Taraana turns paler; Daraja sits down beside him and slips her arm around his waist. He stiffens for a moment before relaxing into Daraja's embrace. Each keeper's life ended messily; each one's death is an escape. None of them were more than thirty years old when they died.

Finally, we get to the handkerchief with the unraveling embroidery. The faded threads tell the tale of a keeper named Yasmine. She is the lone woman among the keepers whose tales we read. It is always worse for a woman, and so, too, it is for her. Violence against a woman is so much more than the physical marks on her body. Even Qasim has to take a break between relating all that was done to her, all that she endured. What hurts most is that Yasmine never gives up. She speaks of looking for human conjury that will help her. Every day she gets up determined to escape, determined to find that conjury, determined to reclaim her life and her body, and take revenge. Her hope persists until her tale abruptly cuts off. She died hoping.

Qasim finishes his tale with a wobble in his voice and wet eyes. We, however, don't cry. We are too angry to.

"Why?" Paheli stands up, knocking the chair back so it falls to the ground with a clatter. "Aren't the Keepers of the Between important? Don't they have power of their own? Why are they treated this way?"

Ferdinand jerks at the violence in her voice. He shudders, and we wonder if Paheli has managed to kill someone simply by questioning him. Finally, he breathes out in a gasp and we relax. "I, too, have wondered the same thing, child. Eckle told me in confidence that they only gained power once they bonded to the Between. Before that, they, though not hunted like the keepers after them, were powerless. Unlike the keepers after them, however, they had a mentor, an old magic user whose primary purpose was to educate them."

"Where is that magic user now?" Valentina asks.

"He died some years after Eckle came into power, or so Eckle told me," Ferdinand says. "Eckle was very, very old. They felt as old as the Between sometimes. If they hadn't chosen to fade, they would still be walking the corridors."

"Mama Magdaline, the Keeper of the Green, told us that the Between is very important to the health of the magic the middle worlders are dependent on," Talei says, interrupting the old man's musings. "So why do they treat Keepers of the Between like this? It doesn't make sense."

Qasim steeples his fingers and takes a breath before speaking. "You're probably aware of or have even experienced that discrimination humans face from middle worlders. The Keepers of the Between always begin as humans, so their importance has always been debated." He raises an eyebrow in question, and our expressions must answer him because he continues. "Plus, Mama Magdaline is but one voice, perhaps the only contradictory one on the Magic Council. From what I've heard, not all middle worlders believe that magic is refined in the

Between. They think it a simple corridor that makes traveling convenient."

"Eckle died a long time ago, and no other keeper has bonded to the Between in the interim. The middle worlders think nothing has changed," Ferdinand adds.

"That's not quite true, though, is it?" Paheli says. "The Dar, our enemy, said magic is decreasing both in quantity and power around the world. Could that not be an effect of not having a Keeper of the Between?"

Ferdinand doesn't say anything, but the expression on his face is loud, making words unnecessary.

"Couldn't you speak for the need of a Keeper of the Between to the Magic Council?" Paheli asks.

"The members of the Magic Council are the ones hunting the Keepers of the Between," Qasim says. "The Dar you mentioned— he sits on the council as well."

"We know that," Ligaya says with an impatient sigh. "What other power can we appeal to, though?"

"Can't you try speaking to the normal middle worlders, then? I know you are human, but perhaps if you did, some of them may surprise you and listen." Widad is earnest.

"I can't step out of the library," Ferdinand replies, his voice thick with frustration. "I remain alive within the walls of the library, but if I take so much as one step out, I will turn to dust." The old man looks at Taraana, who sits with his head bowed. "My sincerest apologies, keeper. I can offer you nothing but a haven here in this library. If the Between falls, so will we, but until then, if you need it, this can be your home."

Taraana looks startled at the offer, but before he can say a word, Paheli speaks.

"Thank you for the kind offer, but Taraana's home is with us," she says. "We will keep him safe, and *we* will be his haven."

Once, we wrote suicide notes.

Dear World, we wrote in the dust, in any ink we could find, and, when we were desperate, in drops of our blood.

Dear World, I am angry and I am hurt. I cannot. Be. Am. Are. Exist any longer. Language has failed me. I am unwanted in all tenses.

Dear World, why do you not care?

Dear World, I can no longer hold this pain inside of me. I need to spill blood—yours, ideally, but mine will do just as well.

But before we could take the step that has no take-backs, Paheli found us.

Have you ever noticed how, in an argument with a woman, a man, on the losing side, will start casting aspersions on a woman's sexual behavior? He will call her a slut or a bitch or both, as if her intelligence is compromised either by the number of times she has sex or by the number of men she has sex with.

Walking in Wicked Ways or
The Importance of Balık Ekmek

Qasim leads Ferdinand away, leaving us to linger over the artifacts curated in the library. No one else in the library seems inclined to approach us, so we spend some time sitting in silence, gathering our thoughts, mulling over all we have learned.

Finally, Paheli stirs from the pensive silence she retreated into. Taraana is sore at her, but this has not stopped him from returning to her side. He just doesn't talk to her.

All of a sudden Ligaya stands up and stomps her foot. We frown at her actions; we are still in the library. "I'm sorry!" She sits down and bounces in her seat. "I got too excited."

"Why?" Valentina says.

"Because . . . THIS LIBRARY WAS CREATED BY A KEEPER OF THE BETWEEN!!!" Ligaya screams in a whisper, then coughs.

We wait for her to regain the strands of her sanity.

"So?" Valentina again, with her one-word responses.

"So? What do you mean, 'so'? Do I have to explain? Can you not figure it out yourself?!" Ligaya gesticulates.

"Well," Valentina replies. Then smiles at Ligaya's visible frustration.

"Fine. I'll spell it out for you. To be able to create a library this huge and this complicated out of magic means"—Ligaya pauses for dramatic effect—"the Keeper of the Between. Is. Super. Duper. Powerful."

"That's *after* the keeper bonds with the Between, Ligaya," Etsuko says, her voice cool like always. "Might I remind you, Taraana is currently powerless and vulnerable?"

Taraana flinches and we glare at Etsuko.

"Sorry," she mumbles.

"Let's go look for a burning door. Maybe if Taraana bleeds on a burning door, the bonding will happen?" Areum asks with shining eyes.

Talei snorts. "Do you think it's so easy to find a burning door? That we can turn a corner and it will spring up in front of us? The Between stretches on in all directions forever. We need time to look for a burning door."

"Plus, the Between isn't exactly safe for us right now," Sevda adds. "While we have been able to defend ourselves thus far, there is no guarantee Baarish won't send forces who will be able to overpower us. Can we confidently take risks with our safety? With Taraana's?" Sevda has been gradually distancing herself from us recently, so we are surprised by her comment. Not at the content of her comment, but at the fact that she made it.

"Let's look for human conjury," Kamboja says. She glances at Paheli. "Wasn't that what you were trying to do in the voodoo store? Did Qasim read you Yasmine's handkerchief earlier?"

"Did you already know that human conjury might help us fight Baarish?" Daraja asks Paheli. "How exactly will it help? What does it do to middle worlders?"

Paheli's tendency to keep things from us has, on more occasions than one, provoked us into arguments.

She looks at us without speaking for a moment. Her eyes are dark and her face devoid of the smile that we almost take for granted. "The first thing we will do is go to Istanbul and look for Baarish's errant granddaughter, Tabassum Naaz. When we find her, we will try to persuade her to ally with us. She has already helped Taraana twice, so it's not a stretch of the imagination to believe she will do so again. There were a few stores in Istanbul that carried authentic conjury when we last visited them. We will visit them again. If we are unsuccessful in locating human conjury in Istanbul, we will travel to Chefchaouen, to that store we found conjury in three years ago. If that store too doesn't have any, we will go to Marrakech. I seem to remember coming across a store selling authentic conjury in the souks there some years ago." She pauses to let her words sink in. "I'm not sure if we can really use human conjury against middle worlders. But it can't hurt to find out for certain. Does anyone have any other questions?"

"Do I give up trying to bond with the Between?" Taraana asks.

"Of course you don't," Paheli replies. "Lalie is still looking for that middle worlder who worked in the Library of Alexandria.

She might have some concrete answers for us. If you want, we can look for a burning door for you to bleed on, but I fear Baarish is going to intensify his search for you."

"It would be better for us to have a plan of action, a way of countering him, before Taraana spends more time in the Between," Talei says.

We all nod in agreement.

"Anyone else have anything to say? No? Let's go." Paheli gets to her feet and leads the way up the stairs to the floor containing the door to the Between. She signals to a man dressed in the same loose white tunic and pants that Qasim was wearing, and he nods, bowing slightly.

We stand, momentarily tense, in front of the black door leading to the Between. We worked hard to unlearn fear; we are not going to let it define our days again, but oh, we remember how it feels to live with fear's clammy touch. None of us miss those days.

Paheli opens the door and we step into the Between.

Talei leads the way to the door that will open up to Istanbul. Before Talei can pull open the door, though, Paheli halts her. She turns to Taraana, who immediately stiffens.

"Have you ever had any run-ins with any middle worlder based in Istanbul?" she asks him. "Do you know?"

He shakes his head. "I've never been to Istanbul before. Assi told me the city is too crowded with middle worlders, so I stayed away."

"All right." Paheli gestures to Talei to open the door and she does. Or she tries to. But the door is stuck again. Once again, it takes Taraana to pull it open.

We exit the Between in the Beyoğlu District in the European half of Istanbul, not far from the apartment we own on Istiklal Avenue. However, our first destination is the magic shop in Balat, the Jewish quarter of the city located in the Fatih District.

Taraana seems starstruck by Istanbul. He looks around at the architecture and landscape with bright eyes.

"The city is overflowing with magic," he whispers, his fingers closing around Paheli's. She looks at him with some exasperation.

"Are we friends again?" she asks him.

"No. Maybe," he says distractedly, his eyes moving around.

Istanbul, once known as Constantinople, is a city with deep roots, and, just like in Byblos, people have left their histories sunken into the stones of this place. A fact that the citizens of the magical world don't usually acknowledge—like Mama Magdaline said, human lives generate the magic middle worlders live on.

"Can you tell the difference between refined magic and crude magic?" Talei asks Taraana as we walk. "Like, is the magic on the streets here crude magic, or has it been refined by the Between?"

Taraana's face contorts in a frown as he considers her question for a minute. Then he nods self-consciously. "I have been able to do that since always. It's just that I didn't have the words to explain what it is I am able to feel. To me, refined magic is like breathing in clear mountain air, while crude magic is breathing in smoggy air."

"How much of the magic on the streets is crude magic, and how much is refined?" Kamboja asks. "Can you tell?"

Taraana purses his lips and Paheli glances at him. He looks

down at her and smiles before replying. "A little more of the crude compared to the refined."

We ponder over this as we make our way through the streets. It takes us forty minutes to get to Balat; we manage public transport quite well without being visible to humans. Like us, Taraana can choose his visibility at will. The day is a fair one, and a clock somewhere chimes three in the afternoon when we get off the bus.

Balat is a series of narrow streets and alleys with tall and equally narrow pastel-colored houses on either side. The houses are rather dilapidated and could do with some maintenance and a new coat of paint. But the air is filled with light and the shouts of children playing; a bright blue sky stretches overhead, and the waters of the Bosphorus Strait glimmer in the distance. Laundry flutters from clotheslines strung high up from the third or fourth floors. To complete the picture, every house has at least two window boxes from which flowers and other greenery spill gleefully over.

We follow the magic to a narrow, three-storied building located halfway up an incline. The house is pale yellow with white trim; a rainbow of roses blooms in a garden box in the lower window. A flight of stairs is located immediately outside the second door, which is the one we need. The house looks nothing like a shop from the outside; the door is closed and covered with a metal bar, which, despite the roses, adds a forbidding demeanor to the place. We know better than to be intimidated, though.

Paheli simply turns the knob and the door opens inward. We enter the store and take a much-needed moment to orient ourselves. Clocks cover every surface of the establishment; modern clocks with asymmetric shapes, vintage ones with yellow faces, Gothic cuckoo clocks made of black metal, and Turkish clocks with tile faces featuring the most beautiful Arabic calligraphy. They are all ticking, and the din is incredible. We have been here, so we knew what to expect, but Taraana's jaw drops open and his eyes go round. The proprietor is black-haired with turquoise eyes ringed by gold eyelashes; she is sitting at the counter, working on yet another clock. She has a weathered, stern but not unkind face. She looks up briefly when we enter.

"We have a bag full of Between diamonds." Areum throws the first volley. "Are you interested?"

"As if you need to ask," the middle-worlder woman replies dryly. Her name is Miray. Though her manner is brusque, she is not unfriendly. Or at least, she hasn't been hostile to us before. Things can change. They have before.

"Oh my, who is this?" She puts down her tools when she sees Taraana, who admittedly is not making any effort to hide himself. He spares the woman a glance before returning his attention to the clocks.

"He is one of us," Valentina replies with a too-long stare at the middle worlder.

Taraana beams at her words, and the sun comes out in the musty dark store.

"Are these for sale?" he asks Miray.

"Indeed, they are." Miray holds up the cogwheel in her hands. "I am willing to sell you whichever one you choose."

"Do you really want to buy one?" Paheli asks Taraana.

"Why not?" Taraana replies.

"These clocks allow the buyer to reexperience bits of their past. And you cannot choose which bits you reexperience," Daraja says gently.

Taraana pales at her words. "I . . . Sorry. I no longer want one."

Miray looks at Taraana again. She puts down the cogwheel and opens a drawer beside her chair. She rummages around in the drawer for a while before pulling out a thin rectangular box. She hands it to Taraana, who opens the box to reveal a pair of spectacles.

"I got this from a magic user as payment for a clock." She sees our baffled looks and elaborates. "They will make an effective disguise for him. I don't know who he is, but the stars in his eyes are very conspicuous. They might attract the wrong sort of attention."

Taraana takes the glasses out of the box and puts them on. Immediately, his appearance changes into that of a rather rakish boy who still has dark hair and dark skin but with no magic that we can sense. These spectacles make him into a beautiful but very ordinary human. When he wears these, middle worlders won't give him a second glance. Probably.

"Will they do?" Miray asks.

"Why are you helping us?" Kamboja gives the middle worlder a suspicious look.

"Oh, don't worry. That isn't free. I will make you pay for it." Miray smiles with all her teeth showing. "Now, shall we bargain?"

Ten minutes later we are done with business and on our way to the reason we came to Istanbul. And no, we are not talking about Baarish's granddaughter.

Taraana's glasses give us and him a reprieve from hiding. Obviously, we are still not completely safe, but to be a Wild One, you have to be comfortable with walking on dark roads. The road *to* becoming a Wild One is dark.

So, we catch a bus to Eminönü and make our way to the western side of Galata Bridge. The place is full of people enjoying the day and the food we have come searching for.

Whenever we come to Istanbul, we ensure that our first meal of the day is the balık ekmek sold from the restaurants located on the boats tied up at the quay. These boats, decorated with golden trimmings and intricately detailed figureheads also painted gold, pitch either gently or roughly depending on the weather. The servers who sport jaunty red hats seem to have sea legs and maintain a steady flow of conversation with the customers they serve. The only thing on their menu is the balık ekmek, which is a fish sandwich composed of freshly caught grilled mackerel and vegetables, and a beverage made from the salted and spiced juice of pickled carrots.

We cast an illusion of safety and feast, laughing at Taraana's delight, the taste of the sea, the hum of the magic, and the freedom, false though it may be, to enjoy all of it.

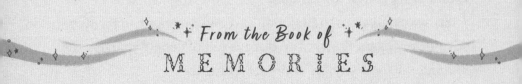
KAMBOJA
CITY OF ORIGIN: JAKARTA

I was a part-time friend

a full-time girl and a glass

half full. Open-toed stilettos and the whisper

of city pavement. I was that journey

of orange rinds and too-rich chocolate in dark, musky

hotel rooms. I was a five-minute love; scheduled between

the featured program and the sponsored commercials.

Words and trickery; I was a book waiting to be read. I was

midnight and I was the last hour before dawn that stretches into

an insomniac eternity. One heartbeat to culmination and I

was the time back when nights used to be only about the dark.

Looking for the Needle in the Haystack

I.

By the time we get to our apartment on Istiklal Avenue, daylight has slipped away, taking with it the fair weather. The door to what we'll call home here opens with a ping after Ligaya enters the passcode in the mechanical lock. The air inside is musty, so Talei walks over to the large windows in the central living room and opens them. We are on the third floor in one of the narrow buildings that line the avenue. Fresh air tinged with gentle rain wafts in.

The place is magically enhanced like our home in New Orleans and adjusts itself to meet our needs. Paheli throws herself down on a rug in the living room and stretches.

"I," she announces, "am exhausted."

"Here, I will lend you my lap," Taraana says, in an unexpected moment of generosity.

"What?" Paheli sits up in alarm. "Why?" She doesn't appear to appreciate it.

"So you can take a nap," he says, almost as if he is entirely without guile.

Paheli stares at him for a full moment before she turns and looks at us, her face bewildered. Valentina is trying, unsuccessfully, to stifle her giggles at the look on Paheli's face.

"Is he trying to flirt with me?" Paheli asks sotto voce.

We look at Taraana, who is looking confused.

"I don't think so," Sevda says. She grins. "I think he really just wants you to use his lap."

"You can't say things like that!" Paheli scolds Taraana.

"What did I say?" Taraana frowns, looking lost.

"Do you make it a habit of offering girls your lap? What's wrong with pillows? Do you have something against pillows?" Paheli's cheeks are definitely red. This is very entertaining.

"No, you are the first girl I have offered my lap to." Taraana runs a hand through his hair so tufts of it stick up. "Nothing is wrong with pillows. I just don't know if you have any here. You don't want my lap?"

Paheli opens her mouth, perhaps to deliver some pithy response, before closing it without uttering a word. This is the first time we have seen our Paheli so completely at a loss. Perhaps we shouldn't be enjoying this so much.

"I think we need ice cream. I will go buy some!" Paheli stomps out of the room, and soon we hear the front door close.

"What's wrong with her?" Taraana asks no one in particular.

"Forgive her, she doesn't know what to do with feelings,"

Areum replies, with a big grin on her pixie face. "She hasn't had them very often."

"What feelings?" Taraana asks.

We look at each other for a moment.

"Oh dear," Daraja says softly.

II.

We wake early in the morning and make our way to our favorite restaurant a few blocks away. We sit on benches at a trestle table at the back of the restaurant that is all but groaning under the weight of the food we ordered.

Widad enjoys Turkish cheeses the most. She loves the pungent taste of Tulum but will always choose the fiery flavor of smoked cheese over it any day. Daraja and Areum adore sucuk, a spicy sausage served in thin slices along with bread and cheese. Kamboja's favorite is an egg dish called menemen, which contains tomatoes, green peppers, and spices. It smells intoxicating and we all demand bites, which Kamboja grudgingly gives. Valentina eats simit, which is a fancy name for a pretzel-type bread coated with sesame seeds. We all enjoy börek, which is made of layered phyllo pastry and filled with meat, potatoes, greens, or cheese. To help wash it all down, we drink countless cups of black tea from Rize.

Replete, we set out to look for the middle-world creature who acts as a fount for all sorts of information for us and probably many others. Like the Greenich in Beirut, we give him Between diamonds in return for information.

The sidewalks are full of humans and middle worlders, so we walk in groups of two and three with Taraana and Paheli at the forefront. With Miray's glasses on, Taraana looks like any other exceptionally beautiful eighteen-year-old. Thanks to us, he is smartly dressed. He walks with his hands in his pockets and his shoulders stiff, ready for the world to bare its teeth at him at any second.

We spent most of last night at a hair salon. We weren't solely following our whims, though a large part, we don't deny, was indulgence. Our changing facades function as disguises in case Baarish has managed to lay his hands on our descriptions. Apart from Taraana—we couldn't convince him to color his hair, as he is a bit of a purist where some things are concerned—we all sport new dos that make this morning look brighter and us more colorful. Paheli's waist-length hair is now a pale lavender, and she seems smitten with the way it looks.

"Do you remember that song that was popular a few years ago?" she said this morning while admiring herself in the mirror. "The one that made girls loving themselves sound bad?"

We did not. We have better taste in music.

"Humph," she said when we told her as much. "It isn't as if I like that song. It was just so difficult to avoid. I happen to love myself very much."

We first look for our informant in the Hagia Sophia. Unlike the Greenich, our informant in Istanbul has no fixed location, which makes the business entirely inconvenient. He is not in the Blue Mosque, where Taraana is bedazzled by the domes and spires of the house of worship. Finally, we check Topkapı Palace and find him lingering in a courtyard there. He is sitting on the floor with his hands pressed to the ground and his eyes closed. Probably absorbing the magic in this place.

There are too many middle worlders around for us to approach him as a group without drawing unnecessary attention, so Paheli separates from us and sashays over to him. She sits down in front of him and waits until he opens his eyes. This middle worlder's name—well, he calls himself Hizrat. He and Paheli have a history neither of them wants to talk about, but their bond is undeniable. Even if a long time passes between their meetings, they pick up the threads of their friendship and continue for however long we are in town. He is very tall and limber with curly black hair and eyes the color of the full moon. Though he looks to be no more than twenty, we know his years contain centuries.

We watch as Paheli asks him a question, receives an answer, and passes him a pouch containing a Between diamond. He says something else to her, something not related to her question, and we watch as she laughs in response. When Paheli laughs, our world brightens.

"Who is he?" Taraana says, his voice low. There is a scowl perched like a crow on his eyebrows. "Is he—no, is Paheli—no, I mean—"

"No," Valentina says.

"Maybe," Etsuko counters.

"Really?" Taraana's eyes are wounded.

We narrow our eyes at Etsuko and she grins. "I'm joking."

"What?" Paheli, who has returned to us, asks. We turn to her as one. "What did I do?" Taraana is looking at her aggrievedly.

"Nothing. There is nothing going on. With anyone," Valentina says, especially to Taraana. "What did Hizrat say?"

"He's actually not sure if the person he knows is the person we're looking for, but he told me to check a tea place in the Grand Bazaar after sundown," Paheli says. "There're still a few hours before then, so let's check out the store that sold conjuries in Dilan Souk."

"Do you meet him often?" Taraana asks as we make our way out of the palace.

"Who?" Paheli frowns.

"Never mind. Let's go," Taraana says, beaming again.

We spend some time in Dilan Souk looking for the conjury store without finding anything to reward our efforts. It's as if the place never existed. We exit the souk when the shadows are lengthening and the skies are a blue particular to the time after sundown.

"I am exhausted." Widad groans, sitting down on a bench outside the souk.

"Why don't Talei and Valentina accompany me to the Grand Bazaar? The rest of you can go home," Paheli suggests.

Taraana's reaction is instantaneous and expected. "Absolutely not!" He is furious. "Why do you always try to exempt me?"

Paheli's usually unruffled mien falters before her eyebrows draw together in the most magnificent scowl we have ever seen from her. "Listen, has it not occurred to you that you are in danger? Yes, I know that you are going to say that this girl saved you, but it has been a long time since then, and who's to say she is of the same mind now?"

"I can protect myself!" Taraana says, leaning down so he and Paheli are nose to nose.

"I am sure you can. However, I am not willing to risk you. What if Baarish is there? What if there is someone else who recognizes you there? We'd be delivering you to them with all but a bow on top!" Paheli replies, standing on tiptoe to glare into Taraana's eyes.

"Do you two need a room?" Valentina asks delicately.

They turn to us with equally infuriated expressions.

"I am going with you!" Taraana crosses his arms.

"You are not." Paheli crosses hers.

"How about we do this?" Talei says. "If we do find the granddaughter at the Grand Bazaar, and she is agreeable to hearing what we have to say, we will ask her for a formal meeting. Once we have ensured that her ambitions align with ours, you can reveal yourself. Does that work for you?"

Taraana hesitates, then replies grumpily. "Yes. You had better come back to me," he says to Paheli, catching her by surprise. She stares at him, her eyes shocked at his words. And then, to our continued amusement, she blushes.

"I will return to *the apartment* obviously," she says to him. "Not to *you* specifically. Goodness, why do you say these things? Let's go, Talei! Tina!"

She practically runs away, with Talei and Valentina following her at a slower place.

"They'll be okay, right?" Taraana asks us anxiously.

"Yes," Daraja says, putting her arm around Taraana's waist. "Let's go eat some dessert. If it makes you feel better, we won't save any for Paheli."

Paheli: The Peculiar Crackle in the Electricity

My cheeks are so hot I might die. Can a person die by blushing? Because I think I'm about to try.

Ugh. Why—no, HOW can that boy say things like that without realizing the effect his words can have on poor, unsuspecting girls like me? Is he really that pure? I know he meant nothing other than "be safe," so why couldn't he have just said "be safe" instead of the remarkably dangerous "come back to me"?

Excuse me, my face is on fire.

"Why are you so embarrassed?" Valentina says to me as soon as she catches up.

I give her a Look. Valentina has been with me the longest, even though I have, on more occasions than one, suggested that she go out and live her life fully, as she should. But I suppose once you have been through what we have been through, normal loses its flavor.

"It's not like you haven't been tempted to dally with boys here and there," she continues, intentionally oblivious to my state of mind. Plus, excuse me again, I may have been tempted, but I have never acted on those temptations, not that there is anything wrong with acting. And temptations. I'm just saying.

"Do you honestly think getting involved with Taraana would be a dalliance?" Because I don't.

She's silent for a bit as we walk toward the Grand Bazaar.

"All right, I don't think dallying with him is a good idea," she says when we are about five minutes away from the shopping mecca.

"Thank you," I reply loftily.

"But he obviously has feelings for you," she continues without so much as a by-your-leave, entirely ruining what little peace I had managed to wrest for myself. "What are you going to do about it?"

"Pretend his feelings don't exist," I reply promptly. "Denial works brilliantly for me."

"I didn't know you were the stick-your-head-in-the-sand kind." Valentina can be quite acerbic at times. Lots of times. Almost always.

"Yes, I feel a keen kinship with ostriches. I don't fly either, you know."

"Maybe you should try out for a career in stand-up comedy someday."

"Is it my wonderfully lavender hair?"

"We are here." Talei interrupts our conversation.

We turn and look at the magical entrance to one of the oldest markets in the world. The human hours are from the morning till early in the evening, but for the middle-world citizens, the Grand Bazaar never closes. Invisible to human eyes, a separate entrance exists for middle worlders. These gates are protected by their region's ruler, not that we know much about him. All of us, but especially Valentina, are allergic to authority. The two guards at the entrance both look like they need bathroom breaks, so we walk past them quietly without making a single attempt at provoking them.

I am suddenly glad that Taraana is not with us right now. Danger blooms in all corners here, and though his glasses hide a lot of who he is, I'd much rather not tempt fate, because fate is not as resistant to temptations as I am. We don't know how long Baarish's arms are.

Anyway, it is almost eight in the evening, which is when the human vendors lock their stores and make for home.

We keep our heads down and walk past groups of middle worlders standing just inside the entrance. They don't give us a second look, and we're glad to be beneath their notice.

A whiff of perfume scents the air; the sound of voices haggling over items; stores filled with light pouring from intricately crafted lamps, exquisite tea sets, luxurious rugs, glinting jewelry, mounds of baklava, and so many other things. I almost wish Taraana were here. He would be just as dazzled as I am.

The magic is so potent here that I feel like I'm drowning in it. Would Taraana glow brighter here? How would he like this place? I wonder.

Why do I keep thinking about him? My brain seems to be growing maudlin in its old age.

"Where do we look?" Talei whispers to us.

We follow the magic through streets, around corners, and into a narrow alley, which has teahouses on either side of it. I am forever amazed by the sheer size of the Grand Bazaar. Very little light spills from the teahouses onto the main pathway, and no other creature, human or magical, is visible in the dimness. Hizrat told me Tabassum Naaz usually whiles away her evenings at one of these teahouses, though personally I can't see the attraction. How much tea can you drink?

I look at my sisters and they look back at me; their confidence in me scares me, but I take a breath and walk into the alley. There are walls around us, so we can retreat to the Between in case of danger, but I prepare a scream anyway. We all tense when a low, masculine laugh reaches us. Talei sucks in a breath and clenches her fist. I realize my mouth is open and the scream is building in my throat.

I close my mouth. We all have nightmares. Ours are just a bit realer.

"Let's go." I put on my most brazen mask and stride ahead, determined not to let the fear have me. I will not be afraid.

I enter the first teahouse we come to, and my sisters follow. It is a tiny place; there are only five small tables inside, and all of them are occupied by middle worlders who bless us with their attention.

We could have done without their blessing. The proprietor has eyes found more often in a snake. I hold his stare for a long moment before he suddenly breaks into a smile I find more disturbing.

"I'm afraid you will have to wait for a table," he says. He has a snake's tongue, so his voice curves around his letters in interesting ways.

"I am not here for tea," I tell him politely. "Is there someone called Tabassum Naaz here?" I pitch my voice so the patrons of the teahouse can hear.

"You will find her next door," a not-human boy says. He has red eyes. There are flowers blooming under his light green skin. I nod a thank-you at him, and we leave without making eye contact with anyone else.

The teahouse next door is a bit larger and more welcoming than the first one. Warm gold light pours out from a chandelier dangling low in the middle of the room. The corners are covered in dark, but the middle seating area is cozy. The patrons of this teahouse seem to be younger and more human-shaped. Music hums in the background, providing an accompaniment to the many conversations occurring simultaneously.

The proprietor has a welcoming smile that fades slightly when she sees us. But she recovers her composure and waves us toward a recently vacated spot in a darker corner of the room. We sit down, keeping our eyes to ourselves at least until we are settled in with cups of mint tea into which we have added liberal amounts of sugar.

"There," Valentina says, her eyes trained on her cup. "That girl bears a resemblance to Baarish."

I turn and look. In a group made of boys is one girl. They are all dressed similarly in formfitting pants and vests. The girl has golden hoops in her ears, a treasure of rings on her fingers, and Baarish's nose, which she has decorated with a gold stud. She is fair, with large dark eyes and black hair scraped back from her face in a tight braid. Also, and very importantly, this girl is staring at Valentina in the same way a lion stares at a particular delicacy before gobbling it up.

Hmm.

Perhaps the girl senses my eyes on hers because she looks at me next and not as kindly. Her companions follow her gaze, and all of a sudden, I feel something alien press against my conscience— someone is trying to use magic to read us. Obviously, the magic fails to uncover the mysteries we present. The girl's stare increases in intensity; it is a wonder I am not on fire. So, of course, I smile at her as sweetly as I can.

In the next minute, without any word from the proprietor, the other patrons of the teahouse exit the place, and the door to the establishment is closed and barred. Oh dear. This girl is entirely too easy to provoke. We don't move from our spot, affecting an interest in our teacups and the conversation we are not having. We are master pretenders.

"I have heard about you," the girl says, getting up from her seat. She speaks as she weaves through the tables toward us, her companions faithfully behind her.

We turn as one toward her.

"What do you call yourselves? Ah, yes, the Wild Ones." Her tone mocks the title I bestowed on us. I bristle slightly. The girl catches it and her sneer widens. Good. She'll give more away if she thinks she has the upper hand. "I was wondering if you would come to me."

"Why is that?" Valentina asks, her voice lazy and disinterested. The girl starts, as if she didn't expect Tina to talk. Her gaze snags on Tina's lips, and her cheeks are suddenly dusted a soft pink. Hmm.

"Well . . ." She pulls a chair from a neighboring table and straddles it, resting her chin on the chair's back. She smiles and says no more, seemingly content to stare at us. Well, stare at Valentina.

"Send your dogs away, would you? They make me want to scream, and bad things will happen if I scream," I say to the girl, with my politest smile. She holds my gaze for a minute before nodding at her companions. They move away from us, hugging the wall across from our seat.

"Are you willing to talk?" Valentina asks.

"It depends on what you want to talk about," the girl replies. She reaches out a hand and hooks a finger around Valentina's pinkie. I hold my breath and steal a look at my friend. She is staring at the offending digit with a fascination that makes me afraid for the future of that finger.

I clear my throat noisily and Valentina pulls her hand away. The girl grins.

"Do you remember that boy? The one made of stars?" Talei says.

All lightness drains away from the girl and she leans back, her face suddenly fierce. "I have no idea what you're talking about," she says, crossing her arms. She needs to work on her poker face.

"You may not remember him, but he remembers you." I keep my voice casual. "He would like to talk to you. Tomorrow at one at Kultur Cafe in Taksim."

"He's here? Are you out of your mind? Why have you brought him here?" She hisses, pitching her voice so only we can hear her.

"He is not for you to worry about," Valentina replies. "We protect our own."

"Then why are you talking to me?" the girl demands. She has a point.

"If you are Tabassum Naaz, we have a proposition for you," Talei says. I observe the girl.

"If I *am* Tabassum Naaz, talking to you would mean an automatic death sentence for me. My grandfather does not suffer traitors." Her voice falters.

"Pretty late for you to worry about that, isn't it? You should have considered it before setting Taraana free all those years ago," I tell her. "Besides . . . from what I've heard, your grandfather wants to kill you regardless.

"If you do decide to talk to us, we will be at the stated place tomorrow for one hour after the promised time. We will wait." I get to my feet. Valentina and Talei follow my lead.

"I didn't say you could go!" The girl stands up too.

"Would you like to try and stop us?" Valentina smiles at her and the girl looks away.

Well then. Things are getting remarkably interesting.

When we return to the apartment, the girls are waiting for us. Taraana is conspicuously absent and I admit it, okay? Not seeing him causes me undue panic as it turns out he just went to take a shower.

My bowl of ice cream and I are the only ones remaining in the living room when he returns. His slightly long hair is curling at the tips, and his soft cotton T-shirt clings to his slender frame. He sits in the chair opposite mine, smelling lemony fresh and utterly irresistible. I have the urge to sniff at him and restrain myself with a heaped spoonful of choconut ice cream.

"You are back," he says unnecessarily.

There is no reason in the world for him to be as attractive as he is. To me. Absolutely no reason.

"As you can see," I reply, focusing all my attention on the ice cream. Okay, I lie. I'm pretending to attend to my ice cream. The truth is somewhat different. He smells good, all right?

"Did you see her?" he asks hesitantly.

I take a deep breath, quash my libido, and tell him what occurred earlier that evening. Somewhere during my narration, he moves to sit beside me. By the time I finish talking, he is practically glued to my side.

"Do you think she'll show up?" He is afraid to hope. He is also too close. I inch away.

"We'll find out tomorrow."

We sit in a contemplative silence. Well, he is contemplative. I'm trying to figure out the best way to extricate myself from this situation. Being alone with him is bad for my heart.

I fidget and finally decide that sleeping is a good idea. I go to pat Taraana's shoulder to bid him good night, but he turns at that moment. His gaze captures mine. Holds it. "I want to be strong in front of you." His voice is a murmur in the silence that suddenly returns to us. "I want to show you all my best sides." He sits up. Licks his lips nervously. A pulse ticks under his eyes. I feel like that deer frozen in the headlights. Any minute now I will go flying over the windshield. "I want so many things, Paheli. I want to wake up in the morning and not feel afraid I won't last the day. I want to walk in the streets without caring about who is looking at me. I want many things, but out of them all, I most want you. However, I keep getting confronted by the limitations this world imposes upon me." A tear, just one, escapes from his eyes and falls on my hand. He breathes in. Oh no.

"Not now, but someday in the future, if"—he swallows—"if I make it, do you think you could love me?"

I stare at him, still channeling that deer, still frozen in the headlights. He touches my cheek once. I do not explode. He leaves the room. I topple over.

Ten Degrees Past Despair

We wear different shades of red lipstick and our fiercest expressions to the meeting. Paheli's not at all sure the girl will show, but Taraana is hopeful.

Hope looks good on him.

We arrive at the narghile café thirty minutes before the designated time and are shown into the room we reserved the day before. Despite the early hour, the café is as crowded as we expected it to be. The more humans around, the easier we can mask ourselves, which is why we chose the place we did.

The private room is one of the few the café keeps reserved for the most affluent of their customers. Sumptuous rugs, tasteful wall hangings, and intimate light provide the perfect atmosphere for the narghile, or as the West refers to it, hookah. Chairs are set in a semicircle at the back of the room with a wide coffee table set in front of them. The narghile occupies the place of prominence on the table, though none of us, apart from Sevda, have acquired a taste for it.

Paheli is curled up beside Etsuko, fairly humming with nerves. Valentina sits beside Daraja, who is next to Etsuko. Taraana sits on the other side of Paheli, with Ghufran next to him and Widad next to her. Kamboja and Areum are too restless to sit and are playing chess set up in a corner. Sevda and Ligaya are standing over their game, giving them spectacularly unhelpful advice.

Talei shrugged when we asked her how the meeting last night went; we translated that particular shift of her shoulders to mean that no blood was spilled but the situation was tense. Talei's shrugs are masterfully eloquent.

The designated hour arrives with the chiming of the clock on a wall in the room. We order some seriously sweet milkshakes and a lot of desserts and continue waiting.

Forty minutes pass. The dessert sits a bit too heavily in our stomachs. Will she come, this girl we know nothing about? Will she side with us, or will she bring her grandfather with her? We don't know. The tension rises and Sevda moves to lean against a wall, her palm pressed to it, ready to call a door into the Between.

"She's not coming." Valentina is the first to give up. "Let's leave."

"She will be here," Taraana replies. "I know she will."

"How can you be so sure?" Ligaya asks. She has dressed up entirely in black today, so we have been careful of her. When one of us wears black, it is a signal to the rest of us that our nightmares are running rampant. That our words will be sharp, maybe draw blood, but that we do not intend to hurt. Not really.

"Wouldn't you want to know what happened to someone you saved?" Taraana answers, and Ligaya turns away without replying.

"Not if it means meeting him would place him in danger," Paheli replies instead, and gets to her feet. "Let's go."

"Giving up on me so soon?" a voice says from the doorway. We all turn. What had been empty space just one second ago is now filled by a tall girl dressed in black jeans and a black vest. We wonder if she, too, is having a bad day. Her hair is pulled back in a French braid, and her lips are as red as ours. Her expression, however, is far more relaxed.

She comes into the room and the door bangs closed behind her. The click of the lock is audible. She looks around at all of us, her gaze lingering on each of our faces. When she gets to Taraana, her eyes widen and her composure slips for a brief second before she forces her features back into the pleasant mask she is wearing.

"I am Tabassum Naaz, here at your request. What do you have to say to me?" She moves over to a chair in front of the narghile and drops down on it. She picks up the narghile pipe and breathes in deeply before exhaling the smoke.

Her every move is designed to broadcast her fearlessness, but what she doesn't realize is that all of us present are fluent in the language of fear. We recognize the pulse of it in her throat, in the tic under her ear, and in the little tremble in her fingers that she doesn't think we see.

"What terrible deed have you done to deserve exile from your family?" Valentina asks.

As an opening gambit, it might be a bit harsh, but the girl doesn't flinch. "Why do you think I owe you any answers?"

We look at Paheli, waiting for her to enlighten all of us. "Well," Paheli says, "we can't run from your grandfather forever, so we have decided to fight against him." Paheli picks up a drink as pink as her hair used to be and sips it before wrinkling her nose at the sweet taste. "One of the ways in which we can do that is to change the patriarch of your family. So, um, considering your current persona-non-grata status in your family, we've called you here to ask whether you'd like to help us."

All artifice falls away from Tabassum Naaz. Her eyes sharpen. "What exactly do you mean?"

Paheli awkwardly scratches her cheek. "Was I not clear? We are going to keep Taraana safe. To achieve that goal, we need Baarish without power. From what we've observed, the majority of his power comes from his title as the Dar. So, if he's no longer the Dar, he won't have as much access to power."

Tabassum Naaz is shaking her head long before Paheli finishes talking. "You do know that my grandfather is but one person who seeks to exploit the keeper, right? So even if you manage to disable the Dar, there will be someone else to replace him."

We don't trust Tabassum Naaz yet, so we won't tell her that we plan to find a way for Taraana to bond to the Between before we have to worry about the other middle worlders who desire him.

"I believe in tackling only one problem at a time. Right now, that problem is your grandfather," Paheli says, with her eyes dark. She's thinking about the children in cages. "By the way, did you know that your family is involved in child trafficking?"

Tabassum Naaz blanches. We wait for her to verbalize the denial her lips open to deliver, but, in the end, she says nothing. Her shoulders sag; a terrible defeat tugs down the corners of her lips.

"They were also attempting to harvest magic off the children. We don't know the details, but perhaps you can find out." Paheli doesn't give Tabassum Naaz a chance to recover from the first blow and neatly deals her a second one. When the other girl just stares at her in a daze, she continues. "The actions of your family don't implicate you. We don't think you're in any way responsible for the evil they're doing. However, now that you do know of their misdeeds, if you still don't act against them, you will be an accomplice. Perhaps an unwilling one, but an accomplice none-theless. Have you ever seen a child trapped in a cage? Treated as if she is less than a human being? Some of us here *were* one of those children." Paheli stares straight at Tabassum Naaz, who seems unable to hold her gaze for more than a moment.

She leans forward, placing her elbows on her knees. Her eyes are stormy. Perhaps there's a hurricane within her. "I know it's a weak justification, but I really didn't know." She drags a hand across her face. "I've been pushed away by family for as long as I can remember. I don't have any conflict with you wanting to fight against my grandfather, but . . . do you know who he is? If it was so simple to kill him, he would have been dead years ago. It isn't as though he is lacking in enemies!"

"We are not murderers. We don't plan to kill him. We just

want him to stop being the Dar," Valentina says.

Tabassum Naaz grins suddenly, showing off her sharp white teeth. We wonder if she's related to a shark. "You don't have to pretend. You can kill him. I don't care. He has hated me ever since I was born. In fact, until I was five, my parents kept me hidden because they were afraid of how he'd react when he found out about my existence."

Widad passes her a plate of baklava, and we lean in closer to listen.

"When my father finally took me home, my grandfather tried to kill me. Only"—she takes a bite of the dessert and grins—"he couldn't. I was protected by some kind of magic he didn't understand. That pissed him off immensely, and my existence became even more like sand in his eyes." She eats some fries with relish. "I turned sixteen, and the waters of the rivers and the lakes started talking to me. I discovered I am a magic user. He almost lost his shit then."

"You're his heir?" Paheli asks, her eyes shining with glee.

"Yep." Tabassum Naaz grins back, and for a second, they're almost friends. "Everyone believes that he has the power to choose his heir. In fact, most of my cousins are counting on it and suck up to him, trying to get into his good graces and be chosen as the Dar. Only when the rivers and the lakes started talking to me did I understand that the position of the Dar is chosen by the magic."

"I suppose he didn't take you being chosen as heir too well?" Valentina asks.

Tabassum Naaz's smile is very warm as she looks at Valentina. "You could say that. He tried to kill me again, and when he didn't succeed, he threw me out of the house, saying my behavior was wanton. He tried to have me killed by others, but magic is strange. It reads intent, and every time he tried to hurt me, it rebounded on him."

"But he can still hurt your parents," Talei says, and the smile disappears from Tabassum Naaz's face.

"Yeah. Which is why I'm here, living in a place I'm not familiar with, trying not to draw attention to myself." She rubs her face and grimaces. "It sucks."

"Since you're his heir, can't you replace him?" Paheli asks, her eyes wide with the same hope glinting in Taraana's.

A strangely bitter smile lifts Tabassum Naaz's lips. "It doesn't work that way." She sighs. "The only way to instate a new Dar is to remove the old one. And the only way to remove the old Dar is to kill him or have him drop dead. And I don't think my grandfather is kind enough to do that."

A shocked silence fills the room. Murder is not one of the choices on our list.

Tabassum Naaz smirks at us. "So, when you say you want to remove him from power, I really don't mind. In fact, I would thank you. But you are overestimating your skills. It's like you're dogs, growling at a mountain. You might annoy the mountain, but in the end, you will be buried by it."

"Is there really no other way than for him to die?" Paheli asks softly. "He was in prison for a long while. Can't we send him back there?"

"The people currently in power, whether in the middle world or on the Magic Council, are all his allies. He has enemies, but none of them are going to act soon. The chances of removing him from power now are slim to none." Tabassum Naaz shakes her head.

"So, what are we supposed to do? Live life running from one city to another?" Kamboja bursts out. "How long are we going to run?"

"I . . . I can leave," Taraana immediately offers.

"Nonono, I didn't mean that, Taraana," Kamboja says, her voice wobbling.

"What did you mean, then?" Daraja's voice is cold. "We've only just experienced a portion of what Taraana's life has been. Have you forgotten that it's because of him you're even here now?" All of a sudden, everyone is speaking at once. Our emotions are sensitive and our tempers easily ignited.

"You will all shut up for me," Paheli says, her voice loud enough that everyone, including Tabassum Naaz, falls silent. Valentina glances at her, but she is lost in her own thoughts.

"At this moment, I don't have a concrete plan or any way to act against your grandfather. This may not be the case in the future. Will you help us when we need you to?" Paheli asks.

"I won't risk my parents," Tabassum Naaz says. "But . . . if I can help without putting them in danger, I will."

"Are you sure?" Valentina again.

"At this moment, yes."

"Aren't you worried that your cousins will try to kill you to gain favor from Baarish?" Etsuko asks.

Tabassum Naaz smiles the sort of smile we associate with dark corners and sharp knives. "I am my grandfather's granddaughter. I have more than my fair share of his ruthlessness, not that I would ever do what he did . . . what he's trying to do," Tabassum Naaz says, more earnestly than she has said anything before. She meets Taraana's eyes for the first time and bows her head to him.

"Thank you." He smiles at her. "I wasn't able to say these words to you back then."

"You don't have to thank me," Tabassum Naaz says angrily. "I am the last person who deserves your gratitude. My family owes you a debt." She leans back in her chair as if exhausted and waves a hand. "Are you sure you can keep the keeper safe? As I said, my grandfather has many allies, even here." Tabassum Naaz looks at Paheli and shakes her head. "I didn't risk my life twice to set him free for him to be caught again, you know?"

"How did you manage to do that?" Valentina asks curiously.

"Well, I overheard my uncle and my grandfather talking about the keeper. So one day I followed them to where he was keeping Taraana. I don't know how I managed to do it, honestly. I was a lot of braver as a kid than I am today." She makes a face at Taraana. "I freed him, but the next day I heard that he was caught again. I was so mad, but I was determined not to give up on him."

"I'm glad you didn't," Paheli says. She squeezes Taraana's hand.

Tabassum Naaz shrugs. "I didn't inherit my grandfather's evil gene, thankfully." She gets to her feet. "I will take my leave now and wait until it is my turn to move. Ah, just so you know, if you get caught, this conversation never happened. I don't know you and we have never met." Tabassum Naaz moves toward the door, then stops and whirls toward Valentina. She whispers something in Valentina's ear, throws us a smile, and is gone.

"What did she say to you?" Paheli asks as soon as the door closes behind her.

Valentina's cheeks are scarlet. "She said that if I have an itch, she'll be happy to scratch it for me."

"And do you?"

"You should worry more about *your* itches than mine," Valentina says primly, and effectively shuts Paheli up.

"What are we going to do about Baarish?" Sevda asks. Her voice is soft but her question is loud.

"Let's not worry about that right now," Paheli answers, her fingers briefly on her eyelids, which flutter down as if to underline her exhaustion. "We can figure out the logistics when we have a weapon with which to fight him. Currently, we have nothing." She thinks we don't see the coldness in her eyes, but with Paheli, we have learned to step softly, cautiously, so we don't say anything.

Paheli continues. "I know you are all upset and unsettled. I have no quick fixes with which to appease you. But hey, this is not the first time we've faced mountains, right? We will bring him down, one way or another. Anyway, let's change the topic. All this talk about Baarish is giving me an upset stomach."

"Are you comparing Baarish to expired food?" Taraana asks.

"No. Not expired food. Just something that doesn't taste good," Paheli replies.

"Like peanut butter?" he says with a grin.

Paheli narrows her eyes. "This conversation is over."

Listen.

Sometimes we wish for things and people we never had but other people take for granted. Like:

A mother who worries when you don't come home at night. A father who is neither a gaping absence nor only present in the marks on our bodies. The luxury of nights not fragmented by nightmares. Bodies that are ours alone.

Sometimes we wish for impossible things like that.

The Fault in the Stars

Midnight. Somewhere in Beyoğlu, Istanbul.

The darkness has depth and the scent of magic is heavy in the air. We walk the cobbled streets on light feet, veiling ourselves with shadows. Paheli is on a mission, and we know better than to stop her.

Each of her missions yields a Wild One. We were all once such missions.

We do not consider ourselves heroines of yore. We are not strong like the superheroes people love. We do not intend to save humanity. Far from it, in fact.

We simply help girls. We help them escape, we listen to them when they need someone to listen, and we hug them when they need comfort that comes without conditions. We set up safe houses around the world and keep them funded.

We help them because once, Paheli helped us. She brought us out of danger, listened to us, comforted us, and gave us the space and the resources we needed to heal. All of us have spoken to professionals versed in the science of broken hearts, hurting minds, and invaded bodies. We are works in progress.

We don't know what drives Paheli to go one step further than us to help other girls in need. Thanks to Eulalie, she has a spell that sends her a summoning whenever she is in the vicinity of a girl who might become a Wild One. A girl who is hanging on to life and sanity by the last strand she can muster. A girl who has been betrayed by those she considers most dear. Paheli tastes the pain and she yields to its summoning.

We left Taraana in the apartment. He wasn't happy, but he didn't protest. Perhaps he read the haste in our hearts. He is there, and for the moment he is safe.

Walking swiftly, we leave the revelry in the main streets for the quiet blanketing the residential areas of the city. Paheli leads the way.

It is a clear night. Stars, what we can see of them, glitter in the sky. Paheli stops in front of an apartment building. We stop with her. She looks up, and for a moment we see nothing. Then we do and we wish we hadn't.

We make our way to the roof—the door to it is ajar, banging in the wind. It is cold; our breaths steam. The girl is framed against the night. She stands at the very edge of the roof, poised as if to fly. She is about seventeen and slender, with thin brown hair.

Our footsteps are silent, but she must sense us, because she turns. We stand in front of her, a collection of broken girls. She looks at us, but she doesn't seem to see us. The sounds of the city are muted. A cat yowls somewhere.

Paheli steps forward. The look in the girl's eyes sharpens and she focuses, for the first time. She doesn't say a word, though. Her silence is a question.

We have all stood on precipices much like this one. When you get this close to self-destruction, words no longer have strength. How did Paheli reach us? How did she persuade us to retreat from the edges we cleaved to?

We cannot remember.

"I am Paheli," she says, and sits on the wall right next to the girl. "Why are you here?"

The girl stares down at Paheli, her expression frozen in a grimace of grief. "Why do you want to know? Do you collect tragic stories or something?"

"You could say that. Do you have one to share?"

The girl turns back to face the night, the city, and the sky. "I was raped by my brother-in-law." She takes a deep breath. "When I told my mother, she told me it was my fault. It must have been something I said or did or wore that gave him the wrong idea. That led him on."

She stops. A car honks in the street below.

"I was sleeping in my bed in my room when he raped me. I was supposed to be safe there. Safer *there* than anywhere else in the world." A sob punctuates her narration. "A month later, I found out that I was pregnant. They wouldn't let me get an abortion. Said they would send me to my aunt's place to have . . . that."

She takes a wheezing breath and thumps her chest with a fist. "I heard them talking this morning when they thought I was still sleeping. My sister, that man, and my parents. My sister can't have children, and that man needs an heir. My parents didn't want my sister to be abandoned by that monster, so I was elected to be a sacrifice.

"I snuck out of the house today and went to the doctor. But you know what? They said I needed my guardian's permission. Why? It is *my* body. Why do I need to have anybody's permission to do anything with it? I can feel that thing in my womb. I would much rather die than let it grow within me."

"So, you are here," Paheli says, turning to look at the city glimmering in the distance.

"Yes. And you? Why are *you* here?" the girl asks.

"Me? I was raped by the man my mother sold me to." The girl turns to face Paheli suddenly, looking at her as if for the first time. "And those girls back there? They all have similar stories. We don't compare notes." The girl turns to us. Her eyes are wide and her cheeks tearstained. "Do you want to come with us?"

"Where will you take me?" the girl asks.

"Away from here. You won't ever need to return to this city if you don't want to."

The girl's lips quiver, and she barks out a sound that is perhaps meant to be a laugh. "You know what hurts the most? Everyone I thought I could unconditionally call my own betrayed me in the most terrible of ways, and yet I still love them. I still want them to love me. The thought of never seeing them again horrifies me. Even though they hurt me so badly. Even though they are *still* hurting me, I can't let them go! It's tearing me apart inside." The girl brushes her tears away with the back of her palm. "If I go with you, will I stop hurting so much? Will this pain go away?"

Paheli chooses her words carefully. "Eventually the pain will dull. Eventually it will ease. It will take time, but it *will* happen."

The girl shakes her head. She gives us no warning. Just turns her back and takes a step. The moment slows. Paheli scrambles to grab hold of her.

An absence of sound. Then:

A crash. A car alarm. A window opening. A sudden scream.

We didn't even know her name.

The Blue City in the Mountains

I.

We leave Istanbul the same night. We gather Taraana and the few belongings we are loath to leave behind, open a door into the Between, and step through. We will not return to this city for a while. Not until the unnamed girl is a memory and not a recent experience.

How many unnamed girls are there, do you think? How many unnamed girls disappear due to emotional and physical violence done to them?

How many girls are there who are on the brink of a fall, falling, or fallen? How many of their stories will we never hear? Do you ever wonder that?

We do. We think about these girls all the time. We wonder what their names were. What they dreamed of. What they could have been.

II.

The number of words in a pen full of ink, the number of flowers in a hive full of honey, and the number of turns in the mazelike streets of Chefchaouen; these are the things we most love to ponder to keep the grief at bay.

Have you ever been so sad that everything tasted salty?

It is early morning when we arrive in Chefchaouen. The alley we step out into is narrow, blue, and deserted. We don't talk as we walk single file to the place we call our own in the old town. The buildings here are interconnected, and as we open the door to the house that belongs to us, we can hear the sounds of people in the houses nearby, waking up and readying to meet the world outside.

Chefchaouen is located in the Rif Mountains of Morocco and is known as the Blue City due to all its houses and buildings at least partially painted the shade of blue we associate with a lament. It has narrow, cobbled streets that frequently change into stairs, alleys, and dead ends. It is a place where stories breathe and become legends. Magic loves this city; it is the only place where doors to the Between manifest not simply as upright rectangles on uninterrupted walls but as actual doors with all the design that fancy magic can grant them.

Taraana hasn't asked us any questions. Perhaps he has read our hearts and knows not to. We close the door behind us and stand awhile in the parlor, listless in our grief. Paheli catches Valentina's hand, and they look at each other in wordless communication. Valentina nods, so Paheli drops her hand and separates from us. The skin under her eyes is bruised. She pauses for a moment and her eyes snag on Taraana. Her mouth moves as if she is trying to work up the nerve to say something, but then her shoulders droop. She disappears into a bedroom on the other end of the house without a word.

Taraana stares after her, his face worried.

"Leave her be," Valentina says. Outside, it has started to rain. A light drizzle that feels custom-made for the way we feel right now. "She needs time."

"She will blame herself," Daraja says. "She always does."

"This is not the first time we have lost somebody," Ligaya tells Taraana. She stomps to a chair and throws herself on it, burying her head in her arms.

When you lose something or someone, your life becomes a series of sharp corners and razor edges. No matter how much care you take when navigating it, you will get hurt and you will bleed. No one knows this truth more than we do.

"So, what do we do now?" Areum asks in a small voice. She and Kamboja are holding each other.

Valentina purses her lips and thinks. "Talei, Areum, Kamboja, and I will go exchange some Between diamonds for money. We'll get some food on our way back. The rest of you, get some rest. We'll be back soon."

We slip out of the house and into the pale blue brilliance of the city. The cobbled streets are wet and slippery; pedestrians hurry up and down the roads with heads bowed against the rain. We keep ourselves invisible from the humans and our eyes out for middle worlders. Chefchaouen is not unfamiliar to us, so we navigate its streets with ease.

Every time someone leaves our ranks and returns to the

human world, we come here. Because the stars are limited in number, Paheli encourages us to move on when we are ready to face life and the world again. When one of us removes the star from her palm, she is able, once again, to walk beyond the limits of the cities. She becomes wholly human again. She forgets us and the time she spent with us as a Wild One.

She will pass us on the streets sometimes and look at us with a look that says she once was us but is no longer and cannot understand why. We become the color she sees in the corner of her eye and the name on the tip of her tongue that she can't quite ever fully remember. We are the nostalgia she feels when she sees a group of girls, and we are the lights she thinks she sees on the darkest nights. Every time a Wild One leaves, it feels as though we have healed the wings of a wounded bird we found. There's sorrow, but there's happiness, too.

We walk briskly up a narrow street of stairs and reach a store that has its door wide open. Because it is raining, no wares are displayed immediately outside, but tables set right by the doors are laden with lamps in different sizes and shapes. The lamps sold in this store illuminate a person's truth whether they want it illuminated or not. We stay away from them.

After Talei exchanges Between diamonds for Moroccan currency, we find some restaurants a few streets from our house and place an order that has the manager peeking at us. An hour later, we make our way back with carefully packaged portions of chicken, beef, lamb tagines, couscous, pastillas, meat skewers, a variety of soups, and, especially for Taraana, eggplant with garlic.

When we get back, the living room is empty but for Taraana,

who is sitting at the edge of his seat, his eyes turned in the direction of the room Paheli has cloistered herself in. We exchange glances before Talei takes pity on him.

"Could you call Paheli out? Tell her to come and eat," she says. Taraana beams at her and is gone before she has finished talking.

Paheli: Disharmony in the Attics

I sense his attention before he even takes a step toward the room I have barricaded myself into. It is as though some newly discovered nerve stretches between his mind and mine. I have been able to feel him thinking about me. His concern feels like a balm, perhaps a Band-Aid, not very useful but comforting nonetheless.

He opens the door so easily and steps inside without hesitating. I lie on the bed with my back turned toward the door. I don't move as he comes closer. I don't move as he climbs into the bed beside me. I don't move as he slips his arms around me and moves me closer to his body. So close I can feel his heart racing. He tucks my head under his chin. At this moment, he demands nothing from me and, instead, offers me his warmth, his comfort. I am greedy so I take both.

The silence is loud between us. It usually is. There are things in it that I need to tell him and things that he needs to tell me, but right now, all I can think about is that girl on the rooftop, that girl I failed. My sisters think I feel guilty and they are right, in part; I do. Was it something I said that spurred her on? Pushed her to take that final, conclusive leap? Could I have done things differently? Said something else that would have convinced her to ally with us? I will never know.

But I am not so guilty as to believe that she was up there because of me. Her presence on that precipice wasn't my fault.

When I left Eulalie for the first time, I asked her for a spell that would help me identify girls like me. I didn't think there would be so many of them. I didn't think I wouldn't be able to help them all. Eulalie cautioned me against using the spell even as she gave it to me. She warned me that such spells exact an emotional toll that few are able to pay. I didn't give her words as much thought as I should have. I needed a purpose, and playing a hero gave me one.

The truth is, I am no one's hero. Not even my own.

You see, even though I pretend to be altruistic, all the girls I save have one thing in common: they were betrayed by their parents, their mothers in particular. Just like I was. And every time I fail to save a girl, it is as though I am failing to save myself.

The girl in the dumpster a couple of years ago was me. The girl last year who returned home to certain death was me. And that girl who fell from the building yesterday was also me. I mourn them, but to be honest, I am mourning myself.

I turn around in Taraana's embrace and face him. Looking at

him hurts me, somehow. My heart feels too full, too full of thorns. His eyes contain no censure, even though I know he can feel everything that is in my heart. I run a finger down his face and his eyes flutter closed. He is too good for me, and me, I am bad for him. I will corrode his goodness.

Knowing this makes no difference. I continue lying in bed with him when I should be outside, making decisions, pretending to have answers. I let him hold me when not a few days ago the idea would have made me run in the opposite direction.

"Why do you insist on getting closer to me?" I ask him.

He opens his eyes and the stars in them peek at me. I look at him and am surprised anew not just by his beauty but by how familiar, how *dear*, he has become to me.

His presence is slowly becoming a necessity to me. How did I survive all these years without him? How did he live without me?

These feelings scare me.

Is this love? How am I supposed to know? Or do these feelings exist because of his tear that I wear on my palm? Will my attachment to him disappear once I take it off?

"What are you thinking?" he asks, pulling away. A frown upsets the symmetry of his face.

"Can't you tell?" I sit up and run my fingers through my hair. Or I try to. My hair is too tangled for me to succeed.

"No. I can't read your mind, Paheli." The way he says my name always startles me. There is a history in the way he says it, a wealth of meaning I don't get. Am I supposed to?

"It's nothing. I am thinking about nothing. No, that's not true. I'm thinking about how I'm hungry but how I don't want to go out of the room because, well, because. I don't have a reason, but you don't always have to have one, you know? It's okay to not be strong all the time. I'm giving myself permission to be sad. I'm going to stop talking now." I get off the bed and move to the small vanity on the side. I locate a hairbrush and, without thinking too deeply, throw it to Taraana. He catches it and raises an eyebrow.

"Brush my hair."

My mother used to comb my hair. It was the one thing, apart from my blue eyes, that seemed to give her pleasure. She would spend a long time brushing it.

I kept it short for years after that last day I saw her. I hacked it all with a blunt knife I found somewhere. I got Eulalie to buy me contacts because it was difficult for me to look into the mirror and see my blue eyes staring back at me.

But time, you see. It passes. I let my hair grow again and came to terms with my blue eyes. I started loving parts of my body. My odd feet, my bony fingers, my clavicles, my waist . . . my hair. I learned to belong to myself.

Taraana holds the hairbrush awkwardly. He brushes my hair as if he doesn't quite know what to do.

"How are we going to use human conjuries? Won't Baarish know what they are? He will kill us before we can use them on him," he says.

I rub my lips, thinking. "I don't have all the answers, Taraana, but you know, conjuries are the one thing that makes middle worlders vulnerable. So, I'm not sure how we're going to use the conjuries or even if we *can* use them, but we have nothing else. We have to see this through. Do our best to find something."

Taraana stops brushing my hair and turns me around by the shoulders.

"What?"

"What if we can't find any?" he asks with his eyes downcast.

"We will," I tell him. Then, graciously, flick him on the forehead. He grabs my hand in protest. "Look, we know for sure that these things exist. They're rare but not impossible to find. If it's too difficult for you, you can give up. I won't. If one place, one city, doesn't have them, I will go to another one. I will keep on looking until I find something we can use. I will keep you safe. I promise. Okay?" He doesn't respond, so I pinch his chin. "Okay?"

"Yeah. Okay."

"All right. Now stop staring at my lips. Let's go. I'm hungry."

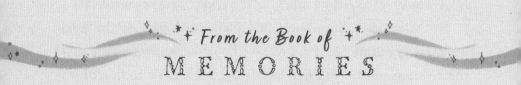

From the Book of
MEMORIES

VALENTINA
CITY OF ORIGIN: PARIS

I was once a king.

Paheli: Continued

We leave the house when the sun dips beneath the horizon and the city lights up; the night sky is enthralled by the pale luminescence of a half-full moon. In other words, it is night and the moon is out when Valentina and I slip out of the house, ignoring the protests of our sisters and Taraana. They want to accompany us, but we'd rather not take the risk.

The air is nice and cool and people are out and about, enjoying it. I glance at Valentina as we navigate the narrow sidewalks of Chefchaouen. As usual, she is perfectly put together. Her lips are a signature red, her eyes hooded to hide their cold depths, her long, skinny boots cover half of her legs, and her clothes are all exquisitely crafted.

"Is my beauty so great that it rendered you speechless?" She smirks at me.

I side-eye her. "Your beauty doesn't, but your narcissism might."

Her smile broadens. "I have it so I flaunt it."

"Too bad Tabassum Naaz isn't around to appreciate it," I say, and am rewarded by the deepening color in Valentina's cheeks.

She clears her throat. "Do you know the way to the store?"

"Yeah." I quicken my steps. "The place isn't that far. Just over half an hour's walk from here."

"Have you figured out a way to use conjuries against Baarish? Is it even possible to use them? Won't he recognize them for what they are?" Valentina asks me things that Taraana was asking me, and I haven't magically gained answers in the few hours that have passed since he did.

"No, I don't know, and maybe," I reply. I don't mind being short with Valentina because when you've been companions with a person for more than three hundred years without killing them, you tend to go beyond familiarity-breeds-contempt. We're into familiarity-breeds-comfort territory now. Heh. "I can't make plans until I know what manner of conjury we're dealing with."

Before we cross the street leading to the mountain on which the conjury shop is located, we come across an old man sitting on a low stool in a corner. In front of him is a stove on which he's cooking msemen, which is a thin, square-shaped pastry. We've eaten a lot today, but neither of us can resist the call of the msemen, especially when it's drizzled slightly with both butter and honey. We treat ourselves and promise to keep it a secret from the girls.

I don't know which of us notices the preternatural quietness in the streets closer to the store. No couples linger in the shadows being annoyingly mushy, no family strolls the streets exuding their harmony, no one except us and shadows. Valentina nudges me and I nod at her. We slip into the shadows cast by the buildings, which seem stoic fortresses that will admit no one.

"Magic?" Valentina raises an eyebrow.

I nod. What else could it be?

We haven't been to this conjury store for a few years now. Well, it is wrong to call it a conjury store, as the primary products offered are pots and pans. The old shopkeeper sells conjuries on the side, probably to beef up his thin profits. He didn't have many things the last time we saw him, but what he did have was authentic.

We reach the steep steps leading up the hill to the store, and the infrequent streetlamps choose this moment to flicker out. My heart quakes once; oh, the familiar stench of fear. I squeeze Valentina's hand tightly, and we creep up the stairs, walking lightly. There is a big tree in front of the store; its branches spread outward in a silent supplication to the sky. It must look beautiful during the day, but right now, it is sinister. Still, it casts deep shadows that shelter us from the eyes of the middle worlders we see standing in front of the conjury store.

Two not-human middle worlders are having an intense conversation while eight scaled creatures stand beside them. Four of these scaled creatures have blue scales (or what looks like blue in the semidarkness), and four have silver scales. We're far enough away for them to not notice us and close enough to make out some of their words.

"... a coincidence. How did you know this shop sells conjuries?"

one not-human middle worlder says to the other one.

"We're . . . keeper . . . here." Valentina and I straighten when we hear the words. We don't need to fill in the blanks to understand who the middle worlder is talking about. "The Dar's servants . . . smell . . . conjury." Well, that's bad news.

"Where's the shopkeeper?" Baarish's servant has thin lips and narrow eyes.

"He isn't in town," the other middle worlder replies.

"That's too bad. If he returns, have someone remove him." Is "remove" a euphemism for murder? Because that's what it sounds like.

"Set the place on fire. Everything in the store must burn," the other middle worlder commands the blue-scaled creatures. I'd like to see them reduce the aluminum, iron, and steel to ashes. "Can we help you hunt down the keeper as thanks for informing us about this conjury store?"

"Please," Baarish's servant replies.

"It's the least we can do. Our master considers Baarish a close friend. If you'll follow me, I will take you to dinner at the mansion, and tomorrow morning, we'll begin our hunt." The middle worlder nods at the blue-scaled creatures and turns to go, and Baarish's servant and the silver-scaled minions follow him. We duck behind the tree trunk and stand still, not even daring to breathe when they pass the tree. Nonetheless, both middle worlders stop; we hear their footsteps cease. My arm itches unbearably at this moment.

Someone steps closer to the tree and I ready my scream. At this moment, there's an explosion inside the store, and the place catches fire. Whoever was trying to look into the shadows of the tree changes their mind, and we hear the sound of people walking away quickly.

Then we feel the heat emanating from the building. It is a magically set fire, so it doesn't spread. We feel the moment the magic that was cast around the area breaks; it feels like a bubble popped. We can suddenly hear things that we couldn't before. The sound of the TV, radios, and soon, someone's scream. Doors open and people come streaming out, holding buckets of water.

Not that the water will help. This is not a fire set by humans, so it's not a fire that can be put out by humans. Everything will burn, though not everything will turn into ashes.

We find an elderly woman sniffling outside the store, her large eyes reflecting the flames currently consuming the old building.

"Do you know the shopkeeper, Grandma?" I ask her.

"Yes, I do. Poor Mahmoud. First he lost his wife, and now he's lost his store. He's going to be devastated." The old woman wipes her tears away.

"Do you know where he is at this moment?" I ask carefully. The old woman gives me a look at the question. Perhaps I look harmless, because she tells me.

"He's with his son, Farroukh, in Marrakech. Farroukh runs a store in the old market, and the old man often makes trips to spend time with him and his grandchildren now that his wife is gone. Poor man." The old woman sighs heavily and shakes her head.

"Do you have the contact for Mahmoud's son, Grandmother?" I ask. The old woman shoots me a suspicious glare.

"It's just that we think the fire was deliberately set with the intent to hurt the shopkeeper. We think it might be safer for him to stay at his son's house for the time being instead of returning to Chefchaouen," Valentina says in a gentle voice.

"I understand that you have no reason to trust anything we say, Grandmother, but we mean the old man no harm. In fact, we want to keep him out of harm's way," I tell her.

Perhaps we convince her, because she nods and leaves to make the call. We watch until we can no longer see her before we swiftly make our way back to the house. We need to be gone before the new day dawns and Baarish's servants begin their hunt.

The Politics of a Body, the Politics of Pleasure

Once, in the early hours of a pale London morning, we ran into two girls fleeing their home. This was nothing out of the norm for us. Running into girls fleeing from places they called home is a specialty of ours. It is the reasons they run away that keep us listening, keep us shocked.

The elder of the girls was called Dawa and the younger one, Zainab.

Over cups of hot cocoa we brewed in the kitchen of our apartment, we listened to their story.

Dawa told us of midnight and a conversation heard through the cracks of a door. Her parents spoke of home, of Sierra Leone, of a place where their childhoods resided, and of their plan to take the girls back. For a vacation, they said. To learn your roots, they insisted.

And perhaps they did intend that, but the biggest reason they were taking the girls "home" was to get them circumcised.

Genital mutilation.

"My sister doesn't know what it means," Dawa said. "I have heard stories, though. One of our cousins died after the procedure because the tools used weren't sterilized. My mother called it an accident. A mistake."

Uncircumcised women are considered dirty. As if a woman's ability to achieve sexual pleasure makes her unnatural or deviant.

Do they not consider that if the God they profess to serve wanted women to live without sexual pleasure, they would be born without clitorises?

We gave aid to Dawa and Zainab, but what about those countless others? Who hears their screams? Who answers their pleas for help?

What rhetoric convinces people, *mothers*, to perpetuate this particular violence against girls?

The world continually tries to steal a woman's right to her own body—who she allows to touch her and who she doesn't. They take it one step further and try to remove the pleasure that belongs wholly to her.

Does this not make you angry?

Can you blame us, then, for wanting to burn the world down sometimes?

Even when the break is in the heart, the body bears evidence of it. You know what we're talking about. Of course you do. Being a girl, a woman, means being fluent in the languages of pain and power. Knowing what hurts and how much and if you have the ability to endure it.

Ever notice how many derogatory terms are actually words that describe female bodies? Yes, we are talking about words that you may have used yourself despite being a girl or a woman, perhaps not realizing that all you are doing is being complicit in the way the world recognizes women not as people but as bodies: bodies to objectify and to police.

Feminism isn't a four-letter word.

You know what is?

Rape.

The Medina, the Riad, and the Red City

If cities have hearts and pulses, the ones belonging to Marrakech would be ticking frenetically. Time, so as not to be squandered, is defined by haste here. We, still drunk on the blue of Chefchaouen, are disarmed entirely by the chaos in the Medina of Marrakech. The Medina, in case you don't know, refers to the part of a Moroccan city that belongs to the Arabs.

The door leading to Marrakech is, thankfully, not too far from where we enter the Between. Still, we are on high alert as we walk the short distance. Paheli and Valentina told us of the events that occurred the night before. We're all anxious, and though at this moment we see no enemies, we can feel them, nipping at our heels and hastening our steps. Funnily enough, it seems as if the Between is as tense as we are; the sound of it is muted, and the golden light in it shines so bright that no corners are left unilluminated. Taraana, as usual, is glowing like the sun at noon in the Between.

We keep an eye out for a burning door. Perhaps we will encounter one and Taraana will bleed on it, forging a bond with the Between. But alas, we are disappointed. However, we reach the Marrakech door without incident and walk through it into a narrow street in the Medina, not far from the Jemaa el-Fna where people gather to buy and sell goods and food. It is midmorning and the air is filled with the scent of exhaust, food, and spices. To blend in better, before leaving Chefchaouen, we changed into caftans, while Taraana is wearing a cotton djellaba with a pointed hood that he refuses to pull up. He has his spectacles on, however, so we are somewhat reassured of his disguise.

Though the city is entirely new to Taraana, it is familiar to us. Returning to Marrakech always feels like putting on a well-loved dress. We have spent a lot of time in this city, learning its softness. Enough time that it has acquired the tangy flavor we associate with home. It's true. We look for the scent of home in every city we travel to.

An abundance of middle worlders call Marrakech home. Something about the Red City makes the magic here intoxicating. The Medina is like a wonderland. Not the pale and cultured Wonderland Alice walked in, but a Wonderland that is wilder, one whose song gets underneath your skin and heats your blood. The streets of the Medina are labyrinthine, bordered on either side by mud-brick ramparts often shaded red by dust or paint.

We navigate the alleys and pathways of the Medina, avoiding

mopeds, bicycles, and carts pulled by donkeys or horses. The streets are crowded. We're visible to humans at this moment as we walk quickly, in twos and threes, drawing glances from the middle worlders present but nothing more. We keep our eyes empty of recognition, and no matter how fantastic the physical expression of the middle worlder, we don't look. We won't look at what the humans can't see.

The muezzins have started the call for Zohr prayer when we finally leave the main thoroughfare for the emptier streets of the residential areas. Here, we can smell food cooking and hear voices in the middle of conversations. Our steps quicken. Taraana keeps pace as we all but run around a corner, through an alley, and out onto the other side, before finally coming to a stop in front of a heavy wooden door that leads to the riad we call home in Marrakech.

A riad is a traditional Moroccan house built around an inner courtyard. Ours is a particularly large one. Paheli steps forward and bangs on the door, which opens a minute later. A human woman stands on the other side. Her name is Ahlam; when she sees us, her lined face becomes wreathed in smiles. Ahlam and her family are the custodians of the riad and the administrators of the halfway home we run from it. She welcomes us and ushers us inside without asking any questions.

Ahlam's grandmother, Bushra, was a Wild One. She didn't want to forget us when she left the Wild Ones, so we asked Eulalie for a spell that would allow her to remember. It wasn't a decision we made easily, but we don't regret that we did. Working with Bushra and with the money we earned by selling Between diamonds, we purchased this riad, which became a home for us and a haven for those who have nowhere else to go. Here, like in other halfway homes we run around the world, we employ therapists, doctors, and other staff who help women seeking aid without asking questions or making judgments.

We watched Bushra as she found love, had children, grew old, and finally crossed the veil. Out of all the halfway houses we have opened, this one is the most precious to us because it belonged to Bushra, who lives on in the legacy this place represents.

We enter the riad and Ahlam closes the door behind us. We follow her through the front door, through a hall, and into the inner courtyard that is an even mix of tiled floors surrounding garden beds. The house has three floors as well as an accessible roof. The second and third floors have verandas with railings that look out onto the inner courtyard.

The courtyard garden is Ahlam's pride and joy. Lemon and orange trees have been planted strategically in the corners. The floor of the pool in the middle of the courtyard is decorated with Zellige tiles. The air is heavy with the scent of oranges. Benches and rugs laden with cushions are strewn all around the courtyard.

"How long will you be staying, bibi?" Ahlam asks Paheli once we are seated and inquiries about her and her family's health have been made.

"Not very long," Paheli replies. "Have there been any problems here?"

Ahlam shakes her head. Her husband and sons usually keep to their section of the riad and function as security when there is need for it. "Half of the rooms are empty. Sadly, I don't think that will remain the case for long."

Though not on any official list of halfway homes, word has spread among humans of this place's existence, and oftentimes there will be a knock on the door at odd hours of the night followed by a soft plea for assistance. No one is ever turned away.

Ahlam returns to us after asking the kitchen to prepare a meal, and we talk to her. She understands, perhaps as much as she can, that we're not strictly human, but she doesn't ask questions that she knows we won't answer. That's why, apart from a second look at Taraana, she doesn't mention his presence. We're familiar with each other, however, so there's a world of things to talk about. We spend an hour in conversation.

"Could you do us a favor, Ahlam?" Paheli asks the woman as she is about to return to the kitchen to check on the progress of the meal.

"Of course," Ahlam replies with a sweet smile.

"Could you ask around and see if there's someone called Farroukh selling goods in the old souk? Could you let us know where exactly his store is?" Paheli asks.

"I will, bibi. The information should be ready for you by tomorrow morning," she answers readily.

Paheli thanks her and she leaves. A few minutes later, she returns with the first of the many dishes the chefs in the kitchen have crafted for us.

We indulge our appetites and our senses on freshly baked bread, bastille, kefta, meat skewers, salads, and couscous. Sated, we make our way to the wing of the riad reserved for us.

Instead of individual rooms, our space in the riad is a long, wide room with beds and bedside tables separated by screens at intervals. Sort of like a high-level dormitory. A separate living room furnished with chairs and a dining table located right beside the dormitory is set aside exclusively for us. We gather in this room while Ahlam has the dormitory freshly cleaned.

"It is obvious from the middle worlders' actions that human conjuries present very real threats to them," Valentina says, returning to the conversation we have been having since we left the city.

"I told you, Assi said human conjury unravels middle worlders," Taraana says.

"That's probably the reason Yasmine wanted to use it against them," Kamboja says, mentioning the keeper whose object we read in the Library of the Lost.

"It makes sense now," Etsuko says, tapping her lips.

"What makes sense?" Areum raises an eyebrow.

"The disappearance of the old woman who sold potions in Moscow. The old man in Tunisia who went missing after his stall caught fire. The witch whose body was found hanging from a tree in her backyard," Ligaya says. "And these are only the ones we know of. Who knows how many conjury makers they've killed so far?"

"They're ruthless," Talei whispers.

We slip into silence again.

"I'd like to talk to you all," Sevda says when five minutes have passed. We know she is unhappy, has been unhappy ever since we decided to throw in our lot behind Taraana, but she didn't say anything, so we kept our silence. Perhaps she is ready to speak, so we give her all our attention.

Sevda takes a deep breath and looks at Paheli. Her smile is wobbly. "I have spent a lot of time agonizing about this and I . . ." She stops and hesitates, biting her lips, collecting her thoughts. "I'm ready to leave." She stops again. "I am pretty certain I am. I can't—I mean, I no longer want to live like this."

"What do you mean by 'this'?" Kamboja says in a dangerously low voice.

Sevda clenches her hands into fists and squares her shoulders. "Returning to the real world will be scary, and I'm honestly not sure I'm ready to, but"—she bites her lips again—"it's much scarier to live as a Wild One right now. Running from one place to another without knowing if we're going to get caught. Having to hide. Feeling powerless. This kind of life is way scarier. I can't do it. I'm sorry. You've all given me so much love and support, and I know I should suck it up and stick around, but I can't. I'm so sorry." Sevda's eyes are full of tears. "Do you hate me?"

"Why would we hate you, Sevda?" Paheli says before anyone else can speak. "Being here, being wild, is not a permanent way of living." She looks at the rest of us, and we all avoid her gaze. "The Wild Ones is sort of like a bus. We get you from one point of your life to another." She pauses. "At least it's supposed to be."

We glance at Taraana; he looks stricken by guilt when this isn't his fault.

"I said in Agra that it's never wrong to put yourself first. You have the right to your fears, to your desires, to your dislikes. It is never wrong to want to be safe." Paheli smiles at Sevda.

Sevda's light brown eyes overflow with tears. "I feel like I'm betraying you all."

"Just a little," Etsuko says, and we glare at her. "I'm being honest!"

"I'm sorry." Sevda bows her head.

"Don't be sorry," Kamboja says. "Be brave."

"She *is* being brave," Daraja replies. "Do you think it was easy for her to speak up right now?"

"When do you leave?" Ligaya asks.

"You don't have to leave to avoid this conflict, you know. You can just stay with Eulalie in New Orleans," Talei says.

"No . . . Though I'm scared and I probably wouldn't have made this move if we weren't running from Baarish, it is time. I want a family. I want to fall in love again. I want to stay in one place. In Marrakech," Sevda says. "Is that okay?"

"Yeah, don't worry about it," Valentina says, getting to her feet. Her face is blank, as is Paheli's. Neither of them shows how they really feel about Sevda leaving. They must have done this many times before. "Come with me. I will make a call to Eulalie. She'll send you all the things you need to live in the human world."

They leave and for a second, we look at the place Sevda was standing in, her absence pulsing painfully for a moment. Then we recalibrate ourselves, change the positions we're sitting in, take up slightly more space, and we are fine. All right, we're not fine, but we will be. We've learned to let go easily.

"Where do I sleep tonight?" Taraana asks suddenly.

"With the rest of us. Where else would you go?" Areum retorts, raising an eyebrow.

"With all of you?" he repeats, eyes wide.

"Yes. Do you have a problem with that?" Ligaya says with a grin.

"Well . . ." Taraana peeks at Paheli, flushing. "Not quite?"

"Half of us don't consider you romantic material, and the other half know where your affections lie." Talei chucks him under his chin, and he buries his face in his hands.

"Am I that obvious?" he mumbles. The tips of his ears are very red.

"Yes." Daraja giggles.

"Why doesn't she seem to get it, then?" he asks, glancing at Paheli.

We pause and consider her. She is lying on the floor of the living room with her eyes closed, pretending to be asleep. We know she is fully aware of the conversation happening around us.

"You should ask her that," Kamboja suggests with a naughty grin.

"You should not," Paheli replies, immediately opening her eyes. "You should not ask her that at all." She sits up.

"Ask Ahlam if the rooftop is free," she says to us. "Let's celebrate Sevda tonight before she leaves."

Paheli: The Atlas Mountains, the Cozy Rooftop, and the Confession, Possibly of Love

Night falls abruptly in Marrakech. We head for the open rooftop of the riad. Someone is playing the oud somewhere, and from a distance we can hear the beat of a darabukka. The air is full of movement, and the night is full of pockets of adventure we would be having if Baarish weren't after us.

Instead, we stay in and we celebrate Sevda under Marrakech's night sky. We celebrate the life she has lived and the life she will live. We celebrate the past she has overcome. We feast on Moroccan oranges and an assortment of baklava. Widad sings a song about leaving, and we sing along because goodbyes are always bittersweet; we will miss Sevda as we miss all our sisters. As *I* miss all of them. Even the ones I can't remember.

I want to miss Valentina, too, but she refuses to leave.

Ghufran puts on music and Valentina dances in the orange lamplight. The night kisses her curves and makes me jealous I don't have any. When we have sung and danced our fill, we sit and talk about the times we have spent with Sevda, the places we have been, the memories we have created. She will forget them all. She will forget me. Eventually, *all* of them will forget me.

Then the girls slip away, one by one or in groups, leaving me alone with Taraana on the rooftop under a sky heavy with stars. We sit on a roofed swing, curled up under the same blanket, gazing at the immensity of the Atlas Mountains, dark in the distance.

Somewhere, a clock strikes midnight. In the street below, someone laughs.

Midnight has a scent in Marrakech. It smells like oranges with faint notes of panic. I take a deep breath but fail to find the peace I am looking for. I haven't planned this out, but I can't keep it in any longer.

"Taraana?"

"Hmm?" He sounds sleepy. This is probably not the right time. Maybe I should wait. No, if I wait, I will throw up all the dessert I ate, and that would be a shame. He opens his eyes and looks at me. "What is it? Do you have to throw up?"

How rude. He doesn't understand a girl's heart. "I have an answer for you," I tell him.

"What? Wait. What?" He sits up straight and stares at me with a panicked face. Good. I'm not the only one panicking right now. Hah.

"Do you want to hear it?" I can't believe I'm doing this. I haven't been a teenager for a long time, on the inside, I mean, but it feels like I'm one right now. My heart is about to give up the ghost, all the ghosts that haunt me, any minute now. My hands are cold and my mouth is dry. This might be the stupidest idea I've ever had.

"Yes. No. I don't know!" he says helplessly.

"Fine. I will keep it to myself," I say, and sniff. I am secretly glad, though.

"No, no, I didn't mean that. I want to know." He catches my hand. There goes my secret gladness. "Please?"

"First, can I tell you about myself?" I pretend I can still stop. I can still walk away.

He nods; the stars in his eyes are glowing.

"I . . ." Wow. This is going to hurt. "I was in a very dark place the day you tossed me the box of stars. I don't know if I'll ever forgive you for seeing me at my lowest, though in all the ways that matter, I'm glad you did. Do you know what I mean?" He nods. I continue. "I escaped into the Between right after, but I knew nothing about it. I stayed there for a week, cowering in a corner. Shattered. Hurt both physically and emotionally. Eulalie was the only one who stopped and asked me if I was okay. She insisted on taking me out and to her home. She took care of me. Nursed me. Held me in her arms when I cried and stopped me when I tried to die. I owe her as big of a debt as I owe you, and yet, I can barely answer the love she shows me." I meet his eyes and almost cry at the softness in them. "I'm broken that way.

"Eulalie is nothing like my mother. My mother, that woman . . ." I swallow and try again. "My mother sold me to a rich man who raped me. And Eulalie is nothing like that. She would never do anything like that. In my mind, I know that, but my heart, you see? My heart is convinced that if I lower my walls and let her in, she will hurt me. It has been so long, and I am still scared that she will hurt me. And you . . ." I clench my fists. "You are the best person I know. You are good. In a really horribly sincere way. And I am not. I am not good, nor do I intend to be. No, don't say anything. Hear me out. I didn't kill the man who raped me, but I made him wish he were dead. It was entirely too easy to do. Hurting him gave me pleasure. I am not sorry about that. I *won't* be sorry about that.

"And, I'm just saying this, but if it turns out that there's no way to defeat Baarish other than by killing him, I will make that decision. Because that's how bad I am." I turn away from Taraana. I am afraid to meet his eyes, so I address his chin. "So, the answer to your question, if you still want it after everything I've said, is that yes, I could love you. Maybe I already do a little. I think I could try? The thought terrifies me, and I can't promise a happy ending. Do you still maybe . . . want me?"

His arms are around me long before I finish speaking. I press my face into his chest and listen to his heart thunder.

DARAJA
CITY OF ORIGIN: BENIN CITY

When I think of my father
a wounded lion in
my chest
roars and roars.

Souks, Spices, and Survival: A Guide into Chaos

Sevda's gone when we wake up the next morning. The only thing that remains of her is the star that she used to wear on the palm of her hand. She has left a note that simply says, *Thank you, and I'm sorry.*

We stare at the note for a long moment. All of us have different feelings and for a brief second, our sanguinity slips. Then we look at Taraana, who is all but dripping with guilt and concern, and we smile at him, reassuring him, and in the process reassuring ourselves. Valentina says that Sevda's in one of the rooms meant for the women for whom the riad is a haven. We don't go to see her.

Eulalie magicked her papers over, and when Sevda wakes up, she will have a new identity and enough money to start a new life wherever she pleases. She won't remember us, nor will she remember the life she escaped from. A new narrative, one of her own choosing, will take the place of her old one.

We break our fast in the courtyard under a piercing blue sky. A long table is packed with freshly squeezed fruit juice, mint tea, bread, pancakes made from semolina, eggs, various kinds of jams, goat cheese, honey, olives, and pomegranates. The flavors are sharp, and each bite reminds us that we are alive.

Ahlam comes to us after we finish breakfast. Her sources have found Farroukh, and she offers to send a guide to take us to his shop, but we refuse the help. So she simply tells us the vicinity in which his shop is located. We ask Taraana to stay behind, but he is adamant on accompanying us. Since Baarish's creatures still think we're in Chefchaouen, we concede to his demand.

Half an hour later, dressed in airy caftans and a djellaba in Taraana's case, we venture out of the riad, toward the fabled souks of Marrakech.

Wandering the souks of Marrakech is like taking a walk through a zoo where the animals have escaped. Sheer, unadulterated chaos. The souks are Aladdin's caves, filled with immense treasure and some junk. We have spent many hours in here previously, willingly losing ourselves in its labyrinthine landscapes.

We walk on the right side of the road to avoid the constant traffic. The motorcyclists are not particular whether the road they use has pedestrians or not; there are many near-collisions as we walk from our riad to the entrance of the souks. The din in the city is gaining momentum, and though the Jemaa el-Fna is mostly empty at this hour, the afternoon will bring the street performers out in force. When the sun sets, the food carts will open for business, and we will be present to provide them with some.

The souks are not entirely untamed wilderness. They are frequently organized by the products they have for sale. Some sell all the types of olives you will ever want to eat; some sell mounds of spices in fantastic colors and with sharp smells; and others sell shiny things that make our hearts beat faster. Taraana, as usual, is looking around in wide-eyed wonder, his starry eyes visible to the world. Valentina pinches him and he puts the spectacles back on. There are numerous middle worlders around, but there are just as many humans in the area. No one seems to have paid him too much attention, so we relax our vigilance slightly.

The plan was to go straight to Farroukh's store, but we get distracted along the way and spend a couple of hours browsing. We sample desserts and street food to sate our hunger during lunchtime and go farther into the souks. We come across a stall that sells nothing but empty birdcages carved in the most exquisite of patterns. Taraana won't step close to one, so we move on to a stall that only sells wooden spoons. We are visible to the human proprietors of these stalls, and they give us grievously wounded looks when we don't purchase anything. So, of course, Daraja goes on a shopping spree; her soft heart is easily moved.

"Wasn't there a conjury store here the last time we visited?" Areum asks Paheli. "Let's go see if it's still there."

She nods. "Yeah, it was in the area that exclusively sells beads. But I don't remember what the conjurer's name is."

"I do," Valentina replies with a twist of her lips. "Bahir. I remember him and his anguish really well."

"It wasn't that bad!" Paheli protests. "Only the conjuries made of paper caught fire."

"The majority of them were made from paper, Paheli," Etsuko says patiently.

Taraana turns his head so Paheli won't see him laughing, but Ligaya snitches on him.

"I'm not laughing *at* you!" he says, laughing at her.

"You are lying, aren't you?" Paheli glares at him.

"Yeah," he replies sunnily.

She turns away after sniffing haughtily and starts walking faster, going ahead of us. "Let's go see if that store still exists." We follow quietly; it doesn't take us long to reach the area where the store was located. Old craftsmen and women sit in tiny stalls squinting at the pieces they are working on. All of us are moved to buy something sparkling from each of the stalls we pass.

Suddenly, Paheli freezes and gestures for us to move back. We obey without hesitation, turning back and retracing our steps without changing our expressions or revealing any distress. Paheli doesn't stop walking until we are at least a kilometer away from the area.

"What was it?" Valentina asks.

"The store was closed, and there were middle-world creatures wearing armor bearing an insignia of some sort, standing guard outside the emptied store," she says with a frown on her face.

"Let's just go and find the son of that conjurer from Chefchaouen. Wouldn't he be our best bet?" Widad asks.

Paheli nods. "At this point, yeah."

"Is that really a good idea?" Talei asks. "Perhaps one of us should accompany Taraana back—"

"I'm not leaving," Taraana says with a particular set to his lips.

"Taraana," Paheli says.

"No," he replies.

Paheli sighs and gives us a look. We, understanding her unspoken request, immediately surround Taraana, hiding him in the center.

Old Mahmoud's son, Farroukh, sells in Marrakech what his father used to sell in Chefchaouen: shiny silver pots and pans. The store is sizable; one side is dedicated to the pots and pans, and the other side sells drinks. We're inured to surprise and accept the strange pairing.

Valentina orders us drinks, and while we wait to be served, we peruse a selection of trays on the side. Most are made from exquisitely carved wood with Moroccan landscapes painted on them. A large number feature the streets of Chefchaouen.

"Look," Kamboja says, pointing to one. The scene painted on the tray is of the Chefchaouen street on which the store selling the conjuries was located. The tree with its branches spread is impossible to mistake. We look at the proprietor, a dark man of about forty years with a pleasant face and a gentle demeanor.

He notices our gaze and, smiling, walks over to us. "Is there something we can help you with?"

"This is going to sound strange," Paheli says, "but did your father's shop in Chefchaouen burn down the day before yester-day?"

The man's face changes dramatically when he hears her

question. His eyes narrow and his hands close into fists. "Did you have something to do with it?"

Paheli rolls her eyes. "Give my intelligence some credit. We are the ones who asked the grandmother to phone you to keep your father from returning home. Did you?"

The man's suspicion doesn't fall away, but the hostility in him eases slightly. "Why do you want to know?"

"We have business with him," Valentina says.

The man looks at all of us, perhaps trying to gauge the threat we present. "Is he really in danger?" he whispers.

"Yeah. If the people who are looking for him find him, they'll kill him," Paheli says, not bothering to soften the blow.

The man's face blanches. "Wh-who is after him?"

"We can't tell you. We'll speak to him, though," Paheli says. "The less you know, the safer you will be."

The man rubs his cheeks; the gesture reveals his anxiety. He doesn't fully trust us, and we can't really blame him. We wait for him to decide. Finally, he does.

"He's in the back room," he says in a ragged whisper. "I don't know if he'll talk to you. My father is . . . somewhat eccentric."

"Please lead us to him," Paheli says. The man hesitates again but then bids us to wait while he checks with his father.

A minute later, he returns. "You may go in," he says to us. Kamboja, Areum, and Ligaya stay behind as lookouts, while the rest of us go through the door. In a dim room with no windows and only a naked light bulb hanging from the ceiling is a very old man hunched over a table, working on something.

The makers of human conjury are usually people with elastic

wills. At least that's what our limited and faulty experience has shown us. They're not particularly strong or brave; they are just able to shift intention from their mind to an object and anchor it there. It's not exactly magic. Not the magic we know. These makers also sense the middle world, but not all of them are able to see it. They just seem to know that there's more to the world than their eyes show them.

The din in the market outside fades, and the air gains a still quality. Paheli sits in the chair opposite the old man, and we stand behind and beside her. The old man peers at us with his bloodshot eyes.

"Who are you?" he whispers. From the pulse ticking under his eye, we can tell he senses something awry about us.

"Let us ask the questions, baba," Paheli says with a smile. She leans forward, elbows on the table, a palm of her hand cupping the side of her face.

"What do you want?" Old Mahmoud says, his fingers drifting to a folded-up notepaper on the table.

"Is that conjury?" Valentina asks, and the old man starts, his fingers retreating from the paper. The question is unnecessary. The paper has a telltale purple aura.

"What are you talking about?" he blusters. "I don't know what a conjury is!" His eyes are wide with panic. Ah, so the old man isn't quite as oblivious to the middle world as we thought. He must have been previously warned by someone.

"We don't mean you any harm," Paheli replies, her voice calm. Soothing, even.

He gives us a suspicious look. "You think I will believe you when you say that? I don't make talismans anymore. Stop bothering me!"

"If you had really stopped making these so-called talismans, baba, they wouldn't have burned your shop down," Valentina says, and the old man flinches.

"They? Who are they? How did they find out? I was so careful!" The man licks his dry lips and his eyes well up.

"They are the ones who walk unseen amongst humans. You must have felt them? Their creatures can smell human conjury," Paheli says. Her voice gentles. "You didn't do anything wrong."

The man wipes his tears with shaking hands. "What am I supposed to do now? My home is gone. The place I have lived in for sixty years is gone. Everything that remained of my wife is gone."

We don't know how to comfort him; our sense of home is tethered more to a person than to a place.

"Well, what do you want with me?" Old Mahmoud asks when reason returns to him. "Are you here to threaten me? I'm telling you, I'm not as weak as you think."

Paheli purses her lips, perhaps gathering her thoughts. "You must have realized by now that we're not as human as you are," she says. The old man shakes his head, denying her words and our existence. "We need you to create a conjury for us."

"My home was burned down because of these conjuries you keep mentioning. I'm never making them one again!" The old man stands up, but his legs are unsteady, so he sits back down.

"Your words would have more weight if this table weren't covered with paper conjury," Talei says sweetly.

"These are just talismans to keep my family safe!" the old man insists.

Paper conjuries won't work for us. They broadcast their identity with the purple aura; there's no way Baarish would pick one up willingly, and there's little chance of us tricking him into doing so.

"Do you have anything other than these paper conjuries?" Paheli asks.

"They're not conjuries, I'm telling you. These are talismans to keep my family safe." Old Mahmoud regains his hostility. "Why should I help you?"

"Without us, you'd be dead right now, old man," Valentina replies. "If we hadn't told the old woman to call your son, you'd have returned home yesterday, and those who burned your store would have burned you."

"You don't have to believe us," Paheli says. "We'll give you a lot of money for your . . . talismans. A lot. Enough that your son no longer needs to run a shop in the old souk, enough that you can leave this country and build a home somewhere else. How about that?"

The old man's expression becomes complicated. Money is, after all, a limited resource, available only to a select few.

"Well?" Paheli prompts.

"What do you want?" The old man gives in. We knew he would. Not many humans can resist the allure of money.

"Something that isn't obviously a conj . . . talisman," Paheli replies.

The old man frowns, thinking hard. "Can you tell if something is a talisman just by looking at it?"

We all nod.

Seeing that, the old man gets up from his chair and rummages in a cupboard in a corner of the room. After a while he picks out a small box and brings it to the table. From the box, he takes out small rectangular boxes, each one wrapped in yellowed pieces of newspaper. He unwraps one and opens it to reveal a pendant wrought in silver with a semiprecious gem in the center. There is no glow to it, nothing that indicates it is a conjury. It looks like a normal piece of jewelry.

"These talismans protect wearers from harm and injury, but to use them, you have to waken the gem first. To do that, you have to speak the word bound to the gem. Until the word is spoken, the pendant is nothing but simple jewelry."

"Demonstrate it for us," Valentina says. When Paheli levels a look at her, she adds, "Please."

Old Mahmoud slides the pendant through a silver chain and drops the chain over his head and around his neck. He closes his palm around the pendant, closes his eyes, and whispers a word. Then he opens his hand to reveal the pendant, which has a purple aura.

"Do we have to touch it to awaken it? Does it have to be on our person for us to awaken it?" Paheli asks.

"No," Old Mahmoud replies to both questions. "Is this good?"

"It is good. It is more than good." Paheli beams. "Sell us all the pendants in your inventory. Take the money we give you and leave this place. Change your name. Change your son's name.

Disappear." She looks at the old man. "We will give you enough money to do that."

The old man nods, but he doesn't thank us. We understand. We have brought him nothing but bad news.

When we step out of the souk, the sun has set and the speakers are broadcasting the azaan for Maghrib. This means the food stalls in the Jemaa el-Fna are open.

Jemaa el-Fna: The Mosque at the End of the World

Magic is thick in places where blood has been spilled. The Jemaa el-Fna, the large square that is our destination, was the site for public executions back in the days of the Almohads, who, according to our understanding, were the nice and kind rulers who did things like public executions. They spilled enough blood in the square that it draws all middle-world creatures in the area, especially after the sun sets.

For humans, the square holds its own attractions. We have sat among crowds of humans, as enthralled as anyone else present, with the tales woven by the storytellers whose rich and rough voices make stories come to life in ways that make your breath hitch and your heart pound. We have seen snakes charmed by the wailing music that charmers play. The chained monkeys set us free, and sometimes we secretly set them free.

The ensuing chaos is *always* worth it.

When we emerge from the souks out into the square, the sun is a recent memory in the sky and the night is fresh and ripe with possibilities. We skirt past the carts selling fresh orange juice and weave through the increasing numbers of people toward the food stalls that glimmer more enticingly to us than a store selling nothing but diamonds would at this moment.

We probably shouldn't be here; we should have returned to the riad with Taraana or chosen a more hidden place to eat, but we are flush with success after finally finding conjury we can hopefully use. We are living dangerously. The crowd around us is composed of locals, tourists, and middle worlders who give themselves away by the liquid way in which they move. We pull Taraana's hood over his head so his face is in shadow. The glasses make him look nothing more than human anyway. We receive one or two piercing looks from middle worlders, but most of them are too busy with their own errands to give us a second look. It should be fine. We're only staying here for the length of a meal anyway.

We stop a moment to appreciate the spectacle of the food stalls that spring up in the Jemaa el-Fna every day after dusk. Each stall is numbered, though the numbers are not in sequence. Stall number five, for example, might be right beside stall number 105.

Imagine a cool October night. The heavens high above are heavy with stars—not that you will have the time or inclination to look up. A million conversations are happening simultaneously around you. Somewhere, a storyteller's deep voice is poised on the tip of a precipice, the pungi of a snake charmer wails plaintively, voices accompanied by a darabukka sing to entice your stomach and your hunger. Meat sizzles on grills, and a thousand different aromas compete to awaken your appetite. Smoke obscures the view sometimes, but your nose is not easily distracted.

We walk around the stalls for a while before choosing one filled with locals. Dinner is a fantastic explosion of intense flavors, and entirely satisfying. After the meal, we get cups of mint tea and start to navigate our way through the crowd.

It is Ghufran who first notices the men. She doesn't speak much, our Ghufran, but you will never find anyone more observant than her. She plucks at Paheli's sleeve, and when Paheli turns to her, she whispers in her ear. Paheli doesn't miss a beat. She doesn't react visibly at all to Ghufran's words but turns slightly so she can look at the men following us. There is nothing specifically conspicuous about them; they are not giving us any more attention than others are. Still, there is the way they don't look at us but still manage to be everywhere we go. Though Ghufran remains the most damaged amongst us, we all have sung the song she sings, and in these men, we recognize the notes of that dreaded music.

We move so Taraana is snug in the middle; they will need to get us out of the way to reach him. We are assuming it is him they want and not us. Well, they will have to work harder if they want us. We have more thorns than Taraana does. Paheli and Valentina look at each other for a long, silent moment. Have they prepared for this inevitability? It seems like we are going to find out.

We are in the middle of the Jemaa el-Fna with no walls imme-diately at hand, so we can't run into the Between. The nearest uninterrupted wall is about ten minutes way, more if the crowds get thicker. Since magic doesn't work on us, will Baarish's men resort to violence? Can they, in the middle of this crowded square? Can we trust them not to?

Well, of course not.

We pass a man with three chained monkeys trained to do tricks. The monkeys are pulling at their chains, and the owner keeps swatting at them. A possibility. Talei, moving so quickly she is but a blur, reaches in and opens their collars, setting them free. Ligaya throws her cup of tea at a passing tourist, while Areum bumps into two women carrying trays of oranges.

The monkeys take a moment to realize their freedom, then flee from their owner and jump onto shoulders. They steal food and throw fruits at people. The tourist with tea dripping down his face looks for someone to yell at. The women with the trays full of oranges wail at the loss of their goods. Someone swears. Someone else bumps into a crowd of people all carrying food and drinks. The moment turns to madness.

In that madness, we flee. Not in the direction we were going but in the opposite. We do not let go of Taraana's hands. Not once. It takes us seven minutes to reach a wall and thirty seconds to enter the Between. It is only when the door shuts behind us that Taraana realizes that Paheli is not with us.

He pulls the hood of his djellaba down and looks around at each of us, as if he has made a mistake and Paheli will somehow appear. His eyes widen and the stars in them dim. He looks at the door leading to Marrakech, and Valentina moves to stand in front of it.

"We left her behind," he whispers. "I need to go get her back."

He moves to open the door, but Valentina won't budge from her position in front of it.

His panic spreads until he is practically shaking from the force of it. "Get out of my way. Please. I *need* to get her back," he entreats. Then angrily. "How could you leave her behind?"

"She will return to us," Valentina says gently. She tries hard, but we can see her uncertainty snag on her words until they are more of a question than a statement.

"How can you be certain of that? What if they take her? I can't let that happen. I will go back." He stands in front of Valentina, as if he will physically remove her.

"Paheli would never forgive us if we let you do that," Talei says. "We didn't leave her behind, Taraana. She *chose* to move in the other direction, perhaps to lead those men away from us. She knows what she's doing. Come on, we need to go before our pursuers enter the Between."

"You do not understand," Taraana says, his head bowed, "and I don't know what to say to make you understand. She wears my star in her palm. I can *feel* her terror right now. Don't you get it? You think she's prepared and strong and whatnot. She's not. She just pretends she is. She's always pretending!" He breathes harshly, on the brink of tears. "I can't. I won't stay here and be safe. Not when she is not here with me."

"It is not that we don't know she's scared, Taraana," Daraja says. "It's not that we don't know she's pretending not to be scared. It is just that all of us here pretend. We pretend so hard that sometimes what we pretend becomes true. We pretend we aren't scared. We pretend we're all right. We pretend we don't yearn for homes and roots. We pretend until we believe it and once we believe it, it becomes true. So, we will pretend Paheli is all right. We will believe she is all right. And she will be."

"I understand that. I do. But you can't ask me to leave her behind." He looks at Valentina, a plea on his face. "Her feelings, her desire to live no matter what, her will, and her strength were the things that made it possible for me to continue living. As long as she wears my star, she and I are connected. I can feel what you all feel too, but with her, it is more intense. Perhaps because my heart is involved. Perhaps because I seek out the connection between us.

"I have loved her without knowing where in the world she was, what she looked like at any moment in time. I have loved her so long that time seems immaterial to me. It was enough that she existed somewhere. That she breathed, felt, and loved. It was enough. I knew if I searched her out, I would put her in danger. So, I didn't until I had no choice but to seek her out. Seek you all out."

He looks at us. The stars in his eyes are lustrous, but the tears don't fall. "And now that I have found her, have held her, I can't continue without her. I know what Baarish does. I can't stand aside and let him hurt her. I will die first."

"Nobody is going to die," Valentina says, frowning. She takes a deep breath. "Paheli will come back to us, Taraana. She is stronger than you give her credit for. She is stronger and wilier than any of us. You need to trust her."

"I do trust her, but you are underestimating Baarish and his desire to capture me," Taraana says. "He will do anything to get me back in his power, and if he finds out what Paheli means to me, he will use her as bait."

"They can't use magic against her," Ligaya says.

"Baarish *never* used magic against me. He just hurt me. Over and over again. Until I didn't know what it meant to exist without pain."

"They won't catch her," Valentina says. "I refuse to consider that possibility."

Taraana is far from convinced. Clenching his fists, he looks at the door leading to Marrakech as if he can will it open. The unseen lights in the Between flicker, and we are reminded that while he may seem helpless, Taraana is not entirely without power. Especially not here in the Between. If he wanted to, he could probably force Valentina to move. That he doesn't says a lot about him.

"What do we do now?" Ghufran says. We have never lost Paheli before. This unanchored feeling is new to us, and we don't much like it.

"We need to start walking before our pursuers enter the Between," Talei says again. Of us all, she is the most anxious. "Where are we going, V?"

"To the safe house," Valentina replies shortly.

"Safe house?" Kamboja echoes. "What safe house?" This is the first time most of us have heard of it.

"Areum." Valentina raises an eyebrow.

"Follow me," Areum says, and, choosing a branch of the Between, starts walking. Taraana takes one last look at the door leading to Marrakech before following her. Valentina leaves last.

Paheli: A Moment in Chartreuse

Bang, bang! How easily the chaos is curbed and the crowds quieted. People stop, one step away from a stampede. Too bad. Now I have to return to fear.

You learn fear all at once, you know. In less than one second, your body will understand all its shades and ken all its depths. Corners will become sinister and the sound of footsteps will become reasons to panic. Darkness will begin to mean more than just the absence of light. A half-second is all it takes to learn fear. But it will take you a lifetime to unlearn it.

Me? I am not there yet, and I have lived several lifetimes. Make of that what you will.

The girls are gone and with them, so is Taraana. I am left as the landmark of a disappeared quarry. I watch as our pursuers realize this fact. I could have gone with them. I *should* have gone with them. But see, there is this quality in me that makes me want to poke at a beehive. So that's what I am going to do. Poke it. Because the fear that I struggle with is 50 percent anger. Anger that even so many years, centuries, later, I still can't walk down a dark road alone without "asking for it." Anger that my female body makes me available for consumption whether I consent to it or not. Anger that those with strength continuously try to use that strength against me. Angry. I am so angry.

I look around. The pursuers are whispering to each other, making sure to keep me in their sight. I pretend that I am not watching them watch me.

One of the pursuers, a not-human man with a beard red from henna, glances at me and then quickly away. I ignore the middle worlder for the moment and help the two human women whose trays of oranges we sacrificed. We pick up their now-trodden fruit. I press some money into their hands and watch the enemy numbers reduce to four as the rest of the men leave to presumably comb the square for the girls and Taraana, who are all hopefully on their way to our safe house.

The middle worlders left to shadow me are doing an abominably bad job of being circumspect. They stalk me as I meander from one food stall to another, though I have no intention of eating anything. The night is full of lights, colors, and scents, and I am alone. This is the first time I have been truly alone in a long while. I don't dislike solitude, but I am wary of how close it skews to loneliness.

"Are you buying?" a stall owner asks me hopefully. I shake my head, give him a smile, and move on.

The red-bearded middle worlder is so close that I could turn around and scream into his ear if I so wished. I don't, though. That would be too easy and too messy. You need not always bloody your hands to win a fight.

Three quarters of an hour pass by with them tailing me around the food stalls. Do they think I am unaware of their presence? Maybe they simply don't care. Maybe they want to intimidate me. Hmm. What do they see when they look at me? Prey? And if they catch me, what will they do? Drag me to their master? And what will he do? Force me to give up the star embedded in my palm? How? Will he torture me? The same way he tortured Taraana?

I turn and look at the red-bearded, not-human man. He is surprised by my gaze for a second, and then he smiles at me. In his smile, I see another man. One I thought I never would see again. I guess it is true what people say. You never forget the shape of your monster, no matter how much time passes since the last time you saw him.

The fear I feel is bigger than I am. It is darker and more malicious. But I am stronger than it is. I will *always* be stronger than it is.

I smile back at the red-bearded man and show him all my teeth. His smile withers at mine. Heh.

I could stretch out this strange play, build it up before letting the cards fall into place. But the night is aging and my girls will worry if I take too long. So, I plunge into the crowds, abandoning caution entirely, and lead my pursuers on a merry chase before I emerge out of the area where the food stalls are and into the space belonging to everyone else. Musicians, storytellers, entertainers, and a vast array of other entrepreneurs have set up shop in all available space here except one.

One square, just a little ways from the line of carts selling freshly squeezed orange juice, remains deserted. No locals venture there. If they have to pass by, they will go around it, keeping a solid distance between it and them. Tourists who stumble into the space leave hurriedly, often with ashen faces. Local middle worlders won't cross it. They have learned not to.

To understand what makes the little piece of the square so vile to both middle worlders and humans alike, you have to understand the history of the Jemaa el-Fna. Particularly the part where it was used as execution grounds. The blood spilled in the square not only gives the magic here an incarnadine flavor, but it also makes the place thick with ghosts.

Ghosts are not common, but neither are they the impossibilities human science labels them as. Any place where emotions are spent in excess becomes fertile ground for ghosts. If the magic in the place is enough to sustain them, they will exist. Usually the magic isn't, but here, it is.

Most of the ghosts lingering in the square are benign, barely held together by some unfulfilled wish or unspoken desire. They are wisps who only require one strong gust of will to dissipate. They have no anchors, so they grow no roots. That is not the case with Farah.

To call her a ghost seems like an insult to the strength of her being, but in the end, that is what she is. I met her, if one can meet ghosts, one afternoon when the storm inside of me was raging harder than the storm outside in the square. The pain, which constructs her, which binds her to this world long after everything she was, has decayed away, seems like a distant echo of mine. She lost her heart and then her life with scarcely a pause between the two. She was betrayed first by her father and then by her husband. Two things remain of her: her name, which she holds on to tightly, and her anger, which she grasps even tighter. She haunts the little piece of the square on which she was executed and exacts a payment from anyone who is unlucky enough to step into the space. She causes humans pain and rips the magic from middle worlders. She doesn't kill them, but without magic, they might as well be dead. She is not searching for absolution; she has no wish to move on to anywhere.

What she and I have is not friendship, not exactly. You cannot be friends with a ghost. What we have is an understanding, a common language that we both speak. A language that anyone who has been violated and known fear speaks.

If I had wanted to escape the men, I could have done so in a hundred other ways. I could have hidden in a corner or blended in with a group of tourists, but we all have things we can't do. I can't let the fear rule me. I will not run away. So, I make sure the men are following and head to Farah's square, stopping right in the middle of it.

The men follow me into Farah's square, crowding me with their physical presence. Since they came so willingly, they must not have heard of the danger this little piece of the Jemaa el-Fna poses. Or perhaps they do not give credence to any rumors they may have heard.

Still, how can they not feel her? Do they not sense her in the frenzied beating of their hearts? One of the four men frowns and looks around, as if something in the air has disturbed him, but the rest are serene, confident of the power they have and think I don't.

"Lead us to the keeper and you will go unharmed," one of the men says. He uses magic to throw up a veil that makes us invisible to all observing eyes. "If you don't cooperate, you will get hurt."

I do not reply.

The red-bearded man steps nearer to me and opens his mouth, and at that moment the air crackles with lightning, though the night sky is clear. The men all freeze—but it is far too late.

She is there in the lack of color in their cheeks, in the swallow of their throats, and in the sweat dotting their foreheads. She is there in the pain that peels their lips back in silent snarls.

See, the magic is ripe in the Jemaa el-Fna, and ripe magic is strong magic. Strong magic intoxicates middle worlders and gives strong ghosts a bite that they usually don't have. I step around the unconscious bodies of the four men and leave Farah to her meal.

AREUM
CITY OF ORIGIN: SEOUL

*Midnight peeked before it passed
and found me with my petticoats up
observing my legs in horrified detail.
When did I become a monster?*

Paheli: On the Frailties of the Heart

I.

It is late afternoon in Gamcheon Culture Village in Busan, South Korea, when I finally get there. The shadows are thick and sunset perhaps less than an hour away. The days are short this time of the year.

It has been five hours since I sent the girls ahead. Two since I left Marrakech. I wonder how they feel without me. Do they feel relieved? Have they realized my presence is unnecessary? Are they worried? Carrying a story on your own is difficult.

Taraana must be angry.

I stop in the thin alley I came out in and rethink my decision to return to the girls and Taraana. I can still run away from him. He must be one or two degrees over angry. How will I face his anger? I halt my steps and look down at my hands. They are not covered in blood, but they may as well be.

That moment on the rooftop in Marrakech. How could I hug Taraana when I don't deserve his embrace? What if I sully him? What if I don't go back? What if I turn around and go back to the Between and—the thought of never seeing Taraana again terrifies me, and the fact that I'm terrified terrifies me.

I am a mess. You heard it here first.

I take a deep breath and feel the cold air cool my insides. Okay. I won't think about all of this here in this stinky alley. I most certainly won't have a breakdown here. I put my chin up and start walking again. We chose Gamcheon Culture Village as the location for our safe house for one simple reason: the area is young enough to deter other middle worlders from settling here. The magic here is too thin to sustain them for long, but it is old enough to easily keep us.

I follow the road for a bit before turning from it to climb the first of several flights of stairs. The corners are hairy and the going difficult, but I make it through with minimal wheezing. Finally, I make it to a house with bright pink walls and an equally bright blue roof.

Gamcheon Culture Village started life as a slum, flooded with refugees fleeing the Korean War. A government initiative turned this town built on the side of a mountain into a tourist destination. All the houses here are painted in happy colors reminiscent of a pastel rainbow, and that is just the first and most obvious way the place was transformed. The walls feature murals or graffiti art; the stairs are decorated with paintings. Art installations invite tourists to take pictures, and small cafés do brisk business serving visitors who need a place to sit down and recover from the many steep hills and stairs that compose the town.

From the front, the pink-walled house appears deserted, which is as it should be. The purpose of the safe house is to give us a place to go to ground. No one knows of this place apart from us and Eulalie. But what if something happened to the girls and they didn't make it here? What if by spending time without me, they realized they don't need me after all? That they are better off without me? What if Taraana got so angry he left? What will I do without them? How will I get him back? Should I even want to? Perhaps it is better for me to be alone.

The front door swings inward at my touch. Breathe, I need to breathe. They will be inside and they will be safe. They will still love me. There is nothing to it.

When I step through the door and into the house, I see no one for a second and my heart cracks like a nutshell in a nutcracker. The next minute there is a scream, and suddenly I am besieged. I manage to extricate myself after a minute only to be immediately subjected to Valentina's glare.

"What took you so long?" she demands. Her eyes are suspiciously bright. She might actually be glad to see me. Wow. My eyes sting in response. I don't know what's wrong with me.

I don't know how to answer her. What do I say? I had to take care of business? My hands aren't bloody, but they may as well be? I don't regret what I did. I just don't like how I feel afterward.

"Taraana?" I ask instead.

Daraja nods at the staircase. "He disappeared into one of the bedrooms when we got here and hasn't come out." She gives me a long look. "He's . . . Well, just be prepared."

"What happened to those men?" Ghufran asks, her hands holding mine tightly.

"They were taken care of," I tell her. She smiles and lets go.

"Go talk to Taraana," Widad says. "He has been slowly going out of his mind every minute you weren't here."

"I don't envy you," Kamboja says, taking a bite of a very red apple.

"Neither do I," Areum says, her lips red from tteokbokki. Where did they get the food from? Weren't they supposed to stay inside?

"The anger this time isn't going to be solved easily," Daraja warns. "Want to take him chocolate?"

"I don't think a tub full of chocolate will help. Not this time," Ligaya tells me with her unkind smile.

"You deserve whatever he says to you," Etsuko says.

I look at Talei. "You have nothing to say?"

"I'm sure Taraana will say it for me," she says serenely.

I look reluctantly at the stairs, but I have no other choice. I will have to dare the dragon's den.

II.

I have been alive for a very long time, and I have met many different kinds of people, but I can honestly say that I have never met anyone who disconcerts me in quite the same way that Taraana does. I am upset by how easily he sweeps away my defenses and leaves me helpless against his direct gaze. I exert a lot of effort to be mysterious, and yet I am transparent to him. It truly annoys me.

I am fully prepared for his anger, you know. I *expect* him to rage at me. I am prepared to battle that hurricane. When I knock on his door, he doesn't respond, so I open it. The room is shrouded in shadow; the only light in the room comes from a window on the far wall looking over the back of the house. Tara-ana is sitting by the window, staring out at the red-streaked sky. He doesn't turn when I open the door, and he doesn't respond when I call out to him.

So, here I am, standing like an elephant in heels in the middle of the room, waiting for the ax to fall. He won't look at me and he won't talk to me and I have no idea what to do. See, this is why relationships are a bad idea for me.

I take a step in his direction, and he gets up so suddenly that I jump back. He turns to face me, and all the words I have prepared to appease him disappear. He looks at me; his eyes travel my face and my body as if searching for some kind of wound. His hands clench at his sides. He lets out a ragged breath, then wipes his eyes with a fist.

I thought he would be angry, but the emotion I sense from him is something more potent, something darker, something I don't have the words for.

"Taraana—"

"I am leaving," he says, cutting me off.

I stare at him, uncomprehending for a second. "Where are you going?"

"It's better if you don't know." He is entirely too calm. His voice isn't shaking, and apart from the earlier show of emotion, his face is composed. It is as though I don't know him.

I swallow. All right, this is serious. "Why are you leaving?"

"The answer is obvious, isn't it?" he replies, turning his back to me. Again.

"No, it really isn't. Look at me."

"I don't want to."

Oh. Ouch.

"I survived well enough without you protecting me, you know." He should maybe just hit me. That would hurt less.

"Look." I step closer to him. After thinking about it, I place a hand carefully on his arm. If he flinches, I may never recover. He stiffens but doesn't otherwise react. All right. "I am not going to apologize for what I did today."

"I am not asking you to." He turns to me abruptly, and I realize how close we are to each other. "You don't think I am strong enough to protect myself. You consider me weak and afraid, and maybe I am both those things. But you, you are cavalier with your disregard for danger. You taunt death as if daring it to try to take you away." He takes a deep breath. "There was no reason for you to stay behind today. No matter how you try to justify remaining behind, the fact is, you could have run with us, escaped with us, but you *chose* to remain behind. Perhaps to prove a point, perhaps to confront your fears. I don't know."

My eyes prickle. Oh no. I am *not* going to cry. I will be damned if I do. He can go if he wants to. I don't care.

That is a lie. Damn it all.

I do care. I care too much.

Do you know how difficult it is to love anything or anyone when your sense of self has been shattered? It took me a long time and a lot of help to even admit to liking the way the sun felt on my skin. I *admitted* to liking Taraana. I admitted that I might even love him someday in the future. Shouldn't that be enough?

Taraana crosses over to the wall, and a door to the Between appears.

"Wait. Wait. Wait." I am all panic.

"Listen." He grabs my hands in his gently. "I know you have your own demons to fight. I shouldn't have asked you to battle mine as well. I'm sorry. You don't owe me anything." He pauses as if fighting the urge to say something else. Finally, he shakes his head. "As for the other thing, I—" He stops. Shakes his head again. Lets go of my hands. Turns away.

If he leaves, I will never see him again. But to ask him to stay will take the kind of courage I only pretend to have.

"Convey my gratitude to the girls. Thank them for being the family I never had."

"Wait, Taraana." Dammit, I am crying. If I am going to do this, I will have to do it all. I wrap my arms around him, forcing him to stop walking toward the Between door. His heart is beating furiously under my cheek. His skin is warm and he smells like strawberry soap. "You can't leave."

"Don't tell me what to do, Paheli." He growls my name. I look up into his eyes and am trapped by the stars that glimmer in them.

"I am going to kiss you now," I tell him, and proceed to do exactly that. I rise on my toes and press my lips to his, and the world explodes in a festival of feeling. Neither of us is familiar with the concept of kissing, but his lips are soft and I like them. I like touching him. I want to touch him as I have never wanted to touch another person. I want us to kiss longer and deeper. Kissing him is like getting that little bit of myself back. That bit of myself I lost so long ago. Our kiss is flavored by tears, though I don't know whose tears they are.

The first thing he says when we finally stop kissing is "This doesn't change anything."

My mouth falls open and I gape at him. "How can you say that?" I demand. Why doesn't he realize how much courage it took me to touch him?

"You will leave me behind again the next time there is danger. Or perhaps you will intentionally deflect all attention, all danger, to yourself because you think yourself dispensable."

"I don't think that!"

He looks at me with those eyes that see too much. I look away from him, but I don't let go of his hand.

"All right, maybe you have a point. A tiny little point, but it's not because you are weak. It's because you are precious to me."

"Haven't you ever thought that *you* are precious to me as well?" he replies.

"I . . ." I look at him, bewildered. I sit down on the bed, and he sits down next to me. Actually, honestly, I haven't.

He sighs and his arm snakes around my waist to pull me softly against him. "I am in love with you, Paheli. When you put my tear on, you unintentionally and unknowingly became my companion. I spent nights curled up in a cage, sometimes hurt, sometimes bleeding, feeling what you felt. The place Baarish kept me was dark; there was never any light, but through you, I could see the sun. Baarish used to talk to me after torturing me for a day. He used to tell me my only purpose in life was to provide him with my tears. He sat on a stool outside the cage and talked.

He told me I was useless. That my parents threw me away. That no one would ever love me. He didn't know that I had you. Your pleasure when you eat mangoes, your anger, your fear, your sadness. I feasted on your feelings. They were so much more than the bleak despair that composed my days."

I am crying so hard, I feel dizzy.

"When I first saw you that evening in Byblos . . . there is nothing I can say here that can encompass the entirety of all I felt in that moment." He cups my face with his hands, wiping away my tears with his thumbs. "Our feelings aren't the same yet. I understand that. I have loved you longer. You are precious to me. Infinitely so. I won't ask you to not take risks or do anything that you don't want to as long as you will realize that I will do the same thing. You can't leave me behind or stay behind unless I am allowed to do the same thing."

I pull away from him and grab some tissues from a box on the bedside table. I wipe my eyes and blow my nose and try to stop crying. It takes a while.

"Well?" He pokes me.

"Well what?" I say, and he glares at me. "Okay, okay."

"Do you promise?" he asks.

"I do."

"Say it."

"I promise." I sniffle.

As a reward, he kisses me again.

Sonagi, or A Sudden Rain

We are still shaken from what happened in Marrakech. We startle easily and huddle together for comfort. Our screams are a breath away and our hands tremble. We hate this weakness immensely, but Baarish has threatened the safety, the security, we have spent decades if not centuries cultivating.

The evening finds us in the living room, with the television blasting cheers from the fans of Apink, a K-pop girl group we all stan. We are seated around a stash of street food Areum and Etsuko went and bought. Taraana has discovered tteokbokki and appears to have found heaven at the same time.

"What are we going to do now?" Apink's song ends, and Valentina turns the TV off.

Paheli pops a piece of tuna kimbap into her mouth, chews, and swallows. It is a delaying tactic of hers that we're familiar with.

"We do an experiment," she says finally. "Before we decide how exactly we'll use the conjury we bought from the old man, we need to know what exactly it does."

Valentina gets up and starts pacing. "Why do I feel like you're not taking this seriously? Those middle worlders last night—they were from Baarish, right? He was able to follow us to Marrakech. Who is to say he won't be able to follow us here? We are sitting ducks here. Isn't it time we made plans?"

"Can't I finish eating first?" Paheli puts another kimbap piece into her mouth and chews with relish.

Valentina glares at her. "Paheli!"

"Fine." Paheli wipes her mouth.

"I don't see why you are being so casual about this. I don't see why you had to stay behind!" Ah. That's the crux of it. Valentina's angry.

"Look, I've just had a difficult time explaining to Taraana—"

"Actually, I don't recall you saying a single thing in explanation," Taraana corrects her.

Paheli glares at him.

"So? What do you have to say for yourself?" Valentina asks, a quivering tone in her voice.

"I'm sorry. Sometimes I need to act in ways that don't make sense and aren't very sensible. I will attempt to do better." This is the first time we have heard Paheli say something like this, and our eyebrows are so high, they might break through the stratosphere and reach space.

"Apologize a hundred more times and I'll consider forgiving you," Valentina replies with a sharp smile.

Instead of responding to her, Paheli walks over to where

Daraja's backpack is, opens it, and grabs the bag containing the small rectangular boxes that house the pendants along with their chains. She takes one out and pops the box open. The semiprecious stone in the center of the pendant glints dully in the light. Paheli holds the pendant in her hands and nothing happens. It really looks like a piece of unmagical jewelry.

"So, we can be sure that human conjuries are dangerous to middle worlders; otherwise they wouldn't be as conscientious about cleaning them up as they are. In fact, not only do they clear up places selling the conjuries, but they also kill the humans who make them. While we know they consider it dangerous, we don't know what they do to middle worlders for sure." Paheli rubs her chin and glances at Taraana. "We've got Assi's word for it, but we need more than that. So, to figure things out clearly, let's see what a conjury does to a Between diamond."

Talei places a Between diamond on a coffee table in the middle of a living room next to the rec room we were in. Then Paheli balances the unawakened pendant on the Between diamond. We take five steps away from the table, but nothing happens.

Taraana takes a breath, closes his eyes, and says the word that's supposed to awaken the conjury.

Five seconds later, the pendant starts glowing purple, and the Between diamond starts melting. In five more seconds, all that remains of the diamond is a puddle, and that too disappears shortly.

Ligaya whistles through her teeth. "That was intense."

"Now I know why middle worlders take human conjury so seriously," Areum says, shivering.

"Okay. I am pleased," Paheli says. "Now all we need to do is get Baarish to hold one of these pendants, activate it while he's holding it, and bang!" Her eyes are shining with a bloodthirsty light.

We stare at her.

"What?" she asks.

"He'll die if he holds an activated pendant," Talei says flatly.

"That's the point." Paheli looks at us, the lightness flitting from her face. "Isn't it?"

"We'd be directly responsible for his death." Daraja licks her lips. "I don't know if I'm okay with that."

Paheli tilts her head. "But you'd be okay with him chasing us, catching us, torturing us, and ultimately killing us?"

"Paheli." Valentina slips an arm around her.

"Do you have any other methods to suggest? I'm not speaking to Daraja alone. If you have any other suggestions, make them. I'm listening." Paheli's face is uncharacteristically serious. None of us are able to meet her eyes.

Paheli turns to Taraana. "Do you have the same qualms about killing Baarish?" Before he can reply, she forges ahead. "Listen, I'm not a saint who forgives people for the pain they inflict upon me and the people I love. I refuse to be a victim. If this means I have to plan for Baarish's death, so be it. I will not let him take Taraana again, and I will not let him hurt one of us."

"Won't bonding with the Between make Taraana more powerful?" Widad asks. "Can't we try that?"

"Taraana has been trying," Kamboja says. "You've seen that."

"But he could try harder," Widad says, and then stops talking at the look Paheli gives her.

"We've been able to escape Baarish thus far not just because of luck but because he hasn't been seriously chasing us. He's playing with us the same way a cat plays with its prey. Once he does get serious, how long do you think we can run from him?" Paheli asks.

"Ideally, Taraana would be able to bond to the Between, gain a lot of power, which would keep him safe from Baarish and his companions." Valentina spells things out. "However, the process of bonding to the Between is more complex, and right now, attempts to do so without attracting Baarish's attention, impossible."

"But Baarish is simply one of many people who want Taraana," Ligaya counters. "Aren't the others on the Magic Council also after him? Are we going to kill all of them? Can we?"

"Probably not," Paheli says. "But as I said, let's take one enemy at a time. If your conscience cannot handle what's going to happen, you can either stay with Eulalie or leave. I promise, there'll be no hard feelings whatever you decide. It is your choice."

"I will always choose myself," Taraana says suddenly. "Between Baarish and me, I mean." He slips his fingers through Paheli's. He offers us a crooked smile. "I have to be alive to feel the twinges of my conscience."

Paheli has made her decision, and it is up to us to make ours.

"How do you propose to get Baarish to hold a pendant in his bare hands?" Etsuko asks when the silence lasts for a beat too long, raising one of her thin eyebrows. She has no problem planning a murder.

Paheli licks her lips at the question and turns to look at Taraana. He meets her eyes, and his face becomes blank for a second before a steely resolve fills it. He nods.

Areum is the first to comprehend what that wordless exchange means. "How can you ask him to do something like that?" Her protest is a wail.

Paheli considers the question for a moment. "You know as well as I do that you have to save yourself. No one else can do it for you."

"I don't *want* anyone else to do it for me," Taraana says. "I have to save myself."

"I think we should talk to Eulalie about this plan. Maybe she can come over," Daraja says. She's the most troubled by the current course of actions.

"Okay," Paheli agrees easily. "I will ask her."

"You're not going to New Orleans!" Ligaya exclaims.

"No, I'm going to call her."

"How?" Ligaya again.

"I'm going to use the telephone?"

"Oh."

"All right," Valentina says. "This is a plan I can live with."

"You're going to have to do more than just live with it, Tina," Paheli says, leaning against Taraana.

"What do you mean by that?" Valentina angles a narrow look her way.

"You will need to go and make friends with Tabassum Naaz," Paheli replies. "Don't give me that look. I know you don't mind getting to know her."

A blush deepens Valentina's dark skin. "Pray tell why I need to do that?"

"We need to prepare a trap for Baarish. It's not like we're really going to let him take Taraana."

"So, you'll have her play double agent?" Valentina replies.

"Yeah," Paheli says. "Ask her if she'd be okay with that. If she isn't . . . we'll do something else."

Valentina nods.

◇◇◇

Eulalie arrives on the same day Valentina leaves for Istanbul. She is out of breath and wheezing by the time she reaches our house, the lack of magic in the area affecting her as much as the stairs in Gamcheon Culture Village. We give her a Between diamond with which to sustain herself. She wraps her fingers around the diamond and absorbs half the magic in it before putting it away.

Her face glows after her intake of magic and she breathes out, relaxing.

"All right, tell me what you are up to now," she says to Paheli, a wealth of suffering in her tone.

Talei is the one who ends up narrating all that has transpired since we left New Orleans. Eulalie listens quietly, her gaze often on Paheli.

"Let me see this pendant," Eulalie says after a measured silence.

"Look at it from here," Paheli tells her. "Be careful."

"Oh, I might think you love me." Eulalie grins.

"I do," Paheli replies softly.

Eulalie looks surprised. The next moment her eyes fill with some emotion none of us are very familiar with. Mothers are a four-letter word to us. We don't say it.

Paheli clears her throat and we point Eulalie to the coffee table where the activated pendant is still lying. It's glowing purple, all but broadcasting its identity. Eulalie looks at it closely before she shudders and takes a step back. "You said you have an unawakened one?"

Daraja hands Eulalie a box containing one. She takes it out from the box and picks it up, turning it over in her hands. "How fascinating. You're telling me that this will become a conjury after the word activating it is spoken?"

"What does it feel like to you?" Talei asks.

Eulalie shrugs. "Like a pendant. I don't sense any malice in it like I do with human conjury."

"Will it work on Baarish, do you think?" Taraana asks hopefully.

"It will more than work on Baarish," she responds. "But you will have to face the Magic Council afterward. They will consider it murder."

"We will deal with them when we have to," Paheli replies. "And technically, it *is* murder, so they wouldn't be wrong." A strange feeling, like a frigid wind in winter, blows through us at her words.

"It's self-defense," Eulalie replies. "Baarish won't let you simply die if he catches you. Mama Magdaline will speak for you. But the reason I made the trip today is to tell you about Wa'ad. Remember, I said I had heard of a middle worlder who was a librarian in the middle-worlder equivalent of the Library of Alexandria?" Eulalie leans back in her chair. We are in the kitchen, cooking lunch. Well, Areum is cooking. We're just hanging around, annoying her.

"No, I don't remember, but tell me more," Paheli asks, pretending to cut up carrots but actually eating them, Bugs Bunny–style. Taraana, who actually is helping, takes over the cutting session, shooing her away in the process.

"She is remarkably erudite and, obviously, well-read. She might know of a way for Taraana to bond to the Between. It can't hurt to ask," Eulalie says. "She's currently in Cairo."

Paheli looks at Taraana. "Cairo, huh?"

He shrugs. "It may as well be Cairo."

Paheli: The Cheese in the Trap

Cairo, the city of a thousand minarets, rising like a phoenix from the ashes of the cities that stood in its place. It has blood on its streets and fever in its heart. Cairo, a refuge to some and a cage to others. The magic here has a smoky feel to it, as if it is born of grief.

The sky over Cairo is a disconcerting blue. The air in the city has the smell of a new day, car exhaust, and spices. Taraana and I separate from the others a little while after we enter the city. They are going to follow us from a distance. Daraja and Ghufran left with Eulalie the day before, preferring to provide emergency relief should we need any.

Our first destination in Cairo is an unnamed eating establishment run by a not-human woman called Tayseir. She has dark hair, brown skin, and eyes the gold of desert sand. She is standing at the front of the restaurant, talking to a customer, and moves aside to allow us entrance. With her kohled eyes and multihued scarves, she is as beautiful as her name. Her smile brightens when she sees us and sharpens a moment later when she notices Taraana.

"Who is this, Paheli?" Her voice makes a song out of my name. "Are you looking for trouble?"

"I hope so," I reply with a grin. I'm always pretending. "I've even sent it an invitation."

My reply gets me a glower from her. I sketch a bow and turn to follow Taraana, who has chosen a table close to the back of the restaurant, away from the light and the inquisitive patrons.

We exchange Between diamonds for currency and, upon Tayseir's insistence, order lunch. No matter what Tayseir cooks, the flavors in her food evoke the taste of the time you were happiest as a child. This is the magic of this restaurant and the real reason I brought Taraana here. He should taste some happiness before bad things happen.

The food arrives and we gape at the bounty being placed on the table. Tayseir has outdone herself.

"It's not often you bring a man here," Tayseir says with a grin, and Taraana raises an eyebrow.

"I have *never* brought a man here!" I protest.

Tayseir laughs and introduces the food. "I have feteer, gollash, fresh bread, bamia, and ful medames. Here is a platter of rice and a jug of icy sharbat. Eat your fill, and if you want more, just tell me."

Taraana stares at the feast in front of him and takes a deep breath, inhaling the aroma of the delicacies. Then he notices that the plate before him is the only one on the table.

"Aren't you eating?" he asks.

"I am not hungry," I reply. He shrugs, then dips a piece of bread in ful medames and pops it into his mouth, closing his mouth to savor the taste. I watch him chew and swallow. A few seconds later, his eyes widen.

"Did you remember it, then, your happiest memory as a child?" I ask, and he nods. "Will you tell me about it?"

Taraana takes a sip of his sharbat. His fingers are trembling, so he clenches them into a fist.

"It's all right if you can't. You don't have to."

"No, I want to. It's just that talking about my family is . . . difficult." He licks his lips. "I had five older brothers and two younger sisters. I don't remember their faces anymore, let alone their names. But there were times when I was still a part of their family. Times when I believed my parents loved me. We never had much to eat, and sometimes one or two bites were all each of us got. But once in a while, very, very infrequently, my mother would get some parantha from somewhere, some sugar and ghee from somewhere else, and she would make malida out of them. Do you know what that is?"

I shake my head.

"It's just leftover parantha torn into pieces, mixed with sugar and ghee and rolled into balls. Three of us shared one, but every bite was eating a little bit of sunlight. The days we got malida were the happiest I ever was. I had brothers, sisters, and parents.

I was loved. It didn't matter that soon we would be hungry again or that my parents would fight or I would be beaten. As long as I had malida days to look forward to, I could go on and endure anything."

He smiles his broken smile.

"When I eat this food, I taste the malida and feel the happiness I felt back then. I think I can even understand why my parents sold me. I was just one and they had so many to take care of. I can pretend they cried when they sent me way. I can pretend they were reluctant but had no other choice, no better alternative. I can tell myself those lies and pretend they are the truth." He stops talking and takes another bite of the gollash.

It takes all I have not to get up, grab his hand, and flee. Away from here. Away from Baarish's men.

"Taraana," I say.

"Yeah?" He glances at me before he returns his attention to the food.

"I won't judge you if you change your mind, so tell me that you have." Please say that you have changed your mind. Please.

He stops eating and focuses on me. "You know I haven't."

I look at his stupidly beautiful face, at the stars in his eyes, at the way he is looking at me, and I find the resolve in me break. I am the stupid one. I should have thought of a better plan. One that doesn't involve him getting kidnapped. Possibly beaten. Hurt.

"I am wearing the pendant. I know the word. It will be okay." Why is he reassuring me when I should be the one reassuring him?

"Why don't you wear more than one?" I ask. "Just in case."

"It'll be too suspicious if I do," he says, turning me down. "One will be enough."

"What if it isn't?" I ask.

"Then you can come and rescue me." He smiles, and my heart twinges so painfully, I almost die right then.

After he finishes eating, we go look for the middle worlder Eulalie told us about. I am extra careful, but I don't see any of Baarish's creatures around.

According to Eulalie's sources, the middle worlder, Wa'ad, is usually found near well-stocked street libraries at around two in the afternoon. We check a couple before we come across a tall, brown, wooden bookcase with glass windows set beside a red bench. She's standing in front of the open doors of the tall bookcase, her head buried in a book. What we see of her looks mostly human-shaped, but as we get closer to her, I notice the moving words under her light brown skin. The words, written in ink, come from many different scripts. I can only identify Hindi, Urdu, English, Arabic, and Korean. Unlike tattoos, which are sedentary on the surface of the skin, her words swim like fishes in a woman-shaped aquarium.

She looks up as Taraana and I approach. The blacks of her eyes are also made of words, and yes, they, too, are moving. Is it too much to ask for middle worlders to have eyes that, you know, don't make me want to scream?

This middle worlder, Wa'ad, looks at me for a long while before she transfers her gaze to Taraana, who is not wearing magic spectacles for once. I watch as her eyes flood with so many words that the whites darken and she turns into a demon. Okay, not really, but I am ready to run.

"Are you the Keeper of the Between?" Wa'ad takes the initiative and moves a step closer. She seems stunned by Taraana. I slip my hand into Taraana's and grip it tightly.

"Yes," he says. "Could I ask you some questions?"

"Of course," she replies with a smile. Yes, her teeth are pointy. Why do librarians need pointy teeth? I have to ask Qasim. "It would be my honor."

The streets aren't crowded in this area, but there's enough foot traffic that I am confident Baarish's servants won't attack us here. Still, I remain vigilant. When you've invited the vampire into your home, you have to be ready to sacrifice your blood.

Wa'ad leads Taraana to an empty bench while I stand behind him like a bodyguard, much like Assi used to. All of a sudden, I have a lot of empathy for her. I hope she's doing okay. I hope we get to see her again soon.

"Have you known any other Keepers of the Between?" Taraana is asking Wa'ad when I start listening to them again.

Wa'ad closes her eyes to think, and the words under her skin start moving faster. It's rude to stare, but goodness, she's better than any TV program I've sat through. Five minutes later, she shakes her head. "I haven't known any Keepers of the Between personally, but there was an entire section dedicated to them in the library." It is obvious that the library she mentions is the only library that counts to her. "Is there something specific you would like to know?"

Taraana's face lights up at her words. "Do you know how a keeper bonds to the Between?"

"Hmm," Wa'ad says, her narrow lips pursing at the question. And once again, the words go in a frenzy around her body. She's wearing a gray caftan that leaves her thin arms bare. The words converge in her palms as she opens her eyes again. A flicker of frustration sweeps across her face. "The Keepers of the Between were a recalcitrant lot, given to secrecy and suspicion. Their power afforded them that right. Though the library had many texts with many hypotheses about the process of bonding, we didn't dare pin down a keeper to get a clear answer. All I know is that during the process, a keeper is remade. It is a physical transformation that makes it possible for the keeper to then use magic." She bows her head. "I apologize for not being able to answer your question." Even though she says that, there is very little emotion present in her tone.

Taraana seems to take her words pretty well. "I have one more question. May I ask it?" Wa'ad motions for him to continue. "How do I find a burning door in the Between?"

Wa'ad blinks and we're subjected to another show of words racing around her body. The spectacle is both fascinating and creepy. "A door in the Between burns when the city it leads to is dying." Oh. I guess that makes sense.

Wa'ad captures Taraana's hand and I bare my teeth. Is she going to try to eat him or something? Instead of fulfilling any of my gory expectations, she says softly, "The Keepers of the Between are the ones who facilitate the conversion of the unrefined magic into forms middle worlders can use. Keepers of the Between usually control the flow of not just magic but also of middle worlders through the Between. The library documented their power well, and the middle world knew to treat them with respect. Things have changed a lot. My efforts to educate the current Magic Council on the importance of the Keepers of the Between have always been ignored."

Taraana nods jerkily. "Thank you for letting me know."

"You are welcome. Be safe," she says, and drifts away from us to browse the books in the street library.

It is almost three when we take our leave of the middle worlder and make our way to the Khan el-Khalili souk. This souk is very much like the souks in Marrakech and the Grand Bazaar in Istanbul. It boasts the same intoxicating sights and smells that we have become so used to in the past few weeks. Everything is the same, but different.

Tabassum Naaz agreed to sing like a canary; she agreed to betray us to her grandfather. If we succeed here, she will be indirectly responsible for her grandfather's death. Even if we don't succeed here, she will find her circumstances changed. She will find a place, if not by her grandfather's side, then near him as the one who delivered the keeper to him. Such a position will afford her the chance to kill him. If we fail, that is, and I don't intend to.

Taraana walks with his hand gripping mine and his face arrested in an expression of wonder at the sights before him. I can tell how much this insouciance costs him, though. His shoulders are tense and his grip on my hand is tight.

We walk through the crowds, being jostled at every turn. The middle worlders attracted, perhaps, by the stars in Taraana's eyes give him long, considering looks that all feel malicious to me.

We have to enter the deserted alley at the end of the path. That's where Baarish's servants are waiting to ambush us.

My steps become slower as we get closer to the entrance of the alley. However, I cannot delay it any further.

"Taraana, we don't have to do this," I whisper.

"*I* have to do this, Paheli," he says. His eyes are bright, the expression in them making my heart crack like china. At this moment, I love him so much, I feel like I will kill anyone who even thinks about doing him harm.

"Why? I will keep you safe, I promise." I all but beg him.

"Because I deserve to walk down a street without worrying about being kidnapped. Because I should be able to sleep without having nightmares. Because I am not an object to be owned but a person with rights and feelings. This might go wrong and I might fail, but, Paheli, I will have tried. I will have fought. That matters to me."

Without caring about the people around us, Taraana leans forward and presses a kiss on my lips. In the next second, he pushes me away and runs into the alley where Baarish's servants are waiting.

I run after him immediately. I'm only a few seconds away, but a few seconds is all it takes. When I enter, the alley is empty. No one is around, not even an oblivious human. I lose all reason and scream his name. I demand that he come back to me. Then I notice it. The pendant he was wearing, our only weapon against Baarish, lying on the ground. I am standing frozen, staring at it, when my sisters arrive.

Paheli: The Maze and the Minotaur

In times of crisis, every second appears an eternity. Some streets over, a car honks aggressively. The sound forms the background score for a moment that will forever be etched in my mind.

"Paheli?" Valentina says, a rare note of hesitation in her voice.

I will fall apart later. I can't afford to right now. I reach down and pick up the pendant on the road. The clasp of the chain it was hanging from is broken. Probably in the struggle when Taraana was taken. Why didn't I ensure the chain was stronger?

"Is that the pendant—" Etsuko breaks off, horror draining her face of color.

I ignore her and turn to the newest member of the Wild Ones. I didn't expect Tabassum Naaz to hang around after she did her part, but here she is. Valentina grabs my arm and swings me around. I don't meet her eyes. I can't.

"Did you tell Baarish not to use the Between?" I ask Tabassum Naaz.

She nods, looking from me to Valentina and back again. "I told him he might not be successful if he took the Between."

"Okay," I say. I am standing here on this noisy, dusty street, but inside, I am falling apart. "All right." I nod to show people I am okay. "And you are sure he is going to take Taraana to"—I pause—"Lucknow?"

"Yeah, he has a longtime lair there. That's where he originally kept Taraana," Tabassum Naaz replies.

I nod again. It makes sense to move my head up and down, pretending I know what I'm doing. And I do. I planned for everything. I am terrified because he is in their hands, without a single weapon to defend himself. But he said he believed in me. He did.

"He borrowed his friend's private jet." Tabassum Naaz continues talking. "The flight from Cairo to Lucknow will take seven hours and twelve minutes."

I nod. Again. It's easy to do. "If we leave now and use the Between, it will take us three and a half hours to arrive in Lucknow. We will be there before him. We can find a way to return the pendant to Taraana."

The girls take my word as fact and don't seem as concerned. All of them, apart from Valentina. I can never have any secrets from her.

It takes a while, but we find an uninterrupted wall. Tabassum Naaz presses a palm on the wall, calls for a Between door, and grimaces as the Between extracts a magic toll from her in return. We enter the Between behind her.

I am conscious of other people having conversations behind me. Perhaps some of them even talk to me, but I can't hear anything or anyone else at this point. What have I done?

Valentina appears beside me. She doesn't say anything. She knows better than to ply me with empty platitudes. We both know better than to rely on false comfort.

Tabassum Naaz walks on my other side. The golden light in the Between is dim today, as if the Between has somehow sensed what has happened to its keeper. An hour passes in silence.

"I finally talked to my parents," Tabassum Naaz says. "Threatened them with outright anarchy if they didn't answer my questions."

I glance at her bright face. "What questions?"

"See, my mom keeps a little red dress, the kind usually worn by babies, in her closet. For the longest time, I thought it was mine."

"But?" Valentina says. I really don't want to know.

"Turns out it belonged to my sister." Tabassum Naaz turns away, not wanting us to see her face. "Did you never wonder why my family has only one granddaughter?"

"We usually don't poke at beehives," I tell her.

"Yeah. I didn't get that memo. He killed my older sister and three other female cousins the day after each of them were born. Threw them in the Yamuna and let the water reclaim the magic in them. He tried to do the same with me, but as I said, the water refused to take me." She laughs, a shrill, tearing sound. "I thought

I would grapple with some kind of guilt over leading him to his destruction, but I don't." She breathes in. "He is a monster and he needs to die. If he survives your attempt, he won't survive mine."

Two and a half hours more of walking takes us to the door leading out to Lucknow. I returned to this city only once before, and that time too, I spilled blood. I look at the door for a long time. I know I need to open it, but my arms feel like they're weighted and won't rise.

Valentina wraps an arm around me and Daraja opens the door. They let me stay in the Between longest.

The city is no longer as it was; time, the most ruthless of them all, has scrubbed all surfaces so the city wears a new face and a new name. But no matter the cosmetic changes, the city's song remains unchanged. I hate it.

Tabassum Naaz leads the way, and half an hour later, we find ourselves in front of the Bara Imambara. I have never seen this place, though I remember the nawabs who frequented the kotha talking about it. Of course, in their conversations, the place was under construction. It is a grand building originally built to house people who gather to worship.

"Come this way," Tabassum Naaz says. "Everyone here is a middle worlder, and I can't magic you invisible since magic won't work on you. What I will do instead is magic the air around you so it is opaque. As long as you stay together within the circle of magicked air, no one will see you."

It is ten in the morning in Lucknow, and the place is not yet busy. We move swiftly and without interruptions and take the stairs to the labyrinth housed on the second floor of this building.

The labyrinth is known as the Bhool Bhulaiyaa and was commissioned to create jobs for people during a drought when work was scarce. It has seemingly no purpose except to get people lost.

Tabassum Naaz seems to know her way through it quite well. "This used to be my playing grounds. As much as the old man hated me, he kept me close for a period of time. I used to tag along with my cousins, who walked as if this place belonged to them. There was one area in which we were forbidden entrance, so of course I was determined to get into it. It was where I discovered the keeper."

We slip between the pillars and stop when Tabassum Naaz holds up her hand. A few meters in front of us is a magically created chamber. It is a sizable place. Half of it lies in shadow. The other half is dimly lit by both the daylight and some lamps that glow a dirty yellow. There are five not-human men sitting on chairs and on the ground, presumably waiting for Taraana.

Tabassum Naaz signals with her eyes and we move past the not-human men, using the darkness their eyes cannot pierce, until we have moved to the other side of the chamber. We can still see into it through the pillars that make up its wall. We gather close to each other, sit down, and wait.

Every second that passes brings to mind a different scenario starring Taraana and pain. I hate myself a million times over for suggesting this stupid plan, for putting him at risk. I wish I could reassure you that everything is going to go as we have planned, but I cannot. Things have already gone wrong. Time, it goes by agonizingly slowly, but finally, we hear sounds of people coming up the stairs and into the maze. We hear the sound of something . . . someone being dragged, and I attempt to get to my feet before the other girls pull me down.

The two not-human men who probably kidnapped Taraana appear, dragging him into the chamber, accompanied by another middle worlder. The other men move aside, and Taraana is placed on a chair in the middle, his legs shackled and his hands tied behind his back. One of them hits him on the head, and I force myself not to march over and kill him right at that moment.

I can't see him clearly; the light is too dim. Perhaps this is a blessing. His head hangs down and his shoulders are slumped. His entire body is an expression of defeat. I hate myself.

"I will go distract them. Try to get the pendant around his neck when I'm gone," Tabassum Naaz whispers, looking at me. I must make some gesture of acknowledgment because she straightens up and walks into the chamber, surprising all the men there.

"What took you so long?" she says to them, not at all intimidated. Her confidence cows them. Perhaps they remember that she's the Dar's only granddaughter.

The middle worlders make some noise about traffic.

Tabassum Naaz waves her hands dismissively. "My grandfather?"

"He went to receive his friends, my lady," one of the men says. "They plan a celebration now that they've caught the keeper."

"I see," Tabassum Naaz says. "I need all of you to come with me. I saw some of the girls the keeper travels with outside, and I can't capture them all alone."

Will they believe her? They have no reason not to, but then again, there's very little reason for them to obey her.

We are surprised when most of the men immediately agree to go look for us. Of the eight middle worlders, only one is left behind. I don't hesitate. As soon as Tabassum Naaz and the other men are out of sight, I break away. Talei takes care of the remaining middle worlder. A scream in his unsuspecting ear. My eyes are for Taraana alone.

His face is covered with bruises. There is a gash on his forehead, and his lips are bleeding. His eyes are closed but I don't think he's unconscious.

"Taraana," I whisper, and he opens pain-filled eyes. I told him I'd be here, waiting for him. He exhales, tension flowing out of him.

Without another word, I put the chain containing the pendant around his neck. "Do you remember the word to awaken the pendant?"

He nods as if he doesn't trust himself to speak.

"I'm here. If you can't do this, say so. I will take you away right now." I don't care about the logistics.

He shakes his head. We hear the sound of voices. "Go," he hisses. "Be safe."

It kills me that he, the one who's shackled to the chair, is telling me to be safe. I run back into the shadows where the others are waiting.

"Did you really see them, my lady?" a middle worlder is asking Tabassum Naaz.

"Yes, they're definitely in Lucknow," she answers. Because she's telling the truth, her voice rings with conviction.

"Hey, where's Jaffar?" Someone has noticed that the middle worlder left behind is no longer at his spot.

The men look for their companion; one of them comes a bit too close to us. Thankfully, Tabassum Naaz calls him away. A few minutes later, making an excuse to search in this direction, she makes her way over.

"What did you do with him?" she whispers to the dark that contains us.

"He's behind that pillar," Ligaya replies, pointing. Tabassum Naaz doesn't change her expression. A quick spell later, the body's gone.

"The Dar is supposed to hold the pendant in his hands, right?" Tabassum Naaz raises an eyebrow.

"Yeah," Valentina replies. "But make sure you don't touch it."

Tabassum Naaz pats Valentina's cheek and gives her a smile. "I won't."

She leaves us to cling to the shadows and walks back to the chamber. The middle-worlder goons mutter loudly about the disappearance of their companion. Someone wants to report to Baarish, but Tabassum Naaz persuades them not to, saying that it will cause him to be embarrassed in front of his friends. The men agree to postpone their report.

Ten minutes later, Baarish arrives with four middle-worlder men who all, to some degree, look like him: hungry for power and entirely without hearts. They don't travel with the entourage we expect. Perhaps they left their attendants in the Imambara below. Baarish's goons set up chairs on one side of the chamber and offer them refreshment in the form of chilled soda.

Baarish, especially, is in a jovial mood. He circles around the chair Taraana is shackled to, looking him up and down like he is livestock. Perhaps, to them he is.

"It was originally my turn to harvest a keeper," one of Baarish's friends says, with a hint of grievance in his voice. "You harvested the last one."

"I was the one who found him, Haaruv," Baarish replies. "So, I get to keep him."

"Well, I don't care who finds the next one. Whoever it is, the keeper will be mine," Haaruv says with a pout. He needs to die too.

Baarish doesn't respond. Instead, he grabs Taraana's chin and forces him to look up. We all shudder. In the next moment, he slaps him so hard, Taraana's face hits the side of the chair. I stuff my hand into my mouth for fear I will make a noise. Taraana jerks forward and the pendant falls out.

He opens his eyes and looks at Baarish. The Dar smiles, triumph in his eyes, on his face, and in his voice. "Did you think you could escape me? Fool. I have caught you, and soon I will catch those girls who prance around the Between. I will reclaim the stars they wear. And you? You can watch as my men pleasure themselves on those girls. Perhaps I won't have to torture you directly, then—"

"Dada-ji," Tabassum Naaz says, interrupting him. "Please don't touch the pendant. It might be dangerous," she cautions. "One of the girls told me it is a talisman that protects the keeper."

Baarish turns and glares at Tabassum Naaz. "Dangerous? For *me*?" He returns his gaze to Taraana and gives the pendant a piercing look. Finding nothing dangerous about it, he picks it up and pulls it free.

I almost forget to breathe. This is the moment, Taraana.

As if hearing my unspoken words, Taraana's lips move, hopefully speaking the word to awaken the magic in the pendant.

"How is this trinket supposed to be dangerous?" Baarish bellows. "Boy, you should know that nothing is going to keep you safe from me. By the time I am done with you, you will be lucky to still be ali—"

Baarish comes to a discordant silence in the middle of the word. He looks down at the pendant he is holding in his hands. It is now glowing purple. He tries to speak again, but his voice fractures and his face becomes tangled up in a frown. He looks at the men he calls his friends, and they jump to their feet and back away from him. Baarish flings away the pendant and it falls to the floor with a thud.

But it is far too late. The damage has been done.

Baarish's skin cracks like the earth in a drought. His mouth opens, but no sound comes out. He turns in silent appeal to his minions, but they are frozen. Then he turns to Tabassum Naaz, his hand stretched out, an entreaty in his eyes.

She crosses her arms and steps back. She is not as unaffected as she pretends, however. Her eyes speak volumes.

The next few minutes are an instruction in pain. One that we didn't need but are forced to endure. At the end, all that is left of Baarish is a pile of dust and the echoes of his screams.

A New Era, a New Dar; the River Sings

We are not monsters, so we aren't indifferent to the violence enacted in front of us. Though we didn't wield the knife, we still killed Baarish. We retain enough of selves to feel the pinch of our consciences. Baarish's friends, however, are another story.

Barely a minute has passed after Baarish's death before the four middle worlders are trying to grab Taraana. Baarish's minions seem shell-shocked and are unmoving. Tabassum Naaz is heaving in a corner. We walk into the chamber and Paheli pulls one middle worlder away from Taraana. He retaliates immediately, throwing a magical force at her. It rebounds, stunning him. Baarish's minions, a monster with its head cut off, decide that we're the enemy they need to fight and come charging at us.

"Protect your ears," Valentina calls to Tabassum Naaz, five seconds before we scream. They wanted magic so we'll give them magic, more magic than they'll know what to do with. The air sparks with our screams; the middle worlders hold their heads and fall to their knees. We scream until our throats are hoarse and no one, apart from us and Tabassum Naaz, is left standing.

Paheli is beside Taraana, freeing his hands and feet from the shackles. She wraps her arms around him, holding him so tight that we worry he won't be able to breathe. But Taraana doesn't seem to mind. He's holding her just as tightly.

We turn away to give them the illusion of privacy and look at Tabassum Naaz who, despite the earplugs in her ears, is still pale and jittery from the force of our screams.

"What will you do now?" Valentina asks her. Baarish's death is hardly the end of our story.

"I need to bond to a river here." Tabassum Naaz leans on a pillar. Valentina grabs her hand and she holds on tightly. "Once I bond to the river, I become the new Dar. Then I will have power."

"Which river?" Valentina asks.

"Any river," Tabassum Naaz replies.

"Gomti River," Paheli says, walking over to us, her arm around Taraana's waist, supporting his weight on one side while Daraja holds on to him from the other side. "We can go there."

"Will you come with me?" Tabassum Naaz asks Taraana.

It would be prudent for us to retreat at this point, but Taraana, looking as though he has just returned from a war he lost, nods. "It would be my honor to accompany you."

"What about them?" Kamboja looks at the bodies on the floor.

Apart from Baarish, none of them are dead. They're not exactly alive, either. The magic in our screams has cooked their brains.

"Leave them here," Tabassum Naaz says. "Someone will discover them eventually."

"Your grandfather?" Areum asks.

Tabassum Naaz shrugs. "As far as everyone is concerned, I wasn't here today. He didn't tell the family that he'd kidnapped the keeper, otherwise they'd have been here too, and things would have been much more complicated."

"And the conjury?" Etsuko asks. We turn to look at the pendant glowing purple on the floor.

"Leave it there," Paheli replies. "Let it serve as a warning."

We exit the Bhool Bhulaiyaa and go down the stairs to the Imambara. Fortunately, Baarish's friends came alone, otherwise we would have had to scream once again. We pile into two vans, previously used by the middle worlders. One of the vans is driven by Tabassum Naaz and the other, Paheli. Whether either of them have driving licenses is not a question anyone wants to risk asking.

Half an hour later we are at the banks of the river.

"It's not a complicated process," Tabassum Naaz says. "I just need to immerse all of myself into the river and submit to its magic." She turns to us. "Just be my witnesses."

We watch as she pulls off her shoes and walks into the river. She continues walking, each step taking her a little deeper, the water covering a little more of her body. She walks until her entire body is submerged in the water. We wait for a long moment, not knowing what to expect. Then, inexplicably, the river gets choppy. Even though it's a hot day with no breeze, little wavelets appear on the surface of the river as if it's in the middle of a storm. Before Tabassum Naaz reappears, the river sings.

Or, more accurately, the magic within the river sings. When Tabassum Naaz walks out of the river, as dry as the moment she walked in, we flock over to her. Her eyes have changed. They look exactly like Baarish's did except less creepy.

"Do you feel any different?" Paheli asks.

As a reply, Tabassum Naaz reaches out and hugs Valentina, squeezing her tightly. Valentina gives her an affronted look, but the smile on her lips is wide. We could get used to a smiling Valentina.

"I feel like I drank an entire liter of coffee," Tabassum Naaz replies. "I know that what waits for me in the very near future is likely to be painful, but I am ready for it. Mostly. I can call on you if it gets too much for me, can't I?"

"We'll send you Valentina," Areum says generously. She grins, unrepentant, at Valentina's quelling look.

We abandon the vans at the riverbank and find an uninterrupted wall nearby. When we enter the Between, Taraana suddenly sinks to the ground.

"What is it? Does it hurt too much?" Paheli kneels by him.

"No, I just thought that I would never travel the Between again. I thought my time was up," Taraana says after a long pause. He shudders.

"I'm sorry. It's my fault that you're hurt," Paheli replies. She yields her spot to Areum and takes a step away from Taraana.

"That is not true," he protests. Paheli shakes her head.

"I will accompany Tabassum Naaz to Agra. The rest of you, take Taraana to New Orleans. Have Eulalie patch him up."

"I can go by myself," Tabassum Naaz says.

"I will take you," Paheli says firmly.

She doesn't give us any chance to protest and leaves immediately, walking so fast that Tabassum Naaz has to run after her.

Valentina sighs loudly. "Let's get Taraana to New Orleans."

"She needs to do something about her habit of running away," Taraana grumbles, getting to his feet with some difficulty. He looks in the direction she has gone. "Their actions weren't her fault."

"When she comes back, you can tell her that. We'll sit on her so she has to stay and listen." Etsuko beams at him.

The Burning Door, the Fallen City, and Taraana 2.0

It takes Paheli five hours to return to us. Taraana, sporting a slew of new bandages on the cuts on his face and arms, sits in the spot nearest to the front door, waiting for her. When she finally enters the house, she looks at Taraana first.

"Does it hurt a lot?" she asks him.

"It hurt more since you walked away," Taraana replies.

"Wow, this is exciting," Ligaya says, taking a seat right beside Taraana before she gets back up. "Wait, wait. Let me get popcorn. Don't continue."

She runs to the kitchen while we try very hard to maintain our serious faces. Honestly, we all want to see this show, but only Ligaya would say so outright.

Paheli scrunches up her face and drops into the chair opposite

Taraana's. "You're going to say you being hurt wasn't my fault. And you are right. It wasn't."

"So?" Taraana leans forward. "If it wasn't your fault, why are you sitting so far away from me?"

"Because we don't need to be stuck together at all moments. That's just gross." Ooh, Paheli, a fatal hit.

"You're lying," Taraana says, leaning back and fixing Paheli in place with a gimlet look.

"I am not. Tina, I told Tabassum Naaz you'd be visiting her next week," Paheli says airily.

Valentina, who was watching the show as avidly as we were, is caught by surprise. "Why?"

"Because I felt like it." Paheli beams briefly.

"Paheli," Taraana says.

"Yes, it wasn't my fault, and yes, I blame myself anyway because I should have known better than to use such a foolish plan. It wasn't my finest moment, and I'm still dealing with how close I came to losing you. Can we not talk about this, please?" She speaks quickly.

"Why not?" Taraana asks.

"Because I saw them hurt you and I keep thinking about how there have been so many times in the past when they hurt you as badly, if not worse, and there is nothing I can do about it. It hurts me." She looks at him and sighs.

"All right. Fine." It is clear the conversation is not over, but Taraana is giving in right now. We nod at him approvingly. "I need to go back to the Between and look for a burning door," he says.

"You're too hurt to go look for a door now, aren't you?" Talei asks.

"Better now than waiting for someone like Baarish to pursue us again," Etsuko replies. "We don't know how many middle worlders are aware of Taraana's existence. Baarish was very blatant. The next middle worlder may not necessarily be as obvious."

"Let's go tomorrow morning," Valentina says. "We need the rest of the day today to breathe and recover from everything that we did. Everything that we saw." We remember Baarish's end again and shudder.

"All right?" Paheli asks Taraana, and he nods before getting to his feet.

"Come with me," he tells her.

"Why?" she demands.

"We need to have a talk about how you continue running away." He folds his arms.

"I thought we already talked about it!" Paheli says.

"No, that was you making excuses and me letting you. Come on," Taraana says very patiently.

"I'd much rather not," Paheli says, and jumps to her feet. "I'm going to go see if Eulalie bought me mangoes."

She runs away and Valentina smirks at him. "Did you think it would be easy?"

He sighs.

The next morning, we return to the Between, determined to search for a door that is on fire. We spend hours looking, sustained by the magic flowing in there. Once in a while, middle worlders pass us by. None of them bother us, though all of them give us narrow-eyed looks. We asked Eulalie to spread the word; we're taking responsibility for Baarish's demise.

"Are you wearing your pendant?" Paheli suddenly asks Tara-ana, and he makes a face.

"You've only asked that question a hundred times today." He grouses.

She narrows her eyes at him. "Are you?"

"Yes!"

We left the awakened pendant on the floor of the Bhool Bhulaiyaa in Lucknow. Fortunately, we have a whole stack of unawakened ones. Until we find a better way to keep Taraana safe, the pendants will have to do.

"I smell something burning," Ghufran says suddenly, and we come to attention. It's true. There's a scent of smoke in the air. We have seen other doors burning in the Between, but we have never felt enough curiosity to investigate them. We should have.

We follow our noses and, thirty minutes later, arrive at a door that is on fire. We stop in front of it, unsure how to react.

The door leads to Aleppo, Syria. We are not entirely oblivious to the happenings in the human world, you know. We have heard the news and listened to the survivors. We have witnessed the death of other cities, but never from the Between.

"It is a city of screams," Taraana mutters. "A city full of the ghosts of dead children."

We share a moment of silence for the people who call the city home.

"Should I bleed on it?" Taraana turns to us.

"Try it," Paheli says.

The flames aren't too large and the heat isn't overpowering. Taraana pricks his finger, steps forward, and squeezes a few drops of his blood onto the flames. We hold our breaths. The lights in the Between flicker, the flames rise up, but a few moments later, the lights return to normal and the flames retreat.

"Why did it fail again? What am I doing wrong?" Taraana stares at the door with not a small amount of frustration. He combs a hand through his hair.

"Wait," Daraja says. She pulls Taraana back. "What if it's us?"

"What do you mean?" Areum asks.

Daraja bites her lip. "Tabassum Naaz immersed her entire self in the water. What if Taraana needs to do the same? The stars we wear on our palms are also parts of him, right?"

"Do we take off the stars and return them to him?" Kamboja asks, staring at her palm.

"What if we add our blood to the fire as well?" Talei suggests. "Give him the box of remaining stars, Paheli, and we'll add our blood to the fire. It's worth a try."

So, we do that. We add drops of our blood before Taraana adds his and step back from the fire. This time, as soon as Taraana's blood hits the fire, the flames leap, but then, like before, they recede.

"It's not us," Kamboja announces very unnecessarily.

"What am I doing wrong?" Taraana looks like he's going to start crying. "Paheli, what did Wa'ad say?" he suddenly asks. "What were her exact words?"

Paheli thinks for a second. "She said, and I quote, 'All I know is that during the process, a keeper is remade. It is a physical transformation that makes it possible for the keeper to then use magic.'"

Taraana bites his lip and glares at the burning door as if it will give him some answers. The next second, without giving us any warning at all, he walks into the burning door. Our screams desert us at that moment as the Between shudders and the lights flicker before turning off. We stand in the darkness, watching as the burning door stops burning. The fire jumps to Taraana, and we realize that the fire is not fire but tangible magic. We watch as Taraana is infused with this magic; he burns with it. It reshapes him from the inside out. The stars we wear on our palms tingle as though they, too, are affected by this change.

The fire burns out after a minute, and Taraana steps back into the corridor. The door is solid again. The lights come back on brighter. The Between trills, and all of us jump at the unexpected sound. A sudden breeze chases away the usual mustiness in the Between, replacing it with the scent of freshly cut grass, the smell we associate with magic.

"Whoa," Taraana says, and turns around to face us. He might be the master of understatement.

We observe him carefully. His appearance has changed, but we cannot say how. His face remains the same. His body is the same. Everything is the same, but somehow, he is completely different. The stars in his eyes burn brighter. His smile is surer. The way he moves is so much more graceful. It is as though his broken pieces have come together to create Taraana 2.0.

We look at Paheli. She is staring at him; the look on her face is inexplicable.

"I can feel the Between," Taraana says to us, his eyes excited. "I can feel all the doors, all the twists and turns. There are seven other doors burning at this moment. Five are in danger of burning. Three doors are being born." He shakes his head and laughs out loud. The sound is catching, and all of us, except for Paheli, are infected by Taraana's happiness.

"Let's go back home," she says, more quietly than we've ever heard her. "Eulalie is waiting for us."

And she is. She's standing in the front parlor, a serious look on her face, and a cream-colored envelope in her hands.

"What is it, Lalie?" Paheli asks.

"Was Taraana successful in bonding to the Between?" Eulalie asks first.

Taraana replies in the affirmative, and only then does Eulalie relax slightly.

"What is the matter?" Paheli asks again.

"'The Magic Council of the Middle World has summoned Taraana and the Wild Ones to explain themselves regarding their actions against the previous Dar of Uttar Pradesh,'" Eulalie reads off the letter she's holding.

Well then.

Paheli: The Beginning of Forever

I wish I could say I am surprised by the summons, but I am not. Not even remotely. What I *am* surprised by is how fast they moved and the fact that they knew to send the letter to Eulalie. I guess we aren't as circumspect in our movements as I thought.

"When?" Valentina asks.

"A week. In Tokyo," Eulalie replies, preempting my question.

"Okay. I will care about it again in three days," I announce to everyone listening, and excuse myself. The girls are gathered around Taraana, and when he is distracted, I slip away. Surely, no one will begrudge me a few minutes to myself.

I am tired.

I head to the conservatory at the heart of the house. The

conservatory is Lalie's most spectacular feat of magic. It is full of lush green plants, several of which are in bloom. She made this place for me after I told her I wanted to go to a jungle. The floors are tiled, and a loud yellow chaise takes the place of honor in the middle. When I sit down on it, I can pretend I am surrounded by the jungle on all four sides. There is even birdsong in the air. The air is redolent with the smell of roses, and a rare peace fills me.

I close my eyes and spend a few minutes trying not to think. Not about Baarish turning to ash in front of our eyes. Not about the role I played in his end. Not about the wounds inflicted on Taraana. And not about him changing. It is a futile endeavor, and I don't manage even a minute of it. Soon I am thinking about not thinking, which defeats the entire purpose.

I feel someone sit down beside me, then smell honeysuckle. Valentina. I open my eyes and she throws a mango at me. I catch it and look at the perfectly ripened fruit in my hands. It's not cake, but I guess it will do.

"Where did you get this?"

"Eulalie picked up an entire box of mangoes for you," Valentina replies, holding up her own mango.

Eulalie. She insists on loving me. Insists on seeing more in me than I can see in myself. Maybe there *is* more?

We eat in silence, Valentina and I. We eat messily. Ferally. Fortunately, there is a tap nearby we can clean up at.

"We're almost at the end, huh?" Valentina says later.

"Of this chapter?" I quip.

"Of this season," she replies. We grin at each other.

"I'm tired, Tina." I lean against her. We have been together ever since I found her on that bridge more than three centuries ago. "Have you ever been tempted to leave?"

She is quiet for a long moment. "Once, I almost did the same thing Sevda did. I was so sure I wanted to go. So sure I was ready. I was going to leave the star and a note and disappear. But the next day we found Ghufran, and with her, I found a purpose. The same purpose you have."

"What if Tabassum Naaz asks you to?" I pull away.

"She knows better than to ask me that!" She is offended. I snicker. "What?"

"It's the first time you didn't deny—" She glares at me, and I zip my lips. For one minute. Then I return to leaning against her and whisper in her ear. "You really like her, huh?"

"It would be a lie if I said I didn't," Valentina says carefully. "But . . ."

"But?" I prompt.

"I'm scared, and I'm unsure whether I want to deal with the messy reality of relationships," she says finally.

"Welcome to my world," I tell her sincerely. She rewards me with a pinch. No gratitude in this world, I tell you.

Valentina gets to her feet and I fall to the side. "Taraana's waiting outside. I will go and tell him it's okay to come in."

She leaves, and I consider jumping in the bushes to hide. Then decide against it because my dignity is already in danger. So, I sit back and start counting to a hundred. I have only reached thirty when I hear Taraana's footsteps.

He even walks differently now. I pretend fascination with the blooms of a bird-of-paradise plant to avoid having to look at him. He sits down beside me, close enough that I can feel his heat but far enough that no part of his body is touching mine.

"I haven't changed that much," he says. Have I mentioned how much I hate the fact that he knows how I feel? "Look at me."

His words are an entreaty, and one I reluctantly yield to. I know I have made a mistake as soon as I look at him. He looks like someone I used to know. This Taraana, so flush with magic and confidence, is strange to me.

"I am still him."

"Stop reading my mind," I snap, and immediately feel bad.

"It's the bond. It has made our connection so much stronger," he replies. "I'm sorry. I'm doing my best not to."

"Try harder." Why am I being this horrible? "Look, I'm sorry. Just leave me alone for a while, and I will be okay."

"No, you won't. You haven't been okay since Lucknow," he says. "It wasn't your fault. I chose to go with your plan, and I am glad I did."

"You almost died because of me." I cross my arms. "I decided to play with your life and you almost died. If Tabassum Naaz hadn't done what she did, you may still have been with Baarish, being tortured." I will hate myself for that.

He sighs.

"Is this where you tell me I am being silly and you were fully on board with my plan so I need to stop imposing my guilty conscience on you?" I say in a rush. "Because, get this, I've already told myself that. And it's not working."

"So, what do you want to do?" he asks.

"What if I take off the star? What if I disappear?" The words are out before I can stop them, and once they are, I can't take them back. No—I won't take them back. Taraana freezes. I risk a look. The heartbreak on his face breaks my heart. Why am I doing this?

"I'm sorry. I'm just angry. Out of sorts. I won't do that." I inch closer to him until I can wrap my arms around this not-Taraana. At least he still smells the same.

"Wait," he says, and separates from me. "If you take—" His voice breaks. He tries again. "If you want to leave, I will let you. Because it is your decision, and no matter how much I want you to stay with me, your life is your own. I want you to be happy, and if leaving gives you happiness—are you going to leave me, Paheli?" He is truly panicked now. I am such an ass.

"No, I love you. I won't leave you unless you do something awful. Like eat my mangoes." I reach for him again. He holds me tight, as if reassuring himself of my presence. "I'm sorry. I'm just upset. I feel guilty. And sad. I *will* be all right. I just need time."

"But you love me?"

"Yeah. Entirely too much," I grumble.

"I love you too. Way more than you love me."

"Ugh. Stop. This is about as much mush as I can handle."

"Okay."

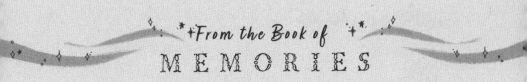

From the Book of
MEMORIES

ETSUKO
CITY OF ORIGIN: KYOTO

I wish I could speak a language,

one in which you didn't exist.

Then I wouldn't feel like a metallic kitchen

on a winter morning:

a blue tabletop, an abandoned jar of cold milk,

the dew on the windows, and

white oblong tiles with a star in the middle.

Clean. And barren.

I wouldn't feel like that.

And when I hear footsteps

I wouldn't think it's you

And when someone touches me on the back

I wouldn't turn around, expecting it to be you

And perhaps when I wake up suddenly

it wouldn't be with your name on my lips.

If you didn't exist,

I wouldn't be like that thick glass; do you remember it,

the one on the window above the front door?

Still intact but with cracks embroidering it.

I wouldn't be like that.

I wish I lived a life

drawn in charcoal

Then how easily I could have reached out

and erased you from it.

Moving One Rock at a Time Will Eventually Move a Mountain, aka Goodbye

The unplanned Magic Council meeting is scheduled for noon in a boardroom in the Peninsula Hotel in Tokyo. We are, of course, fashionably late.

We sail through the hotel doors at twelve thirty, dressed in the brightest colors and the loudest lipsticks. Taraana chose to wear a black suit jacket over a red T-shirt and black dress pants. We put fresh flowers in our hair and some in his, too. He has an unawakened pendant around his neck, even though he no longer needs one.

We choose to be visible to humans and turn heads as we make our way unstopped through the hotel foyer. Our first obstacle presents itself to us in the form of the security consisting of four pairs of middle-worlder men and women. They stand outside the boardroom, their stances aggressive and intimidating. Even their pinkie fingers look threatening. All Taraana does is smile at them and they falter, moving aside without protest.

We walk past them with Paheli leading the way and enter the boardroom unannounced. Immediately, some magic users rise to their feet, protesting our lack of etiquette. We do not pay this squawking any mind and instead stand together at the front of the room, allowing the strongest magic users in the middle world to look at us. Mama Magdaline and Tabassum Naaz are also present in the room. From them, we get reassuring smiles.

The speaker of the Magic Council is an old middle worlder who is the Keeper of the Gold in America. Mama Magdaline told us that he is also purported to be the strongest magic user in middle-world history.

"Are you the group self-named the Wild Ones?" He has a dapper style and could easily be someone's bloodthirsty grandfather. There seems to be a market for dangerous grandfathers, especially in the middle world.

"You could say that," Paheli says.

"And you"—the man turns to Taraana—"are the current Keeper of the Between."

"Indeed, I am," Taraana replies.

"We have asked you here because reports have come to us that you and the"—his pause is full of contempt—"Wild Ones were involved in the demise of the previous Dar of Uttar Pradesh. Were you?"

"Is there any particular reason I need to answer to you?" Taraana looks at the middle worlder lazily.

"If you know what's good for you . . . ," another middle worlder says. Apart from Mama Magdaline and Tabassum Naaz, there are seven other middle worlders sitting at the table in the boardroom. They all resemble Baarish to a certain extent. Imagine a portion of the population glutted on power, privilege, and prestige, and you will know what they look like. If that's difficult, think of politicians, and you will get the idea.

"Why? Isn't Baarish's death good news for you?" Taraana looks around the room. "Now that he's gone, one of you can come after me. Haven't you been hunting Keepers of the Between for centuries now?"

"What are you saying?" A red-haired magic user bangs his hands on the table in front of him with great force. "Do you have evidence to substantiate your claims?"

"I would bring in the keepers before me to testify, but they're all dead," Taraana replies. "Funny, you should know that, considering you were the ones who murdered them."

"Are you going to justify your actions as self-defense?" the Keeper of the Gold asks, bringing the conversation back to a topic they think they can control.

"As I was saying, there's no reason for me to explain my actions to you. You're not worthy of it." Taraana manages to say that without wincing. We practiced with him till late last night.

A moment of shock trembles briefly in the room before anger threatens the existence of any equilibrium these middle worlders still have remaining.

"Why would we not be worthy?" the speaker manages to ask.

"As you said yourself just a few minutes ago, I am the Keeper of the Between. It is not up to you to question my actions. Didn't you know that?" A bland smile flits across Taraana's face.

"You think your position as the Keeper of the Between somehow places you outside the jurisdiction of the Magic Council?" a council member says, looking Taraana up and down, finding him lacking.

"Of course. Did you travel to Tokyo via the Between today? You couldn't, could you? Did you find that no matter how hard you tried, you cannot call a door to the Between?" Taraana leans against a wall and addresses the room. "Perhaps it caused you some inconvenience. Perhaps the lack of the Between made you realize the difficulties of traveling through a world where magic is not equally distributed."

"Are you suggesting you that you had something to do with the Between's closure?" A young middle worlder scoffs. We don't know his name and have no desire to learn it.

"I'm not suggesting anything," Taraana replies, and straightens. "I'm telling you that I have closed the Between."

"Why?" the speaker asks. Unlike his colleagues, his words are measured. Patient. Rather reptilian.

"I've heard that Wa'ad, who used to be a librarian in the exalted Library of Alexandria, has, many times, asked you for an audience. I learned that you, almost all of you, have been unwilling to listen to her," Taraana says instead. "You should have, you know. It would have saved us a lot of trouble."

"Are you going to continue speaking nonsense?" the magic user with the red hair says. Taraana ignores him. We silently applaud.

"Powerful middle worlders like you all should know better than to mess with magic." Taraana clicks his tongue. We went back to Cairo, found Wa'ad, and had a deeper conversation with her after Taraana bonded with the Between. We learned a lot. "Since I am the Keeper of the Between, the Keeper of the Magic, let me tell you exactly what I do. Make sure you listen well because I don't like repeating myself."

All the middle worlders apart from Mama Magdaline and Tabassum Naaz bristle at this point. Our Taraana—we're so proud of his thorns.

"Let me use an extremely prosaic analogy. It's simple enough that even you will understand." Taraana puts his hands in his pocket, looking confident in a way we haven't had a chance to see him before.

"You!" The young middle worlder trembles with rage, but the speaker is more patient.

"Go ahead."

"When drains are not cleaned for a long time, they become blocked. Sometimes, they weaken. Eventually, they rupture. A plumber provides essential service. Similarly, the channels through which magic flows and becomes refined in the Between need a keeper to keep them unclogged. They might survive for a time without a keeper, just like pipes survive for a time without a plumber, but eventually these channels will break down. The Keeper of the Between provides essential service as well." Taraana looks around the room. "That wasn't too difficult to understand, was it?"

"You want us to believe that without you, the Between will

collapse?" A middle worlder wearing too many gold chains laughs.

"Yes. Though I understand that your intellect is severely limited and will perhaps prevent you from believing me." Something dark and very alien slips into Taraana's face. He looks murderous. "I have lived in fear for a very long time. It has twisted me in ways that I don't like. If you persist in challenging me, you will not like the consequences." He looks at each middle worlder in turn. "Consider the closure of the Between my first act of revenge."

The group shifts, clearly uncomfortable with his words. They whisper among themselves.

Again, Taraana smiles. Maybe you won't believe us, but this new Taraana smile is much sharper. Frightening, even. His smiles say he has seen everything you hold hidden in your heart. All your secrets have been bared for his languid perusal.

"We can discuss the importance of the Keeper of the Between later. First, we have to address your crime. Murder is against the law!" a woman with heavy jowls says.

"Is it?" Taraana purses his lips. "Then you might want to investigate the murders of the previous Keepers of the Between. Unless you are suggesting that this law you speak of applies to some more than others?" No one speaks. "You may also want to investigate Baarish's attempts to harvest magic off the children he trafficked. Isn't that against the law too, or was it legal for him to do that?"

An older middle worlder loudly clears his throat.

Taraana doesn't care, and we are proud of him. He addresses the room. "I will close the Between indefinitely. Or perhaps increase the magic toll. Maybe I will allow only a select few people to use it."

"As if that's possible," a council member mutters, loudly enough to be audible to everyone.

"As I keep saying, I don't need to prove anything to you," Taraana replies. "You should do something about your comprehension skills. They're very worrying."

Paheli grins wickedly at his words. She's definitely influencing him in some ways.

The council member, perhaps incensed by Taraana's perceived arrogance, tries to attack Taraana with his magic. Taraana fixes his gaze on the middle worlder's face, and a second later the man slumps in his chair. His companions try to ready their magic, either to attack Taraana or to help their friend, but find their magic refuses to be harnessed.

It was Eulalie who discovered the strange way magic reacts to Taraana 2.0. When magic is worked against the Wild Ones, the spells simply return to the person who cast them, unable to find a place to root in us. But magic refuses to even be shaped against the Keeper of the Between.

Feel free to speculate why. We certainly don't know, and to be honest, not knowing doesn't bother us either. The power this grants Taraana—he calls it freedom. The day Eulalie discovered the reaction magic has to Taraana, he went outside and stood in the sunlight and said it was the first time he felt wholly unafraid to do so.

"What would you have us do?" Tabassum Naaz asks in a perfectly modulated voice, giving no indication that she is the one who came up with this plan.

"Pass laws that will guarantee my safety. Harshly penalize anyone who tries to harm me and mine." Taraana looks around the room with a steady gaze. "I can keep myself and the people I love safe. But don't you think it would be better if I didn't have to leave a trail of bodies doing so?"

Taraana initially balked at using this threat. We got Paheli to persuade him otherwise.

Mama Magdaline looks around the room. None of the council members seem to have anything to say. The middle worlder who dared to move against Taraana is still unconscious. "We will agree to your"—the Keeper of the Green says, smiling slightly—"request."

"Thank you. I expected nothing less," Taraana says, and returns her smile with a sweet one of his own. "Do enjoy the rest of your meeting."

We leave the room and then the hotel.

Have we won? Maybe. Maybe not. The future might boast attempts to do what Baarish failed to accomplish. It might not. We don't know.

Right now, though, we are in a city that is a meeting ground of the modern and the traditional. Where a turn around a corner might lead to a neon alley with bass-thumping clubs or a silent sanctuary full of gardens offering peace. We are in a city where the magic flows in a rainbow and you can be as wild as your heart desires.

And our hearts desire.

Listen.

This is not the end of our stories, and it is not the end of yours, but this is as far as we will take you. As far as we *can* take you. We cannot give you a neat and tidy ending with a bow on top. Life has taught us much, but happily-ever-afters are still unknown to us.

Maybe Taraana and Paheli will find a way to happiness while bickering about everything under the sun. Maybe we'll stumble on it in one of the cities we travel to. Who knows what the future holds?

What we have is our anger and each other.

Aren't you angry, sisters? At being treated the way we are? At having to pick up the pieces of what remains after the world is through with us? At being silenced and abused? At being denied our dignity, our bodies, our voices, and our right to justice? Aren't you angry?

Embrace this anger. Let it fuel your everydays. Defy everyone who tells you that you can't.

Be wild.

Acknowledgments

Every book is a wild ride and *The Wild Ones* more so than any other I have written. First, I have to thank Allah (swt) without whom I wouldn't be possible. Then, I must thank my mother for her hugs, the cups of chai she made me, for the unconditional love she gives me. I'm not certain I deserve you, Ammi, but thank you for being my mom. I love you. I thank my dad, and my bhaiya, Izaz, for being willing to eat sushi with me whenever I asked him, and my bhabhi, Robina, for the trips to the library and for being willing to endure me. My littles, Ruwaiz and Zara, thank you for forgiving me the walks we didn't take and the times I didn't play with you. Thank you for believing Paheli and Taraana exist as much as I do. Thank you to my other bhaiya, Ishraaz, my bhabhi, Farzana, and my nephew, Waizu. Thank you to my niece, Pakeeza. You are amazing and I can't wait for the world to find that out for themselves. Thank you to my aunts, Samrul Buksh and Sadrul Buksh, your snark always made my days bright. Thank you also to my cousins Shafraaz and Sabrina. Sabbo, you're the best sister a girl could ask for.

Thank you to my amazing agent, Katelyn Detweiler, who believed in me and in this book every single step of the way. Thank you for not thinking the book (and its author) too weird. This book (and I) wouldn't be here without your encouragement and the work you did to ensure it sold. Thank you to everyone over at Jill Grinberg Literary Agency, especially Sam, Sophia, and Denise.

Thank you to my early readers Jessica Lewenda, Kate Elliott, Tanvi Berwah, J. Kathleen Cheney, and Nazia Nur. Your encouragement led me to this moment.

No book ever reaches the shelf due to the author alone. So many people are involved at each stage. Thank you to Karen Wojtyla, my editor, for loving *The Wild Ones*. Your insight and suggestions were so necessary and made the book what it is. Thank you for loving Taraana. Thank you also to Nicole Fiorica, whose suggestions and comments helped me look at the story in a different light and thus, made it better. Thank you to Alex Cabal for the beautiful cover and Sonia Chaghatzbanian for the jacket design. They are everything I wanted them to be. Thank you to my copy editor, Rebecca Vitkus. Your eye for detail is exemplary.

The Wild Ones was not an easy book to write. I had to excavate parts of my life that I wished to bury away forever. Some days were much more difficult than others. At those times, I had my own pack, my friends, who, whether knowingly or not, offered me support. Thank you, Teng Teng. For the talks, the snark, and for identifying all those Hollywood people I don't recognize. Karuna Riazi (you are amazing, I love you!), Axie Oh (thank you for reading an early copy and cheering me on), and Kat Cho, thank you. Also, thank you to Karuna's mama who gave me such a warm hug that day in New York that I still think of. Thank you to Roselle Lim and Judy Lin, we didn't eat nearly enough on our retreat. Let's do it again one day when the world makes much more sense. Thank you to Jasdeep for your kindness. Thank you to Shveta Thakrar for being the awesome person you are. Thank you to Janet, your baked goods are my fave, Jane, my fave picture book author, and Yash, my fave person to write with. Thank you to Lana Wood Johnson and Mason Deaver for listening to my mumblings about that certain thing. Thank you to Adib Khorram, Julian Winters, Lu Brooks, Tessa Gratton, Melody, Natalie C. Parker, Rena, and Ronni for listening and advising. Thank you to Sabina Khan. I can't wait to meet for coffee and gupshup soon. Thank you to Rossi, who keeps things real and me humble. Thank you to Laura J. Rinaldi, who I only know through the internet, but whose support and kindness humbles me. Thank you also to Erin, whose enthusiasm and encouragement keep me writing.

Every fortunate author has mentors, and I must mention mine, who have guided me in various ways ever since I started my author journey. Kate Elliott, thank you for cheering me on. You've loved *The Wild Ones* since its first inception. Thank you for encouraging me to keep on trying. Thank you to Rachel Hartman. Your kindness means the world to me. Thank you to E. K. Johnston, who reached out to me and who included me in the writing community. Thank you to Elsie Chapman for your friendship and your wisdom. Thank you also to my Api, Ausma Zehanat Khan, whose grace keeps me going.

Thank you to all those librarians and teachers who champion POC writers. Thank you also, and most fervently, to all of you who read *The Candle and the Flame* and reached out to tell me why you loved it. I am not able to thank each one of you personally, but please know that every single person's words were felt and appreciated. You made me believe in myself, and I can't tell you how much I needed that reassurance.

Finally, thank you to all of the girls out there who are fighting the fight, and being wild every single day. Please remember, you are seen and you are loved. Thank you for being who you are.